KT-132-794

G.I. CONFIDENTIAL

Also by Martin Limón

Jade Lady Burning

Slicky Boys

Buddha's Money

The Door to Bitterness

The Wandering Ghost

G.I. Bones

Mr. Kill

The Joy Brigade

The Iron Sickle

The Ville Rat

Ping-Pong Heart

The Nine-Tailed Fox

The Line

Nightmare Range

Martin Limón

Published by
Soho Press, Inc.
227 W 17th Street
New York, NY 10011

Library of Congress Cataloging-in-Publication Data

Limón, Martin.
GI confidential / Martin Limón.

ISBN 978-1-64129-038-8
eISBN 978-1-64129-039-5

1. Mystery fiction.
LCC PS3562.I465 G313 2019 813'.54—dc23

Interior design by Janine Agro, Soho Press, Inc.

Printed in the United States of America

10 9 8 7 6 5 4 3 2 1

To Violet

-1-

A rifle butt to the face neutralized the bank guard.

Teeth, saliva, and blood flew everywhere. Then, waving M16 rifles, the three American soldiers stormed across the lobby of the Itaewon Branch of the Kukmin Bank, shouting at the female tellers, male clerks, and gray-haired bank manager to get on the ground. They did, kneeling on the floor and raising their hands over their heads. Whether the Korean employees really understood these English commands or had just picked up on the men's frantic hand signals and the swinging barrels of their weapons, every one of them complied.

Two of the robbers hopped over the counter and began pulling 10,000-*won* bills and other cash out of metal trays, stuffing the loot into gunny sacks. The third man kept watch at the front door. Within less than two minutes, the thieves had emptied all the cash drawers, but instead of trying to enter the locked vault, they climbed back over the counter, still clutching their rifles and their gunny sacks now stuffed with ill-gotten lucre. Then, like a well-drilled infantry squad, they backed across the lobby, maintaining a two-arms-length distance and, in good military order, exited the building.

That quickly, it was over.

Some of the tellers and one of the clerks began to cry. Two of the senior women plucked up their courage, came around the counter, and tended to the injured door guard. The bank manager, hands shaking, dialed the Korean National Police. Then he called an ambulance.

When the authorities arrived, they were dumbfounded to hear that the thieves had been American soldiers. The first question they asked was, "How can you be so sure?" The answer was unanimous. The men had been tall and husky; they'd worn fur-lined headgear pulled down low over their ears, but despite the camo paint, they couldn't hide the contours of their faces.

"*Kocheingi*," the employees agreed. Big noses.

The captain of the Itaewon Police Station sighed and put in a call to Yongsan District Police Headquarters. They certainly wouldn't believe it. GIs had never robbed a bank before. Not in South Korea, not even during the chaos of the Korean War some twenty years ago. Of course, back in those days, none of the banks had had any money, at least, nothing worth more than the paper it was printed on. But now, a single ten-thousand-*won* note could be exchanged for almost twenty bucks US.

An amount worth stealing for. An amount worth taking a risk for. Maybe even an amount worth killing for.

"Had any *strange* lately?"

Strange leaned across a Formica-topped table in the 8th Army Snack Bar. His hair was slicked back, his eyes were hidden behind opaque shades, and a plastic cigarette holder waggled excitedly from thin lips.

"What's it to ya?" Ernie replied, looming over the table.

People in the dining area turned their heads toward us. My investigative partner, Ernie Bascom, was tall, slightly over six feet, with sandy-colored hair and green eyes behind round-lensed glasses. His pointed nose swiveled during his occasional visual sweeps, like radar homing in on an incoming missile. For some reason, women found him attractive. Why, I never had figured out. Maybe because he was nervous, fidgety, always looking for someone to arrest—or someone on whom he could focus all his formidable attention. I was even taller than Ernie. Dark hair, Hispanic, no glasses. People's eyes often followed me, too. Maybe they were afraid of getting mugged.

We pulled out chairs and sat opposite Strange.

Undaunted, Strange said, "That bank robbery this morning. How much did they get away with?"

"Ongoing investigation," Ernie said.

"Everybody's talking about it at the head shed. Even the Chief of Staff."

"They'll get their report in due time."

"But if I give them info now, that'll set me up for repayment later. See what I mean?"

Strange is a pervert. He likes to have other GIs—especially Ernie—recount their sexual exploits to him. His real name, according to the plate on his khaki uniform, is Harvey. His shoulder stripes indicate that he's a Sergeant First Class, a senior noncommissioned officer. Titles normally deserving of respect. Ernie and I don't have much of that for him, but we cater to him on occasion because he's the NCO in charge of the Classified Documents Section at the headquarters of the 8th United States Army. As such, he's privy to certain information that we need to conduct our investigations. Not to mention he's a notorious gossip, and despite his obnoxious demeanor, he knows everybody at the head shed. More importantly, he knows what their best-kept secrets are and keeps tabs on what they're up to.

My name is George Sueño. I'm an agent for the Criminal Investigation Division here at 8th Army Headquarters in Seoul, Republic of Korea. Ernie usually deals with Strange, telling him the dirty stories he wants to hear and using pressure and mind games to keep the information flowing.

Ernie reached forward and flicked the tip of the greasy holder dangling from Strange's lips. "How come you never have a cigarette in that thing?"

"I'm trying to quit."

"How can you quit when nobody's seen you smoke?"

"What are you, the chaplain?"

"Yeah. The Church of Ernie." He turned to me. "Pass the plate, Sueño."

"They took about two million *won*," I told Strange.

He whistled. The holder almost fell out of his mouth. "On the black market," he replied, "you could exchange that much *won* for about four thousand dollars. Easy."

Illegal money changers usually offered a better deal than the official conversion rate at a government-authorized foreign exchange bank.

"Not a bad haul for two minutes' work," Ernie said.

"That's all the time they were in there?"

"Precision raid," Ernie said. "The Green Berets would've been proud."

"Maybe it *was* the Green Berets."

"Nah. The Provost Marshal already checked. The Special Forces unit has been out in the field on a joint training exercise since last week."

"That only leaves about fifty thousand other GIs in-country," I said, "that we don't have alibis for."

"Then why are you sitting here?" Strange asked. "Get off your butts and start working the case." When we didn't respond, he looked back and forth between us. An epiphany lit up his eyes. "You aren't *on* the case." He grinned. It was a gruesome thing to see, like a rat having its teeth cleaned. "The

Provost Marshal doesn't trust you," Strange continued. "He's keeping you on the black market detail."

Ernie shrugged.

The two CID agents officially handling the bank robbery, Jake Burrows and Felix Slabem, were brownnosers from way back. They'd do what the 8th Army honchos asked, without exception. And what those honchos wanted was deniability. So far, the official party line was that it hadn't been established that the three men involved in the bank robbery were actually American soldiers. In the early seventies, there were few foreigners of any type living in South Korea who weren't either civilians or service members working for the US military. And there was virtually no tourism. So the thought that the three robbers might've been someone other than American GIs stretched the credulity of even the most gullible. Not to mention that each of the robbers carried an M16 rifle, standard weaponry issued to every American soldier in-country.

The United States military presence here was at the sufferance of the South Korean government, and more importantly, the sufferance of the South Korean citizenry. If the twenty-five million people of South Korea were to suddenly turn against us, the US would have to abandon its only remaining combat-capable presence in mainland Asia. The last of the major military units had withdrawn from South Vietnam just a few months ago, in accordance with President Nixon's policy of "Vietnamization." Leaving Korea as well was something the

American government didn't want to contemplate. Not in the middle of a Cold War, the world divided between the Western powers and the Soviet Union and Red China.

Thus, until proven otherwise, the three men who robbed the Kukmin Bank weren't Americans. A fiction that Agents Burrows and Slabem could tolerate, even pretend to believe. One that Ernie and I couldn't. And that was why we'd been ordered to stay on the black market detail, chasing down Korean military dependents who were buying cigarettes and freeze-dried coffee and imported Scotch at the 8th Army Post Exchange and selling it to black marketeers at twice what they paid for it.

Honest work for us. Sort of. But I doubted that Burrows and Slabem had the skill or tenacity to find these bank robbers, which was likely why 8th Army had assigned them to the case.

"So you two are just sitting on your butts doing nothing?" Strange asked.

"Nope," Ernie said. "I'm seriously considering reaching across this table and slapping you in your fat chops, then kicking *your* butt from here to the parade field."

Strange sat up taller. "I'm a Sergeant First Class," he said. "You can't do that to me."

"Keep mouthing off," Ernie said, pointing his forefinger at him, "and I'll eventually manage to override my respect for your exalted rank."

"That's more like it," Strange said, glancing back and forth between us, unsure if he liked that answer but willing to pretend it worked for him.

"Find out what you can," I told Strange, "about what the Chief of Staff is telling the Provost Marshal."

"Why?"

"Because Eighth Army policy can change direction as fast as a fart in the wind. We want to be ready for it."

Strange glanced at us slyly. "You're planning on investigating on your own, aren't you?"

"You don't have a need-to-know," Ernie told him. "Just do what the man says."

After I bought him a cup of hot chocolate with two marshmallows, Strange promised he would keep his eyes and ears open at the head shed.

"What about us?" Ernie asked as we walked out of the snack bar. "We going to let Burrows and Slabem screw this thing up?"

"Not on your life. These guys, whoever they are, robbed a bank in Itaewon, and Itaewon might as well be our hometown."

"Can't let them get away with crap like that," Ernie said. "Not in our neighborhood."

"No way. We'll catch these guys and make 'em pay for what they did, regardless of whether the Eighth Army honchos like it or not."

"They definitely won't," Ernie said. "Not if it embarrasses the Command."

"We've embarrassed them before."

"Yeah. Which is why we hold an esteemed place on the Eighth Army shit list."

-2-

Night had fallen, and the lights up and down Itaewon's main drag sparkled with a neon glow. Drawn like moths to the bars and brothels and nightclubs, packs of GIs swarmed uphill, hands in the pockets of their blue jeans, nylon jackets with dragons and flames embroidered on the back glistening in the ambient light. Ernie and I watched them go, somehow managing to resist the siren call of debauchery ourselves. Instead, we stood at the base of Itaewon hill, along the edge of the four-lane road that fronted the Kukmin Bank. Crime-scene tape emblazoned with *hangul* script kept the public away, but inside, the bank's lights were still on, and beyond plate glass windows, shadowy figures milled about. Accountants, I figured, doing a precise inventory of what had been stolen.

On either side of the street, shops lined the road, lights on and doors open: Han's Tailor Shop, Kim's Sporting Goods, Pak Family Brassware Emporium, Hamhung Cold Noodles, Miss Shin's House of Leather. Their main source of income was the five thousand or so American GIs who worked on 8th Army's Yongsan Compound less than a mile down the road. And since those GIs were typically working during the day, the establishments of Itaewon, especially the bars and brothels and nightclubs, did most of their business at night. The shops were open until about ten P.M., the bars and nightclubs until the government-mandated midnight-to-four curfew; the brothels, once they locked their front gates, were open twenty-four seven.

Ernie and I questioned the proprietors of every shop within a quarter mile of the Kukmin Bank. We weren't worried about missing the day shift and inadvertently questioning the night shift. In Korea, most shop owners and their employees worked from the early morning opening to nighttime closing, regardless of how many consecutive hours that was. There was no such thing as overtime; to have a job in this beat-up economy meant you held onto it like a hoard of gold. It had been just over twenty years since the devastation of the Korean War, when, as one American bomber pilot famously said, "All we're doing is bouncing rubble on rubble." During the ensuing two decades, circumstances had improved, but not much.

Everyone who worked in the nearby shops had heard about the robbery and was surprised and concerned by it, since the crime rate was so low in Korea. They were especially shocked to hear of the use of weapons.

The South Korean government exercised total gun control.

Only authorized personnel, like the military or the Korean National Police, were allowed to possess or utilize firearms. Penalties for the illegal possession of a rifle or a handgun, much less the use of one in committing a crime, were steep. As a result, even gangsters and other hardened criminals preferred to use cudgels, knives, and other such charming implements. GIs were known to commit the occasional crime with their Army-issue weapon—raping Korean business girls or mugging cab drivers—but no one had ever heard of them robbing a bank.

We found an eyewitness. The owner of Han's Tailor Shop, who oddly enough was named Cho. Because of his profession and the fact that most of his customers were American, he spoke English well. He walked us outside, and we stood in front of his window display of jackets and shirts.

"I was standing here," he said, then pointed two doors down the street toward the bank. "A jeep pulled up onto the sidewalk, there. American."

"How could you tell it wasn't a Korean Army jeep?" I asked.

The Republic of Korea Army, or ROK Army, was massive, almost ten times the size of the US presence, and they had American-made military vehicles swarming all over the country.

"Paint," Mr. Cho said. "Korean army use cheaper paint on their vehicles. Darker green. This jeep was American."

"You saw the soldiers get out?"

"Yes. Three of them. One man stayed behind the steering wheel. The driver."

Ernie glanced at me. So, there were four robbers, not just the three that had been mentioned in the preliminary report by Burrows and Slabem.

Cho lit up a Turtleboat cigarette and took a long drag, and I tried not to grimace at its pungent aroma.

"I wondered if any of them were my customers," he said. "You know, maybe some other time they came to Han's Tailor, bought a suit."

"Did you recognize any of them?"

"No. They wore hats, the winter kind, pulled down low, and their faces were covered with green . . . what do you call that?"

"Camo stick," I said.

"Yeah. Camo stick. Looked like crazy men. All kinds of lines. Black, green, everything. Anyway, they went into the bank."

"Carrying their rifles?"

"Yeah, rifles."

"Why didn't you call the KNPs?" Ernie asked.

Cho studied him for a moment, exhaling smoke through his nostrils. Then he turned and spit on the sidewalk. "I don't trust KNPs."

Under President Park Chung-hee's military regime, the Korean National Police, like most government employees, were severely underpaid. As such, they had to supplement their income somehow. That was usually done with payoffs, mostly minor ones. For example, if someone was caught with a bottle of scotch without an import stamp on it, they could avoid being taken down to the station and having an official report filed on them by paying a "fine" on the spot. A fine that the underpaid police officer would then stick in his pocket. After all, he had expenses, too—feeding his family, paying for his children's books and uniforms, not to mention the tuition charged even for high school. And the massive expenditure if the kid made it to college. Most Koreans didn't resent the police taking money. They'd probably do the same if roles were reversed. But they weren't foolish enough to get involved with the Korean National Police if they didn't have to.

"So the GIs went inside the bank," I said, "and a few minutes later, they came back out?"

Cho nodded. "Carrying bags." He mimicked gripping something heavy at his side.

"What else did you notice?"

"I wanted to see what unit they were in," he said, puffing once again on his cigarette.

I held my breath.

"You know," he continued, slashing a parallel line with his thumb and forefinger, "it's on the front and back of the jeep."

"Right, on the bumper," I said. They always stenciled the unit designation in white paint.

"Yeah. That."

"So what'd you see?" Ernie asked.

"Nothing."

"Nothing?"

"Yeah, nothing. Somebody covered it with black tape."

Damn. "So, we don't know their unit," I said.

"Right."

I supposed it made sense that the thieves didn't want anyone noticing that the vehicle was assigned to, say, C Btry 2/17 FA during the two minutes their jeep was parked outside the bank. According to military nomenclature, this translates to Charlie Battery of the 2nd Battalion of the 17th Field Artillery Brigade and would lead us directly to their place of assignment.

After a long pause, Ernie asked, "Does anybody else know about this?"

"Like who?" Cho asked.

"Like the KNPs. Or like the American investigators."

"No. Nobody came. Nobody asked me anything. You're first."

"But there were cops down the street all day?" I said. "At the bank."

"Lots," Cho replied.

"Can you tell us anything else about the GIs?"

He shrugged and took another long drag on his cigarette, thinking it over. "They're smart," he said.

"Why?" I asked.

He looked at me like I was crazy. "Fastest way to get money."

"Why didn't you ever try it?" Ernie asked. "You work just a few steps from the bank."

Cho threw his cigarette butt on the sidewalk and stomped on it. "You give me a gun and a jeep, maybe I will."

He turned and walked back into Han's Tailor Shop.

I yelled a thank-you at him, and he shrugged and gave a desultory wave. I turned to Ernie.

"You pissed him off."

"How'd I do that?"

"By implying he was a thief."

"Well, he owns a shop, doesn't he?"

"That's not thievery."

"Seems like it to me every time I buy something."

Ernie hated capitalism. He also had no use for communism. I was never sure, really, how he thought the world should be run. Except maybe through playing it by ear, according to the thoughts of *der reichsführer* Ernie.

We walked back toward the lights of Itaewon. After a few steps, a slim figure hopped out of the darkness of a narrow alley. "*Hey!*" she shouted. We turned. She raised and pointed a rectangular object. Before we had time to react, a flash erupted into the night. Both Ernie and I reached for our eyes, blinded.

"What the *hell*?" Ernie said.

The slim figure fumbled with something, shoved it with a click into a metallic device, and the flash erupted again. This time I lurched forward and reached for the shadowy waif, but instead of grasping something solid, all I grabbed was air.

"Relax, big boy," a woman's voice called. "I'm done. Your vision will come back in a second."

"Who in the hell are you?" I asked, rubbing my eyes.

"Just a tourist."

"A tourist? There are no tourists here."

She let out a brief chortle. "There are now."

With that, she trotted briskly away. For a few steps Ernie ran after her, but almost immediately plowed into an electrical pole. I checked to see if he was all right. Embarrassed, he shoved my hand away. I could barely make out the retreating photographer, prancing off down the street, leaving us standing immobilized like two dumb giants.

"Witch," Ernie said, gallantly eschewing the B-word.

-3-

"Where in the hell you two guys *been*?" The next day, Staff Sergeant Riley, NCO in charge of the Criminal Investigation Admin Division, gave us his usual warm greeting.

"Doing what we're supposed to be doing," Ernie said. "All freaking morning. Chasing down dollies and busting them for black market violations. Where the hell you think we've been?"

A slight exaggeration. The truth was, after being accosted by our mystery photographer last night, we'd made our way into the heart of Itaewon and discussed the bank robbery case over a couple of beers, which led to a couple of shots of bourbon, which led to a bottle of soju. All of which inevitably led to a horrific hangover this morning that had made us both late for work. We rendezvoused at the barracks, and after driving the jeep through the empty parking lot of the Yongsan Compound Main PX, we could at least claim that we'd been doing our regular duty on black market patrol. After which we'd made it over to the office.

"Burrows and Slabem," Riley said, "are already briefing the Chief of Staff on that bank robbery fiasco. Good troops. Doing their job."

"Brownnosers," Ernie said, making his way toward the back counter and the three-foot-tall stainless steel urn of hot coffee. Supposedly, some years ago, it had been hand-receipted from the 8th Army mess hall. Somebody had once tried to clean the brown crust that encased its innards, but Riley had ordered them to stop, afraid it would fall apart.

I sat down in front of Riley's desk and grabbed his copy of the *Pacific Stars and Stripes*. President Gerald R. Ford was having his usual headaches, and some were speculating that he was getting ready to pardon Nixon. Since those problems were all on the other side of the planet, I set the paper down. "Are the honchos still claiming the robbers weren't GIs?"

Riley had turned his attention to a stack of paperwork in front of him. "Yep."

"Pretty far-fetched."

"As long as it stays out of the newspapers, they're happy."

The Park Chung-hee government had total control over the South Korean press. More than a few reporters who'd crossed the line with anti-government rhetoric had been arrested and charged with sedition. The rationale was that with over 700,000 bloodthirsty North Korean Communist soldiers stationed thirty miles north of Seoul, ready to invade at the drop of a bayonet, the people of South Korea had more to worry about than freedom of the press. They had to think about survival. Niceties like James Madison's First Amendment would have to wait. And wait. And wait.

A snippet of pulp stuck out from beneath Riley's desk blotter.

"What's this?" I asked, reaching for it.

Riley slapped his hand down on top of it. "Nothing," he said.

"If it's nothing, why are you so nervous?"

"Mind your own business," he said.

High heels clicked down the hallway toward us. Miss Kim, the tall, elegant admin secretary, entered the office. She nodded to me and took her seat at her desk behind her *hangul* typewriter. After fumbling with some paperwork and propping it against a wire holder, she rolled a blank sheet into the platen and started typing away.

I joined Ernie at the back counter. He had gone silent—the uneasy truce between him and Miss Kim still ruled the office, sort of like the détente between North and South Korea. I supposed she'd never forgiven him for his wandering ways during their brief relationship. He hadn't bothered to apologize, after all.

I pulled myself a mug of hot coffee and sat with Ernie on the folding metal chairs at the wooden field table.

"Are we gonna tell 'em?" I asked.

"Tell who what?"

"Tell Riley and Burrows and Slabem and the Provost Marshal about the fourth GI—the driver—and the fact that they covered up their jeep's unit designation."

"Screw 'em," Ernie said, before glugging down more coffee. "I say we keep working on the case ourselves without sharing anything."

"The information could be important to their investigation."

"They don't want it to be important," Ernie replied. "All they want is to be able to claim that our pure-as-driven-snow American soldiers had nothing to do with this. We tell 'em that it was GIs who robbed the bank, and they'll blame us for bursting their bubble. As if the entire robbery was our fault."

I watched Riley shuffling his documents and Miss Kim pecking at the keys of her typewriter. "These guys could strike again. After all, it was so easy for them this time."

"Except for the bank guard."

"Yeah. Except for that."

"Otherwise, they were pretty lucky," Ernie said.

"You know it and I know it. But they may not know it. This time, an old man lost some teeth and ended up with a broken jaw. Next time, it could be worse."

Ernie stirred his coffee.

"I still say screw 'em. They don't want our help, they don't get it. The KNPs didn't even bother to canvass the area. They know the deal. The Americans and, therefore, the higher-ups in the Korean government—their bosses—want deniability.

They want to be able to say it wasn't American GIs. Tens of millions of dollars in US aid are hitched to that story."

Actually, it was hundreds of millions. Both economic and military aid was provided by the US government to the South Korean regime in order to prop them up as our bulwark against Communist aggression. Bad publicity in the States could ruin all that, turn the American public and therefore Congress, which controlled the purse strings, against the US military presence on the Korean Peninsula. An eventuality that the honchos of the 8th United States Army would go to great lengths to avoid.

"So they're investigating with one hand tied behind their back," I said.

"Yes. Which is why they put those bozos Burrows and Slabem on the case. You're the only GI in Korea who speaks Korean. And you and I are the only two law enforcement officers with enough gumption to venture out into Seoul and ask questions. The other guys can't even read the signs, they think people are talking bad about them every time they hear a foreign language, they aren't limber enough to squat over a Korean toilet, and they hate the smell of kimchi. They're *morons*," Ernie said, warming to the subject. "The only two real investigators Eighth Army's got are you and me. And we're sidelined; they've relegated us to wandering around the PX and the commissary, busting housewives for selling a jar of maraschino cherries to black market mama-sans."

I sipped on my coffee, set it down, and said, "Yeah, yeah, *yeah*. But other than that."

Ernie sighed. "Screw you, Sueño."

Riley rose from his desk, hiked up his pants, and walked out into the hallway. I listened to his footsteps, figuring he was headed to the latrine.

"Hold on a minute," I told Ernie, as I rose and walked toward Riley's desk. There, beneath the blotter, was the little piece of pulp. I carefully slid it out. A newspaper. The *Overseas Observer*. It was a single fold tabloid type, like the *Stars and Stripes*, but this periodical was definitely not Department of Defense authorized. I held it up to the light. Covering most of the front page was a gorgeous young woman kneeling on a beach, beaming at the camera and wearing nothing but a leather bikini that accented her voluptuous curves.

Miss Kim glanced in my direction, saw what I was holding, and quickly turned back to her work. I liked her a lot and did my best to treat her well, especially after Ernie's betrayal. I quickly refolded the newspaper, carried it to the back of the room, and plopped it down in front of Ernie.

"All *right*," he said, ogling the bathing beauty. "The *Oversexed Observer*. I used to read this rag all the time in 'Nam. The honchos hate it."

"They won a court case against McNamara," I said. "So the PX has to sell it."

"I see Riley's a fan."

Ernie picked up the paper and thumbed through it. It was twenty flimsy pages with plenty of photos. And plenty of ads for liquor, hair cream, cigarettes, sports cars, even mail-order jewelry, complete with instructions on how to have the perfect engagement ring mailed to your girl back in the States. The headlines were salacious: COLONEL BOFF'S PRIVATE. TENNIS COURT FIRST, THEN PERIMETER DEFENSE. GI CONVICTED OF FRAGGING CO.

All the stuff that would never be covered in the *Stars and Stripes*.

"How do they get these stories?" Ernie asked.

"Shoe leather," I said. "And leaks from inside the military."

Plenty of GIs were pissed off at the Green Machine and willing to pass confidential information to the *Overseas Observer*, even though they could technically be court-martialed for violating a standing order. To wit, all reporters and other media inquiries were to be referred to the local command Public Affairs Office.

Riley stomped back into the office, surveyed his desk, noticed that his blotter was slightly askew, and glanced back at us.

"Hey," he said, "what are you doing with that?"

"Wrapping fish," Ernie said.

Riley marched toward us, holding out his palm. "Give it here."

"Ix-nay," Ernie said, still reading. "I'm improving my mind."

Riley snatched the newspaper, but Ernie held on, and a loud ripping noise tore through the office. Miss Kim stopped typing, stood up, grabbed a tissue from the box in front of her, and briskly swept out into the hallway.

"See what you've done," Riley said. "You've upset Miss Kim. And you ripped my paper."

"You're the one who ripped it," Ernie replied.

"I haven't even read it yet," Riley said.

"Sueño will buy you a new one."

Riley glanced at me.

"Sure," I said. "When does the next issue hit the stands?"

"Sunday," Riley replied.

"All right," I said. "The next *Overseas Observer* is on me."

That seemed to calm the waters. Working with Scotch tape, Ernie and Riley pieced the *Oversexed Observer* back together. It was great to see the boys cooperate. The girl in the bikini probably had something to do with it.

Three days later, on a Friday, Riley answered a call from the MP desk. He listened for a while, repeating, "Yeah." And finally, "Roger that." He slammed down the receiver.

"Bascom! Sueño!" he yelled, though we were only a few feet away.

"What?" Ernie said.

"Hat up! Your presence is required immediately, if not sooner."

"What are you talking about, Riley?"

"Another bank. This one ain't good."

"What do you mean, not good?"

"I mean somebody's dead."

Ernie and I looked at each other. "Somebody like who?"

"Korean civilian. That's all I know." He gave us the name of the bank and the district, grievously mispronouncing both. Still, I knew what he meant. The Daehan Bank in Dongsung-dong. Miss Kim stood up and helped me find it on the large office wall map of Seoul.

"Okay," I said. "Got it."

Ernie and I slipped on our coats and our headgear and left the office. In the parking lot on the way to the jeep, Ernie said, "Why are they sending us and not Burrows and Slabem?"

"Maybe they're through dicking around."

"That'll be the day."

Ernie started the jeep and we roared out of Gate Seven and into the overcast afternoon, heading north toward Namsan Tunnel #3, which would lead us to Dongsung-dong on the far side of downtown Seoul.

-4-

The body had already been taken away.

Still, there was no doubt that someone had been killed. Not only was there a sticky pool of dried blood behind the teller's counter, but all the remaining staff were either crying or comforting one another. As we walked in, men in black suits and women in white skirts and blue waistcoats stared at us through tear-filled eyes. Some of the men mumbled inaudible curses. Women grabbed their handkerchiefs and turned away. The hatred was palpable. Someone who I suspected looked very much like us had just killed an innocent bank employee.

In the back office, a command post of sorts had been set up. A broad-shouldered man in a dark suit, with gray at his temples, hunched forward, interviewing the man I presumed was the bank manager. One of the Korean police officers stepped forward and whispered something in his ear. He sat up and turned around. We made eye contact and nodded to each other in recognition. Inspector Gil Kwon-up, better known as Mr. Kill, Chief Homicide Inspector of the Korean National Police. He whispered something back to the officer, who hurried toward us.

"Outside, please," he said, motioning with his hand.

"We want to look around," Ernie said.

"Okay. But quickly, please."

The pool of blood was behind the counter at the last teller window, next to the wall. The front door was about ten yards away. From the front door to the teller window, at an angle and past stanchions, it would've been a difficult shot. Had the woman resisted when the thieves were collecting the money?

Alongside scattered sprays of loose coins, several cash boxes lay on the ground, having been pulled from their drawers and turned upside down. At the work station with the pool of blood, the cash drawer was still intact.

"They didn't take her money," Ernie said.

"You're assuming it's a *her*," I said.

"One of the tellers," Ernie replied. He had a point. Korean society was patriarchal to the point that most frontline customer-service personnel were women.

Mumbled conversation around us grew louder.

"Please," our escort policeman said, once again motioning toward the exit. This time we acquiesced. As we moved away from the blood, a ray of light glanced off a large heating and cooling unit halfway to the front wall. A wicked dent, accompanied by a long scratch, had been plowed across its metal surface. I touched the wound. The edge was sharp, and dried paint flaked off beneath my finger. The damage was recent.

Outside, our KNP escort lit a cigarette. Neither Ernie nor I smoked, so we sauntered toward the line of blue KNP sedans. Bemused passersby gawked at us. Foreigners were often seen near the American military bases, but if you wandered a couple of miles away from the compound, you became a novelty, something like a rare animal or alien from Venus.

"Mr. Kill's here," Ernie said. "So where's Officer Oh?" His female assistant.

"You've got me," I said.

Ten minutes later, Chief Homicide Inspector Gil Kwon-up emerged from the bank.

"Thank you for coming," he said.

"Wouldn't miss it," Ernie replied.

He stared at Ernie curiously, wondering, I supposed, if he was joking, and decided to ignore the comment.

"I asked for you both," he said.

"Thanks," Ernie replied. "I think."

"The other two investigators, what are their names?"

"Burrows and Slabem."

He shook his head. "They're useless."

"We like to think so," Ernie replied.

"I contacted my superiors, who contacted your chief of staff. That's why you're here."

Mr. Kill had not only earned a university education in

Korea, but had been trained from a young age in the *Four Books* and the *Five Classics*, or the traditional Confucian cannon. He was an expert at calligraphy, ancient literature, and traditional fine art, not to mention the analects of the Great Sage himself. After joining the Korean National Police, he'd been selected for an anti-Communist leadership course sponsored by the US Department of Defense. Under their auspices, he'd traveled to the States for graduate courses in criminology and counter-insurgency at an unnamed Ivy League school. So he was not only brilliant, but also well-educated and could speak better English than most GIs.

Ernie—a high school graduate, and lucky at even that—resented Mr. Kill, sensing their class difference. I'd dropped out of high school during my senior year to join the army and eat regular. But despite my humble beginnings, I had a different take on the situation, seeing Inspector Kill as a valuable source of knowledge. He knew more about crime fighting than either of us probably ever would know. Or for that matter, ever want to know.

"It seems likely," I told Mr. Kill, "that Eighth Army and the Korean government will want to cover up these crimes, or at least keep them from the public eye. Our colleagues, Burrows and Slabem, are better for that."

"You're right. They would be. But the policy has changed. We hoped that these men would strike just once. That they'd keep their two million *won*, have a party, and not take the chance of thieving again. As you can see," he said, nodding toward the bank's entranceway, "we were wrong. Now an innocent woman is dead. Ricochet. The bullet hit the heating unit, dipped, and rebounded at a thirty-degree angle. Caught her in the neck." He pointed to his own throat. "Denial isn't going to work any longer. If these Americans keep robbing, and more people die, word will leak out. We can control the Korean newspapers, but not the international press. And if our own citizens realize we've been hiding something of this magnitude, even President Park will be in trouble."

Which was saying something, since the Park Chung-hee regime was willing to beat people, lock them up, or even make them disappear for publicly opposing government policies.

"So what's the plan?" Ernie asked.

"We're going to catch these miscreants. Bring them to justice before they strike again."

Miscreants. I sometimes forgot how extensive and formal Mr. Kill's vocabulary could be. It was refreshing, something I'd never hear in the barracks.

"We'll take them down," Mr. Kill continued. "By any means necessary."

"You mean dead or alive?" Ernie asked, perking up.

"Yes." He pointed to us. "And your job is to ferret out information on the American compounds. To find them from the inside."

"Eighth Army won't like it," I said.

"They'll have to like it. As we speak, our Minister of the Interior is in discussion with your ambassador to Korea. They'll force Eighth Army to admit the obvious. That these criminals are American GIs who must be stopped at all costs."

When the 8th Army honchos are forced to do something, they feel humiliated and take out their frustrations on someone—usually the lowest-ranking enlisted scum on the totem pole. Which was Ernie and me. But this was nothing new to us. In fact, it was becoming our signature MO.

"Where's Officer Oh?" I asked.

"Canvassing the area. With a task force."

"Something the Itaewon police didn't bother to do."

"No. But I understand you did."

How he discovered these things, I never quite knew. There were Korean National Police stations throughout the country, plus their paid—and unpaid—informants. Still, sometimes Mr. Kill's access to information seemed uncanny. Instead of admitting my surprise, I shrugged. "We had nothing else to do that night."

"And what did you find out?"

I told him.

"A fourth man," he repeated. "And tape on the vehicle."

"Yes, over the unit designation."

"We'll check on that."

"But they'd have to take it off," I said, "almost immediately after leaving the bank. If they didn't, they'd risk being pulled over by a random MP patrol. And they certainly wouldn't be allowed through the gate of any of the American compounds, not with the tape still hiding their unit designation."

There were over fifty US military installations in the Republic of Korea, stretching from the Demilitarized Zone in the north to the Port of Pusan two hundred miles to the south.

Mr. Kill thought about it. "So after the robbery, the thieves would've left the Kukmin Bank in Itaewon and pulled over somewhere to take off the tape?"

"Yes. Probably somewhere not too far away."

"Still a large area to canvass."

Seoul was crowded with millions of shops and homes and government facilities, not to mention people.

"Maybe we can narrow the search area down," I said.

"How?" Mr. Kill asked.

I told him. Or tried to. Before I could finish, one of the female employees of the Daehan Bank, holding a handkerchief to red eyes, stormed out of the double-doored entranceway and headed straight for us. Mr. Kill swiveled, but not in time to stop her. She shoved past him, raised her free hand, and swung her fist toward my face. I sidestepped the blow and her small fist landed on my chest, about as jarring as a tap from a baby. But she kept swinging, her fresh tears throwing off her aim.

"You *kill*," she shouted in English. "You big-nose people kill good woman. She *mother*. Have three children. What they do now? How they grow up?"

By this time, Mr. Kill had grabbed the distraught woman by the shoulders and was pulling her gently away. Other cops surrounded us and stepped between me and Ernie and the woman. Her energy spent, she relented and slouched forward, still sobbing as Kill led her back to the bank.

Standing atop the front steps of the Daehan Bank were the rest of the employees. They'd filtered out and arranged themselves in rows, almost as if posing for a group photograph. Instead of smiling and saying *kimchi*, they stared at me and Ernie with eyes that were red and tearful and angry. Wishing, I imagined, that we big-nosed people had never set foot in their country. Never ripped it in two. Never set Korean against Korean. And never robbed the Daehan Bank.

-5-

Officer Oh finished supervising her canvass of the area and joined us in Ernie's jeep. She sat on the low back seat, knees together, in her KNP uniform of a dark-blue skirt and a light-blue blouse buttoned to the neck. Her regulation pillbox hat with an upturned brim was pinned in front of a clasped fold of long black hair.

Mr. Kill was busy at the crime scene, so he'd sent her with us to look into my theory of the GI bank robbers pulling over to remove the tape from their bumpers.

Officer Oh grabbed the back of my seat, leaned forward, and asked, "*Uri odi gayo*?" Where are we going?

I answered in Korean that I wasn't quite sure yet. As we emerged from the bank's tiny parking area, I told Ernie to take a right onto the main road. What I was looking for were logical places to pull over. Seoul was extremely crowded and the traffic could be maddening, so I searched for a place where someone pulling over and stopping wouldn't be hit from behind and, if possible, where there weren't too many witnesses. After traveling over a mile, I didn't see anywhere that seemed likely. Parked cars lined the road except at designated bus stops.

"Maybe they used one of the bus stops," Ernie said. "That's all that's open."

"Too many witnesses lined up there," I said. "And there are so many buses, one of them would've been liable to pull up behind the jeep and start honking. Or worse, blocked them in so they couldn't get away. Attracted a cop."

He swerved past a truck piled high with Napa cabbage. "You think they pre-planned the getaway?"

"I think so. They probably did a test run beforehand. Everything else about the robbery was pulled off with something resembling military precision."

"Except for the dead teller."

"Yeah. Except for that."

Officer Oh spoke some English, but not nearly as well as Mr. Kill. In the rearview mirror, I could see her eyes darting back and forth between us, trying to keep up with our conversation.

"Hey, turn around," I told Ernie.

He did. Right in the middle of the road. Kimchi cabs—boxy Hyundai sedans—and three-wheeled produce trucks slammed on their brakes and honked their horns.

Officer Oh's eyes widened.

"You trying to get us killed?" I asked.

"Police business," Ernie said. "Time's a-wasting."

Ernie loved breaking rules. To him, having permission to break them was almost as enjoyable as not having permission.

We passed Daehan Bank and kept going. This time, the side of the road was less crowded. There were a few businesses catering to cab drivers, with men wearing rubber boots and holding hoses standing outside of quick-serve chop houses, offering a quick wash while the busy cabbies wolfed down bowls of noodles.

"They could've pulled into one of those," Ernie said.

"Too many eyes," I replied.

Finally, we reached Tong-il Lo, Reunification Road. At the three-way intersection, I said, "They must've stopped here."

Ernie glanced over at me. Officer Oh leaned forward.

"Why?"

"Because when you continue north on Tong-il Lo, you leave the city and hit the countryside. And Division territory."

The US Second Infantry Division guarded the valley that stretched from Seoul to Munsan, across the Freedom Bridge and on to the DMZ and the truce village of Panmunjom. Beyond that loomed North Korea like an ancient terra incognita.

"And Division has MP patrols," Ernie said.

"Plenty of them. And checkpoints. If someone were to have tape covering their unit designation, the MPs would immediately become suspicious."

"Here," Ernie said. He pulled over onto the blacktop parking area surrounding a gas station with a dozen pumps. A huge sign overhead had two Chinese characters that were pronounced "*Sokyu*" in Korean. Meaning "rock oil." Which perfectly corresponded with the Latin-derived word "petroleum."

"They wouldn't want to buy gas," Ernie said.

"No. You can bet they topped off at a POL point before starting this mission."

POL was the military acronym for petroleum, oil, and lubrication. Spots where properly dispatched military vehicles could gas up for free.

Ernie parked the jeep on the edge of the station, and Officer Oh climbed out of the back seat and strode confidently the twenty yards to the sales office. About ten minutes later, she returned. "One of the employees remembers GIs stopping here this morning." She pointed to a spot a few yards from where we stood. "They did something to their vehicle, but the employees were busy and didn't pay them much attention."

"Did anyone see their unit designation?"

"No. They weren't interested. Besides, they couldn't have read it from this distance."

We strolled toward the spot where the GIs had parked. Off the edge of the blacktop, Ernie bent down and plucked something from a clump of weeds. He held it up to me.

A mangled wad of black electrical tape.

As we drove away, Ernie asked, "How'd you figure that out?"

"A documentary I saw on AFKN." The American Forces Korea Network. Since Stateside television broadcasts couldn't reach Korea, 8th Army had its own TV network, AFKN, which rebroadcast US television shows, including plenty of documentaries, along with local military news and public service announcements.

"What? A documentary about how to find GI bank robbers?"

"No. It was about hunters in Africa chasing wounded gazelle. They lose sight of the gazelle and don't have time to study the hoof prints and the broken twigs and stuff, so they trot along, following the contours of the landscape, taking the easiest routes and trying to think like the animal. Some hunters are expert at it."

"George Sueño," Ernie said. "Big game hunter. Should I call you bwana?"

"Can it, Ernie."

We drove to Itaewon to try the same tracking technique, starting from the Kukmin Bank. We weren't sure in which direction the thieves had made their departure, so we'd try both right and left. Navigating instinctively was a little more difficult since we were on the southern edge of the city, farther from the countryside. Here there were more crowds and traffic between tightly packed buildings.

After an hour, we gave it up as a lost cause. Still, Officer Oh thought we'd made headway.

That evening in Mr. Kill's office at KNP headquarters, we went over everything we'd learned from the bank employees. It wasn't much. That the three gunmen and the driver were Caucasian, there was little doubt. That they were American soldiers seemed to be a foregone conclusion. We had estimates of their height and weight, but only one of them seemed any bigger than your average GI. The guy who'd stood watch at the front door and rifle-butted the bank guard and eventually fired the warning shot that ricocheted and killed the teller. His shoulders were broad enough that some of the male employees thought he might be a bodybuilder. Beyond that, we didn't know their hair color or eye color or, because of the camo stick, even the complexion of their skin. All appeared to be clean-shaven, and they'd all worn black GI-issue leather gloves, so the KNP forensic team was unable to recover any fingerprints. Basically, they'd left us nothing.

The bullet that had killed the bank teller was being evaluated at KNP headquarters. Until we had a rifle to match it against, though, it wouldn't do us much good.

At 8 P.M., while we were still going over the evidence with Mr. Kill and Officer Oh, the phone rang. Officer Oh answered it. After listening for a moment, she covered the receiver and said to Mr. Kill, "*Saum-i nassoyo.*"

A fight had broken out.

-6-

The main Seoul railway station, which Koreans call Seoul-*yok*, was a stately old building made of brick with a central round dome that looked like something right out of *Doctor Zhivago*. I'd been told it was a gift from the Russian czar to the Korean king back in the 1890s, when both Russia and Japan were competing for influence on the Korean Peninsula. I wasn't sure if that story was true, but it sounded right, and I liked to wonder about it as I watched the lights around the edges of the roof make the dome glow like a huge orb of polished jade.

The KNP checkpoint was set up in front of Seoul-*yok*. A convenient spot because Tong-il Lo ran down from the DMZ past Seoul Station and continued for less than a mile to the Samgakji Circle. GIs familiar with the city would hang a left there for the short run to 8th Army Headquarters on Yongsan Compound. Plenty of US military vehicles passed through. And because of the bank robberies and the shooting, the KNPs were doing something they hadn't done in years, or maybe ever. Stopping American army vehicles and demanding that the GIs show their dispatch and identification and state their destination and the nature of their business.

In other words, the KNPs were busy closing the barn door long after the horse had escaped.

"I didn't order this," Mr. Kill told us.

"Somebody up top is angry," Ernie said. "It's for show."

Kill's expression hardened, but he didn't reply.

Officer Oh drove us in her blue KNP sedan. When we pulled up to the checkpoint, Mr. Kill climbed out of the front passenger seat. Immediately, a uniformed police officer hurried forward and saluted him. Floodlights illuminated Kill's face as he questioned the officer.

Two GIs, heads lolling, were handcuffed and leaning against a two-and-a-half ton truck. I checked its unit designation: 531 M&S CO. The 531st Maintenance & Supply Company. I flashed my badge and asked them to identify themselves.

"Screw you," one of them said.

"Why'd they stop you?" I asked.

"How the hell should we know? I'm driving with our load, and all of a sudden these guys are standing in our way pointing the business ends of their M16s in our faces."

"You should've run them down," the other GI said.

"Yeah," the driver replied. "Maybe I should have. They

don't have the right to stop the American army. Who the hell do they think they are?"

"It's their country," Ernie said.

"Screw their country. I didn't ask to be sent here."

Ernie offered them both a stick of ginseng gum. The driver stared at the packet with its Korean lettering and drawing of a ginseng plant and said, "You chew that stuff?"

"Good for the metabolism," Ernie said, stuffing a stick in his mouth. "You punch one of the KNPs?"

"Wouldn't you? They started to frisk us."

"Did you have something to hide?"

"Like what?"

"Like reefer. Or maybe a bag full of money."

"I got a bag," the other guy said, grabbing his crotch, "but it ain't full of money."

Ernie and I checked the back of the truck, then the cab and the clipboard with the dispatch on it. Everything appeared to be in order. They were transporting damaged tank and artillery parts to a supply depot to be replaced.

"Just hold tight," I told them. "Don't do anything stupid. We'll see what we can do."

Mr. Kill had finished his conversation with the officer in charge. He stepped toward us.

"They're checking every US military vehicle for money, gunny sacks, rifles, even camo sticks. Any signs at all that they're the bank robbers."

"Too late," Ernie said. "Those guys have already returned to their roost."

Kill nodded his head sadly. "But these Americans resisted, punched one of our officers."

"Is he okay?" I asked.

"Just a bloody nose."

"Would an apology work?"

Kill nodded and said, "It will have to."

I returned to the two GIs and coaxed them toward a solution. After overcoming their initial reluctance, they stood before the officer who'd been hit to offer, if not an apology, at least an explanation.

"If you don't," Ernie said, "ain't nothing we can do. You'll be locked up in a Korean monkey house. Hope you like week-old kimchi and brown rice. When you chew, though, watch out for maggots."

The two GIs looked at each other. Finally, the driver who'd thrown the punch said, "I'll talk to him."

As the GI and injured Korean policeman stood awkwardly in front of one another, I translated. The GI said he wished it hadn't come to this, but once he was getting pushed around and frisked by somebody just for doing his job, it was only natural that he'd lashed out to protect himself. It wasn't his fault. The Korean cops shouldn't have stopped him.

Self-serving nonsense. But I translated his words into Korean with quite a bit of diplomatic license. It came out as something like, *I'm sorry I hit you, I shouldn't have done it, and I'll be sure to show more respect for Korea and Korean law in the future.* I spoke loudly enough so all the cops in the vicinity could hear. Both Mr. Kill and Officer Oh realized that my translation was less than exact but kept their faces impassive.

The wounded Korean officer paused for a moment, making sure that everyone absorbed this abject apology from the obnoxious foreigner. Finally, he nodded his head and barked an order. Quickly, the handcuffs were removed, and the two GIs, mumbling to themselves, climbed back into their truck. One of them was about to say something, but Ernie warned him to keep his mouth shut. Without further incident, the two GIs started the big deuce-and-a-half's engine and sped away.

Mr. Kill told me, "You should be in the State Department."

"Every American soldier is an ambassador for their country," I said. "How long do you think this policy of stopping American vehicles is going to last?"

"Not long, if I have anything to say about it. Or we could wind up with allies shooting one another."

As we made our way back to 8th Army headquarters, I sat in the passenger seat, gazing at the pedestrians still out in droves at this hour of night. Some were male office workers clutching attaché cases, still in their dark suits. Others were women in tight skirts and long-sleeved jackets. Even middle-school students were still out, lugging their backpacks around like brick masons hauling mortar. I've always been astonished at the industriousness of the Korean public. No sitting home staring at the TV for them. They had a country to rebuild.

And then I saw her. Or someone I thought was her.

A small figure silhouetted by the overhead lights in front of the Main Gate. Ernie pulled into the center lane and signaled left.

"What?" he said, noticing that I'd turned around.

She was walking away. Average height by American standards, about five-four. Strong shoulders, not as wide as her hips, though she was slim. Unusually so, in fact. Although she was just a vanishing shadow, I suspected she didn't have an ounce of body fat on her. She gave off the impression that she could have a child in the morning, then outpace everyone in a rock quarry all day. Pure strength, I thought.

"*What?*" Ernie said again, exasperated. "Do you want me to turn around?"

Was I nuts? Was it a case of mistaken identity, or could it really be her? Even if it turned out to be a bust, I had to know. I shouted to Ernie, "Yeah, turn around."

He did, hanging a U amidst a chorus of honking horns. We cruised down the block, Ernie swerving left again, me leaning forward to try to catch a glimpse of the mystery woman, but as we approached the buildings surrounding Samgakji Circle, there were too many pedestrians. Even if she'd been amongst them, I would've had trouble spotting her.

"Slow down," I told Ernie.

He did. Enraged cab drivers zoomed past us.

He turned again, this time pulling off the main road. We cruised for a while through narrow side lanes, crowded with late-night revelers, women delivering laundry, coal merchants shoving pushcarts. If that had been her and she wanted to avoid us, we'd never find her. It was far more likely that it hadn't been her, just a different Korean woman with the same build and demeanor, and that I'd never find her again in this city of eight million people.

"Who are we looking for?" Ernie asked.

I leaned back in my seat. "Nobody," I said.

"Nobody?"

"Yeah," I replied. "I was probably seeing things. I'm pretty tired."

Ernie raised one eyebrow and stared at me for a moment, but kept his mouth shut. He swiveled the wheel and wound us back to the main drag, hung a right, and bulled through traffic, eventually navigating us to the big arch over the main gate of 8th Army's Yongsan Compound. After the MP waved us past the barricades, we entered the relative calm of the base, coasting past the evergreen trees lining the road.

"Home sweet home," Ernie crowed. Within seconds, we passed somber brick buildings and the big flat-cement-block building of the 8th Army Commo Center until we were once again enveloped in gloom.

■ ■ ■

I couldn't sleep.

I threw the blankets off my bunk, swung my feet over, and stood up. Grabbed the keys on the chain around my neck holding my dog tags and quietly opened my wall locker. Reaching inside, I unraveled my pants and shirt and slipped them on, located my jacket, and slid my feet into low quarters. Out in the hallway, I headed for the side door of the barracks and exited, walking briskly toward the Main Gate.

Ten minutes later I was waving to the Korean guard at the Pedestrian Gate and was outside on the main road amidst much lighter traffic. Only a few minutes until the midnight curfew, and anyone smart had already gone home. The dumb ones, like me, were still meandering about with no certain destination.

A ten-foot-high wall fronted the westernmost edge of 8th Army's Yongsan Compound and then changing composition from stone to brick, continued along the front edge of ROK Army Headquarters compound. I stuck my hands in my pockets and walked.

Could it have been her?

There was a chance. She'd contacted me before. What I wanted and what she wanted was to be together as a happy family. Unfortunately, that was impossible as long as the Park Chung-hee regime was in power.

Her name was Yong In-ja. Doc Yong, Ernie and I usually called her. She had been the head of the government health clinic in Itaewon, treating the Korean business girls for all sorts of maladies, including venereal disease and the bumps and bruises and broken bones from their GI boyfriends. Consequently, we'd worked with her on a number of cases. I appreciated her command of English, her vast intelligence, and most of all, her endless compassion for the ones who'd ended up slouched hopelessly on the hard-wooden benches of her waiting room. She and I discovered we had a similar love for books and ancient *sijo* poetry, and although we'd never gone on an actual date, Ernie and I ended up helping her on some of the criminal matters that arose from her efforts to assist her often set-upon underclass clientele.

Eventually, she and I had become intimate. I had hoped that our friendship and affair would result in marriage. And it would have, except for an obligation I didn't know she had. From her parents, she'd inherited the leadership position of a rebel organization based in the southern province of Cholla-namdo. After they'd participated in an overthrow attempt, the Park Chung-hee regime had been hunting them down relentlessly. In their home city of Kwangju, far to the south, they were relatively safe. Anti-government sympathies ran high there, as they had for centuries.

To complicate matters, she became pregnant with our son, Il-yong, the First Dragon. I'd seen him a couple of times, when it was safe, but she'd convinced me that it was better for us to live apart. She could hide successfully in the southern Cholla province, amongst her compatriots, and Il-yong would be brought up safely. But I couldn't look for them. An 8th Army CID agent in a part of the country that drew few foreigners would attract attention. The Korean National Police were everywhere, and they were on the alert for her and her group. If my presence led them to her, she would be arrested, tried in a kangaroo court, and in all probability, executed.

So the Park Chung-hee government, the one the US Army was here to protect, was keeping us apart. President Park was her greatest enemy and threat, and therefore mine, too, though the words could never be spoken aloud. Ernie knew everything, having put two and two together, but we never spoke of my dilemma. He knew better than to bring it up. Why talk about a problem with no solution?

After passing the ROK Army compound, I wandered the streets and back alleys of Samgakji. I'm not sure what I was anticipating—Doctor Yong In-ja appearing from a dark alleyway, our son in her arms? I scanned the shadows, garnering odd looks from old ladies sweeping up the last remnants of debris and locking up the sliding wooden doors of their shops.

Finally, a cop stopped me. He asked me in Korean what I was doing out so late, and I pulled out my CID badge and showed it to him. My get-out-of-jail-free card. CID agents were exempt from the midnight-to-four curfew. After examining my badge by the glow of a penlight, he handed it back to me and saluted. I returned the salute.

But his interruption was enough to ruin my reverie. I was chasing a ghost, searching for a wisp of hope in a landscape where none existed.

I slipped my badge back into my jacket, stuck my hands into my pockets, and, head down, marched back to the main gate of Yongsan Compound.

The next morning was a Saturday, but most Army offices operated for a half day on Saturday. At least for the military people. Civilians—both Korean and American—were off on Saturday since they worked only a forty-hour work week. Riley was in the office reading his *Stars and Stripes*, but Miss Kim's *hangul* typewriter was covered in wrinkled plastic. Without her, the office seemed dour, less full of life. But as it turned out, I was glad she wasn't there to witness what came next.

Colonel Brace, the 8th Army Provost Marshal, was generally a mild-mannered man. Tough, but low-key. This time, when he bellowed from his office, he used the voice of a wounded bull, so loud that Riley snapped his head up and dropped his copy of the *Stripes*.

"Sueño," the Colonel yelled. "Bascom. I want you in my office right now!"

Ernie and I looked at one another. Ernie said, "What'd we do?"

"You got me."

Staff Sergeant Riley never missed a chance to be officious.

He stood up from behind his desk. "*NOW!*" he said, pointing down the hallway. "You heard the man."

"Sit on it and rotate," Ernie told him. But we both rose to our feet and marched down the hallway, condemned men on our way to the gallows. Ernie leaned toward me and whispered, "Deny *everything*."

Which is what I would've done, except I didn't have the chance.

Colonel Brace, wearing his khaki uniform, stood behind his desk with his hands on his narrow hips. The flags of the United States, the Republic of Korea, and the United Nations Command hung from polished wooden poles behind him. He pointed to an unfolded newspaper on his desk. Ernie and I stepped forward to peer at it. "Advance copy. Hits newsstands tomorrow. The PX manager hand-carried it over."

Gazing down, Ernie inhaled sharply.

It was the *Overseas Observer*. There, on a page-three spread, was a large black-and-white photograph. Of us. Me and Ernie. I recognized the place, although the shot had been taken at a sharp angle. We'd been a few yards away from Han's Tailor Shop, and it must've been just after Mr. Cho had returned to his store, when the crazy woman had blinded us with her flash-bulb. In the photo, Ernie and I looked completely caught off guard, having both turned to look at whomever had snapped the picture. In the distance behind us, clearly illuminated by the light of the flash, was a sign in *hangul* with a small-print English translation: THE KUKMIN BANK. That in itself wouldn't have been so bad. So we were standing on a sidewalk in front of a bank. Who cared? But it was the article that made Colonel Brace hopping mad.

The story explained everything. The first bank robbery, the bank guard being slammed in the face with a rifle butt and suffering lost teeth and a broken jaw, the thieves escaping with over two million *won*, and the fact that both Korean and US law enforcement were completely stymied as to the whereabouts of the perpetrators.

The byline belonged to somebody named Katie Byrd Worthington. She was, I imagined, the woman who'd blinded us with her flashbulb when she'd snapped our picture. The headline said it all: GIS ROB KOREAN BANK. And below that in smaller font: BANK GUARD INJURED. MILLIONS STOLEN.

In the body of the article, Katie Byrd Worthington noted that the millions in the headline were in *won* and not in US dollars, but when it came to the *Overseas Observer*, who read past the headlines? The caption beneath the photo identified both me and Ernie by name and claimed that we, the CID agents working the case, were completely baffled. Which was corroborated by, if nothing else, the confused expressions on our faces.

Colonel Brace jammed his forefinger into the photo. "You're making us look bad," he said. "Like morons stumbling around in the night." He waited for us to defend ourselves. When neither of us did, he continued. "And worse: the local AP and UPI stringers are going to pick this up. They won't take it at face value, but they'll look into it and find out it's true. And they'll probably dig up the second robbery and the bank teller's death while they're at it. We are in *deep shit!*" Colonel Brace paused, breathing heavily, as if to regain control. "We had a handle on this," he said, "but now it's ruined. Because of you two."

I was about to explain that it wasn't our fault. That we were just doing our jobs, canvassing the area the way that Burrows and Slabem should've done in the first place. That this *Overseas Observer* reporter, Katie Byrd Worthington, had snuck up on us and practically attacked us to get that photo. If anybody was to blame, it was her. I was about to say all this, but then I stopped. No point. Colonel Brace knew all these things, or at least most of them. Right now was not the time to contradict a bird colonel, not when he was angry and venting hot steam from an open throttle. That was a mistake no veteran soldier would make. In his rage, he was liable to order us to do something he wouldn't be able to take back. Even if he ended up regretting his directive, he'd feel obligated to enforce it, if only to maintain the dignity of his rank.

Ernie, prime troublemaker that he usually was, also kept his mouth shut. Even he knew that when a man with as much power over our lives as the Provost Marshal was angry, the wisest course of action was to pucker up and take the ass-chewing, no matter how unfair.

When Colonel Brace regained a semblance of self-control, he said, "And there's *this*!" He grabbed the edge of the paper and flipped to the front page. As he did, I wondered what story could possibly be more important than armed GIs robbing a Korean bank. What travesty could possibly have won out the contest for the front page?

There were a number of article snippets there, squibs edged around another gorgeous pinup girl. Some concerned Vietnam and others various military bases throughout the Pacific: Guam, Okinawa, the Philippines, Sasebo Naval Base in Japan. But Ernie and I didn't have to scan long to find the article Colonel Brace wanted us to see. Above the fold, above the smiling bathing beauty, there it was, the headline in bold print and in black and white for the world to see.

SEX CONVOY TO THE DMZ

And beneath that a photo of a half-dozen young Caucasian women, most bundled in army-issue winter parkas, elaborate hair-dos waving in the breeze, sitting on wooden fold-down benches on either side of the bed of a three-quarter-ton truck. Two hel-meted American MPs sat hunched in the rear, rifles pointing skyward, faces grim as they guarded their precious cargo.

"What the hell?" Ernie asked, allowing the question to fade into the ether.

"My sentiments exactly," said Colonel Brace.

-7-

Colonel Brace had no idea what to do about the photograph of the women or the accompanying article. According to the reporter, the very same Katie Byrd Worthington, the photograph had been provided to the *Overseas Observer* anonymously by an American soldier who'd been part of the escort team. Although the informant hadn't talked to the women directly, the scuttlebutt was that they were "party girls," as the *Observer* described them, being transported north to the ROK Army III Corps area along the DMZ for a meeting of honchos—not only Korean generals, but also one American general and one or two representatives from other allied nations. The MPs involved groused about having to operate as pimps, but after making the delivery, the entire squad had been given a three-day pass, which largely smoothed ruffled feathers.

"You want us to investigate this, sir?" Ernie asked.

"Hell no. I want you to find this Katie Byrd Worthington and . . . and . . ."

"Dump her in the Han River?" Ernie asked helpfully.

"No. Don't hurt her. Just bring her here. To me."

"If she's a reporter," I said, "the Eighth Army Public Affairs Office must've issued her credentials. All they have to do is pull them, and she won't be allowed on base any longer."

Colonel Brace shook his head.

"Two reasons we can't do that. First, the *Overseas Observer* has lawyers. They'd raise hell back in the States with the Pentagon and with Congress. Second, it probably wouldn't do any good. It looks like this woman, Katie Whatever-her-name-is, knows her way around. Even off post she finds a way to gather dirt." He shook his head again. "There's too many big-mouthed GIs around willing to give her what she wants."

Maybe the GIs would be more circumspect, I thought, if the brass weren't ordering them to transport hookers.

"You want us to *kidnap* Katie Worthington?" Ernie asked.

Colonel Brace pounded his fist on his desk. "I don't mean *kidnap* her, dammit. I just want to talk to her. Find her and convince her to speak to me. That's all I'm asking." He glanced back at the photo. "Somebody's got to put a stop to this."

"What if it's true?" I asked.

"Especially if it's true."

"Will this issue be on the stands tomorrow?" I asked.

"Not if I can help it."

■ ■ ■

On the way out of the CID office, neither Ernie nor I were overly concerned about the hookers being transported up to III Corps. We had the bank robbery investigation to worry about, and to us—if not to Colonel Brace—that seemed like more of a life-or-death matter. I kept remembering those employees on the front steps of the Daehan Bank, staring at me, rebuke in their eyes, anguish in their hearts.

Brace, meanwhile, had to keep the 8th Army honchos happy, and there was nothing they hated more than a scandal—especially a sex scandal. Mainly because of questions the negative press would attract: Were officers misusing funds? Committing infidelities? Ernie and I cared more about bringing our fellow GIs to justice and preventing any other innocent Korean civilians from being murdered. So without telling Brace, we decided to work on our main case before starting our search for the redoubtable Katie Byrd Worthington.

"Three ways," I told Ernie, "we might be able to track down the robbers."

"Name 'em."

"First, find the vehicle. Every Army jeep is assigned to a motor pool and has to be dispatched by a specific soldier. Find the jeep, find the soldier."

"Good luck with that," Ernie said. "There must be two or three dozen US Army motor pools in-country. Some of them with hundreds of vehicles."

"Okay, slow, I admit. But possible with enough shoe leather. And faster if we can find something to narrow the search."

"Like the unit designation," he said, "which we don't have."

"Second, the weapons. Every soldier in Eighth Army has a weapons card with their name and unit typed on it, and they have to turn it into the arms room in order to check out a weapon."

"And there are more arms rooms than there are motor pools."

"Right. I know. A lot of shoe leather. A lot of time. Third is the authorized pass sign in/sign out register."

"You think these guys were on pass?"

"Maybe," I replied. "Or leave. If they were on duty when they robbed the banks, they risked somebody noticing they were missing and getting suspicious."

"Checking sign in/sign out logs at every unit in-country would take forever. Maybe we could issue an announcement on Armed Forces Radio asking supervisors to notify us if they had any men missing during the time periods when the banks were robbed."

"The honchos would never allow it. They're trying to keep this quiet."

"Too late. Katie Byrd Worthington already dropped a dime on them."

"Maybe something more discreet," I suggested. "Like a confidential directive from the Chief of Staff to all the subordinate unit commanders, giving them the particulars of the case and asking them to check who amongst their personnel were unaccounted for during the time of the robberies."

"Yeah. That might work."

"Or it might alert the thieves to what we're up to."

"Yeah. Make them cover their tracks even more carefully than they already have. And at least half the commanders won't cooperate. Few supervisors like to welcome law enforcement into their commands."

"Especially at Division," I said.

Ernie nodded his head.

We knew from hard experience that the honchos of the 2nd US Infantry Division despised interference from the higher headquarters of 8th Army. And they despised anybody like us who wandered into their territory representing 8th Army. It seemed odd that down here on Yongsan Compound, 8th Army Headquarters, Ernie and I were treated like outcasts for our CID positions. But up at Division, we were treated like founding fathers of the 8th Army establishment. Pure hatred.

"So what do we do?" Ernie asked.

"We need one more piece of information to set us on the right track."

"Like what?"

"A unit designation, like you said. Or a report from one of the Division MP checkpoints concerning suspicious activity."

"We don't know that the bank robbers *are* from Division,"

Ernie said. "Sure, they drove from the Daehan Bank to Tong-il Lo. But they might've turned south toward Seoul instead of continuing north toward the Second Division area."

"They might've," I agreed.

"In fact, they might've headed north just to throw us off. They might not be near Division or Seoul at all. They might be from one of the support units down south."

"Or the Air Force," I said.

"Could be. The eyewitness descriptions of their uniforms were vague. And a Korean citizen, even one who served in the Korean military, isn't likely to be well versed in the differences in uniforms between branches of the American military service."

"These guys could even be American or European civilians," I said.

"Don't side with Eighth Army."

"I know, it's unlikely. I mean how would they have gotten the jeep? How would they have gotten the weapons and the uniforms and the camo stick? But it's not impossible."

"No," Ernie agreed. "Not impossible. But pretty freaking unlikely."

"Okay," I said. "Let's assume they're Army. Maybe Air Force. There are only a handful of Navy and Marine Corps assigned to Korea. So Army, most likely. What would you do if you just received your share of two million *won*?"

"Party," Ernie said.

"So maybe we come at this from a completely different angle. Maybe we can find some Cheap Charley GIs who are suddenly spending like drunken sailors."

"Which would require us to check the bars and nightclubs."

"Yes."

"We're good at that."

"I'll say," I said.

"In fact," Ernie continued, "I'd say we're the best anyone has ever seen."

I didn't quibble.

That night, we started with Itaewon. We talked to everyone we could think of: business girls, cocktail waitresses, bartenders, strippers, even the owners of some of the clubs. Nobody had noticed any GIs spending wildly. "All Cheap Charley," one woman told us, waving her hand to indicate the whole of the US military. "Cheap Charley GI, they never spend *nothing*."

That seemed like somewhat of an exaggeration.

To keep up appearances, Ernie and I quaffed down cold OB Beer and watered-down bourbon, and by the end of the night, all we received for our efforts other than a long string of negative reports were two serious cases of inebriation. And in the morning, two hangovers.

Unfortunately, no leads.

Somehow, the next day—a Sunday—Colonel Brace, or perhaps the 8th Army Chief of Staff, had convinced the PX

Manager not to put the *Overseas Observer* on sale. The spot where it should've stood on shelves was empty. That probably wasn't legal, but they didn't call 8th Army 8th *Imperial* Army for nothing. Still, their plan to keep salacious dirt away from the troops backfired. Within hours, Korean boys were selling the *Overseas Observer* outside the gate at 1,000 *won* a pop. Two bucks. And GIs were paying it. Apparently, word about hookers being transported to the DMZ had spread faster than free beer before payday.

At noon, Strange met us at the snack bar, so excited he forgot to ask if we'd had any *strange* lately. Instead, he leaned forward, glancing left and right, and stealthily pulled a folded tabloid out of his back pocket.

"Have you read this?" he asked, shoving a copy of the *Overseas Observer* toward us.

"It's come to our attention," I replied.

"Prime female stuff, on its way north for the enjoyment of our self-sacrificing commanders leading the defense of the Free World. Not that they don't deserve a little R&R. It's just, what's in it for the troops? That's what I want to know."

"Nothing's in it for the troops," Ernie said.

"That's what I mean. It ain't fair."

"Would it be fair if you were invited to the party?"

"Sure. That's all I'm asking, just a little *strange*."

I'd heard enough. "You don't know that this article has any truth in it at all."

"Of course it's true," Strange replied, hitting the tabloid with the back of his hand. "It's all right here, chapter and verse."

"That reporter could've made everything up."

"What about the photo? That doesn't lie."

"You don't know when that picture was taken, or who those women are. You don't even know *where* the picture was taken."

"Look here," Strange said, "those girders in front of the truck. That's Freedom Bridge." The military-controlled bridge that crossed the Imjin River and led directly to the DMZ.

I glanced at the photo. "Could be. But maybe not. There are a lot of bridges like that in the world."

"Look at the unit designation down here," Strange said, pointing to the back bumper of the three-quarter-ton truck. He brought it closer to his eyes, lifted his shades, and studied it. Finally he said, "That's the five-ninety-something MP Company."

"Let me see that," Ernie said, grabbing the paper out of his hands. He looked closely at the photo and said, "Bull. Too fuzzy. You can't make nothing out."

"I've got twenty-twenty vision," Strange told him.

"Then why do you wear shades all the time?"

"To keep the women off me."

"They wouldn't be able to control themselves otherwise?"

"You got it."

"God, you're cracked," Ernie said.

"Tell us," I told Strange, "what's the reaction to all this up at the head shed?"

He looked around again as if expecting a spy to pop out of a potted plant. Then he grabbed his throat and rasped. "Can't talk on a dry throat."

"Hot chocolate again?"

"With two marshmallows."

This time, Ernie got up to buy it. After he left, I said, "Okay, spill."

"Not till I get my hot chocolate."

"*Now*," I said.

"Okay, okay. Don't get antsy." He leaned toward me and whispered, "The honchos are pissed. At the broad who wrote the article, sure, but also the MPs who ratted on their commanders. But there's more."

I motioned for him to go on, but he crossed his arms and frowned like a petulant child. Ernie brought the hot chocolate and purposely sloshed some of it onto the table top. Strange pulled a napkin out of the holder and sopped up the warm brown liquid.

"You're clumsy," he said.

"I'll show you clumsy," Ernie said, knuckling his fist.

"Okay, okay." Strange dropped the second and then the third moist napkin into a thin pile.

"So," I said. "The honchos are angry at the reporter and at the MPs who talked to her. What else?"

Strange sipped on his hot chocolate, set it down, and said, "They're angry at Lawrence of the Frozen Chosun."

"Who?"

"That's what they're calling him up at the head shed. Lieutenant General Abner Jennings Crabtree, Commander of First Corps. In charge of all the divisions along the DMZ, including the ROK Army Third Corps."

"Why are they angry at him? Because of this party?"

"Not that. They could care less about that. Or they wouldn't have, if word hadn't gotten out. What they're worried about is that General Crabtree is getting too big for his britches; he's pointing out flaws in our defensive posture, making his superiors look bad. And he's gone native. That's why they call him Lawrence of the Frozen Chosun. He speaks Korean and everything."

As Strange sipped his hot chocolate again, I said, "There something wrong with speaking Korean?"

"*Yeah*. You ought to know. You start speaking Korean, and pretty soon the Koreans lose respect for you, and sooner than that they're leading you around by the nose and you lose sight of why in the hell we're over here."

He had my attention now. "So why *are* we over here?"

"To civilize the natives," he said. With that he picked up a spoon and shoveled both the soggy marshmallows into his mouth. Once they were firmly in place, he set down his cup and started chewing. Mouth open. I looked away, trying to hide my disgust. Ernie smirked, staring straight at Strange.

When Strange finally swallowed, it seemed like the entire

mush lowered itself visibly down his gullet past three or four roadblocks, like a ship making its way through a canal strewn with muck.

"Korean culture is older than American culture," I pointed out to Strange.

"See? You've gone native. So has General Crabtree. They say he wears a papa-*san* outfit and everything."

Strange meant *hanbok*, the loose cotton pantaloons and tunic covered by a sleeveless silk vest traditionally worn by men of the educated elite known as *yangban*.

"And Crabtree pretty much lives along the DMZ amongst the ROK Army units. The more isolated, the better. Those units guarding the mountain passes between North and South Korea."

"That's his job, isn't it?" Ernie asked. "To make sure the ROK Army is combat-ready?"

"Why doesn't he do that the way everybody else does? The way that makes more sense?"

"Which is what?" I asked.

"By studying reports."

"*Paperwork*," Ernie said, his voice filled with disdain.

Strange sat up straighter. "What's wrong with paperwork?" As head of the Classified Documents Section, Strange lived and died by paperwork.

"Sounds to me," I said, "like this General Crabtree is a pretty good officer."

"Says you. But Eighth Army was out to get him before. With this *Oversexed Observer* article, he's absolute toast."

"Whether it's true or not?" I said.

"Who gives a shit about whether it's true or not?" Once again, Strange rapped the paper with the back of his hand. "This gives them ammo."

"So why doesn't the Eighth Army Commander fire him?"

"Are you nuts?" Strange asked.

"Some people think so."

"Eighth Army can't fire General Crabtree. His father was a four-star general, his uncle a World War II hero."

"So?"

"Revenge. The Eighth Army Commander has two sons and a daughter in the Army. Crabtree doesn't have any sons, but he's got seven nephews, all in uniform with fast-track careers in front of them. You know, it's like they say up in North Korea—you execute one man, you have to execute two other generations along with him. Otherwise, one of the relatives will come back to get you."

"All those nephews are commissioned officers?"

"Every one," Strange said. "It's the family business."

"So what's Eighth Army gonna do about Lieutenant General Crabtree?"

"Let him twist in the wind. See if the legitimate news outlets pick up the story and how they handle it."

"And see if it gets back to Congress?"

"Oh, it'll get back to Congress."

"How do you know?"

"The Chief of Staff purchased twenty copies of today's *Oversexed Observer.* They've already been sent anonymously to powerful people in the Senate, the House, and the Pentagon."

"How do you know all this?"

"How do I know anything?"

"Because you're a genius," Ernie said facetiously.

"You better believe it," Strange replied, ignoring his tone.

"But you can't be sure they were mailed," I said. "You don't have certified return receipts."

"No. But I know."

"How?"

"Because I licked the stamps and put 'em on the envelopes and mailed 'em myself about an hour ago," Strange told us.

-8-

Strange said he'd only mailed the front page of the *Overseas Observer*, thereby excluding the article concerning the bank robberies. Eighth Army still wanted to keep the news of American GIs robbing and terrorizing and murdering innocent Korean citizens quiet for as long as they could. Which didn't seem like much longer, what with Katie Byrd Worthington running around loose.

Before we left, I challenged Strange about being the source of leaks to Katie Byrd Worthington. He was gravely offended.

"She doesn't have a need to know," he said.

"How about us?"

"You have a need to know."

"According to you," Ernie said. "But the honchos might not agree."

Strange shrugged. "I'm a highly-trained, classified-information expert. I make decisions on that basis."

"Under your own authority?"

"You complaining?" Strange asked.

Ernie held up his hands as if to ward off an argument. "No. You're right, Strange. You're right."

"The name's Harvey."

"Right. Sergeant First Class Harvey."

After we left the snack bar, Ernie asked me, "You think he's leaking to this Katie Byrd person?"

"Who knows? I doubt it matters. There are plenty of GIs who would be happy to talk to her. Most of them would kill for a little attention from a round-eye."

"Not me," Ernie said.

I wasn't so sure about that.

"So how do we find her?" Ernie asked.

"I have an idea."

"Don't you always?"

We headed for the office of the *Pacific Stars and Stripes.*

It was in a Quonset hut painted olive drab. Above the side entrance was a colorful sign with two crossed American flags, the logo of the *Stripes*. We tried the door, but it was locked.

"All the news that's fit to print," Ernie said, "except on Sundays."

An emergency contact form taped inside the window listed the names of four Americans. The branch editor was a civilian, and the two reporters were a Specialist 4 and a Corporal, respectively. The NCO in charge was a Master Sergeant by the name of Mortenson Cleveland.

We wandered over to the 8th Army Billeting Office and talked to the Specialist 5 working staff duty. After flashing our badges, he thumbed through his alphabetized file and determined that MSG Cleveland was assigned to Headquarters and Headquarters Company, senior NCO barracks number 7, room 109. It was almost a half-mile walk, and once we arrived, we pounded on the door of room 109, to no answer. Another GI wandered down the hallway.

"You seen Cleveland?" I asked.

"He's probably out."

"Where?"

"He's got a *yobo* in Samgakji."

Yobo was a term of endearment, most often used between married couples, similar to the English word "honey." GIs used it to signify a Korean girlfriend. Samgakji, or the three-horned intersection, was the area of town on the western edge of Yongsan Compound where most of the black troops hung out.

"Do you know his *yobo*'s name?" I asked.

"Who wants to know?"

I showed him my badge.

"What's he done?"

"Nothing. We just need some information."

"From the *Stars and Stripes*?" the guy asked. "I thought their main function was to put a happy face on everything."

"It is," I told him. "But Cleveland might be able to lead us to someone else. It's a long story."

"Are you going to arrest that general up at the ROK Third Corps who ordered the MPs to transport hookers for him?"

"We might," Ernie said. "If we can build a case. At this rate, nothing's going to happen."

The guy thought about it a moment and said, "Her name's Coco. Cute as a button, too. Cleveland put in his paperwork."

Marriage papers. For a GI to marry a Korean he had to receive permission from not only the US Army but also the Korean government, a process that took six to eight months.

"What club does Coco work in?" I asked.

"The Kitty Kat," he said.

At the Kitty Kat Club, the female bartender told us Coco didn't work there anymore. It took some time, but we bought a round of drinks and explained to her that we only wanted to talk to Coco's *yobo* in order to ask about his work. Not to cause trouble. She ripped a sheet of paper from a notebook she had stashed behind the bar and drew us a map.

"She live there," she told us. "Have a room in Hyun-suk Ohmma's house." The house of Hyun-suk's mother.

I thanked her and left a five hundred *won* tip. About a buck.

On the way out, Ernie said, "You're gonna spoil these people."

After a couple of wrong turns, we found the home of Hyun-suk's mother. Like virtually all the homes in Korean neighborhoods, it was surrounded by an eight-foot-high stone wall with a locked wooden gate in the front. But, likewise as with most local homes, during the day the small doorway carved into the gate was open. We ducked through and emerged into a dirt courtyard with a metal-handled pump atop a cement-floored drain. It occupied the center of the small, square yard and was surrounded by a few scraggly rose bushes. The inner wall on the left was lined with squat earthen kimchi jars. Beyond the courtyard, a narrow wooden porch flanked the front of an L-shaped building. One of four oil-papered latticework doors slid open, and a middle-aged Korean woman peered out.

"*Anyonghaseiyo*," I said. "Coco *odiseiyo*?" Where is Coco?

On the opposite side of the hooch, another door slid open and a younger woman with a heart-shaped face peeked into the courtyard.

"Hi, Coco," I said. "We're looking for Mort Cleveland."

Her eyes widened in surprise, but a long-fingered hand grabbed the edge of the sliding door and pulled it fully open. An American GI stared out at us suspiciously.

"Are you Master Sergeant Cleveland?" I asked, stepping forward and pulling out my badge.

"Yeah," he said. "What's wrong?"

He was a thin, smooth-skinned black man, and though he was seated and leaning on his elbow, from the length of his torso I guessed he was fairly tall.

"Nothing wrong," I said. "I'm Agent Sueño. This is my partner, Agent Bascom. We're looking for information on a person we're trying to locate."

"Just a minute," Cleveland said. He slid the door closed. After a couple of minutes of hurried conversation with Coco, Cleveland slid back the door and stepped out onto the porch. I was right. He was tall, about six feet, and very thin. Wearing slacks and a green army T-shirt, he squatted on the porch, reached down, and slipped on his shoes.

Behind him, Coco reappeared, this time holding a toddler.

"Hey," I said, "cute kid. What's his name?"

"Mort Junior," he told me.

So that was why Cleveland was putting in the paperwork.

"Are you guys going to question me here, or do we have to go somewhere?"

"Here's fine," I said.

When he was through tying his shoelaces, Mort Cleveland looked at me and said, "Am I in some sort of trouble?"

"No, nothing like that," I replied. "Just want to ask you a few questions."

Ernie stepped toward the middle-aged woman, who had completely emerged from her hooch and was now sitting cross-legged on her wooden porch, enjoying the show. He asked her "*byonso odi*?" Where's the outhouse?

She pointed toward a narrow passageway behind the hooch. Ernie disappeared into the shadows. I knew what he was doing, reconnoitering the back. That and actually taking a leak.

I sat down on the porch a few feet from Mort Cleveland

and pulled out my notebook. "Have you seen the *Overseas Observer* today?"

"That rag? Hell no. Why, what'd they do this time?"

"Big story. Up north. A photograph and everything. They're claiming that the First Corps Commander had the local MP Company drive a half-dozen hookers up to the ROK Army Third Corps."

"For what?"

"For a party sponsored there by the Third Corps Commander. One that lasted all weekend."

"This is news?"

"Well, it's a little different this time."

"Why?"

"The hookers aren't Korean."

"What are they?"

"Caucasian women."

"Ah," Cleveland said. "I see. The purity of the white race is under assault."

"I guess you could say that. The MPs are angry because they were ordered to act as pimps."

"Without the benefit of getting paid."

"They were granted a three-day pass."

Mortenson laughed. "God," he said. "Leave it up to the *Oversexed Observer* to ferret out a story like that."

"How many reporters do they have in-country?"

"Just one."

"Katie Worthington?"

"None other. Although don't discount the Byrd or she'll bite your head off."

"You've met?"

"A few times. She comes on compound occasionally, snooping around our office for leads on one thing or another. Of course, we never give her anything. Consequently, she hasn't been around for a while."

"Do you have any idea who might've given her this info on the First Corps commander?"

"None whatsoever."

"How about your other reporters?"

"You can ask, but I doubt it. They like their jobs. Get to travel around the country, snag a few bylines. Even if they're not staying in the army, it'll give them a good portfolio when they get out."

"So they wouldn't risk talking to Katie Byrd?"

"I'd be awfully surprised."

The little boy crawled out onto the porch. Cleveland grabbed him and lifted him into his arms. Then he hoisted him in the air and kissed his stomach, the child giggling uncontrollably.

"Your paperwork almost done?" I said, nodding toward Coco.

"We're getting there." He set the boy down. "How'd you know about that?"

"Just a guess."

Ernie emerged from behind the building and flashed me our hand signal for "all clear." We didn't suspect Cleveland of anything. Checking our surroundings was standard procedure. In the business of law enforcement, it paid to be cautious.

"How would I find Katie Byrd Worthington?" I asked.

"She smokes a lot," he said. "Stands outside the office sometimes and shares cigarettes with our photographer, Freddy Chang."

"Korean hire?"

"Yeah."

"You think he can tell me where to find her?"

"Doubt it. But one time she did pass him one of those boxes of wooden matches that Korean hotels give out. It said Bando."

The Bando Hotel had been built by the Japanese prior to World War II, and it was one of the few multi-story buildings in the capital city to have survived the vicious artillery barrages of the Korean War.

"Okay, thanks," I said. "How about other than that? Does the *Overseas Observer* have an office somewhere?"

"No. Not in Korea. The only office they have, I think, is in Germany, where they started."

Which figured, since over a half million US servicemen—not to mention their dependents—had been stationed mostly in Germany, but also throughout the rest of Western Europe, since the end of World War II.

"So Katie works freelance?"

"I'll say. You never know where she'll turn up."

I rubbed my eyes. "Yeah. We definitely know that now." I thanked him and shook his hand. "We'll see if we can track her down."

"What are you gonna do? Lock her up?"

"No. We need to talk to her. It'll probably be a waste of time."

"With Katie Byrd Worthington, nothing's a waste of time."

"What do you mean?"

"You'll see." He half grinned to himself.

I stood to leave and thought of something. "By the way, how'd you get the first name Mortenson? I'm curious."

"Oh." He nodded, not at all offended by the question. "It's my mom's maiden name. Her dad died when she was an infant and she didn't have any brothers, so she wanted to keep the family name alive somehow."

"Sad story," I said.

"Yeah. She's proud of him. He was with one of the segregated black American units that fought with the French army during the First World War. He was awarded the French Legion of Honor. Posthumously."

"No wonder you joined the army," I said.

"Yeah, I guess it was inevitable."

"And your son will carry it on."

"That's why we call him Junior." He reached out and tickled the boy's round tummy, making him chortle.

I thanked Mort Cleveland and nodded to Coco, and we left.

"The Bando," Ernie said. "That's all the way downtown."

It would've been a hike to retrieve Ernie's jeep, and besides, there was little to no parking in downtown Seoul. After deciding to find a cab, we headed for the main road, walking swiftly through the narrow alleys of Samgakji.

On the way, Ernie said, "I feel guilty for not working the bank robbery case."

"We have nothing to go on. Without some sort of break, there's not much we can do. We might as well get this Katie Byrd Worthington business out of the way."

We emerged from the pedestrian pathway onto a two-lane road that led to one of the side gates of Yongsan Compound on our right and left toward the main road that ran north to Seoul Station. A man pushed a wooden cart laden with *yang-pa*, foreign onions, and a small mountain of glimmering green Napa cabbage. He was above us on a slight incline and had apparently not been paying attention, losing his grip, which allowed his cart to roll. Out of his control, it trundled straight toward us.

Just then, a jeep parked across the street and to our right, started its engine and headed in our direction. The cart was still barreling toward us, picking up speed. I grabbed Ernie's elbow and said, "Watch it."

We both stepped back into the pedestrian lane.

As we did, something whizzed in front of us at eye-level like an angry wasp and exploded a portion of the brick wall to our left, turning it into a small mushroom cloud of dust.

-9-

Ernie hit the ground before I did. I suppose it was his keener reflexes from his two years in Vietnam. He yanked at my sleeve as he dove, and I realized vaguely what was happening and fell to the dirt along with him.

The produce cart hit the brick wall and jolted to a halt in front of us, and from between its bicycle-like tires, I saw the jeep pass directly opposite us and keep going. I crawled forward beneath the cart and craned my neck to see what I could of the speeding vehicle. The rear bumper was covered with black tape, leaving no visible numbers or unit designation. The jeep hit cross traffic on the main road and rammed its way forward, forcing kimchi cabs to swerve and honk their horns like a gaggle of startled geese. It completed a sharp right turn and disappeared.

"For Christ's sake," Ernie said. He rose cautiously to his feet, knees flexed, ready to fall back to the ground if necessary. "What the hell was *that*?"

"You're the combat veteran," I said.

He glanced both ways. "Get up. I think we're all clear now. But somebody fired at us from that *freaking* jeep."

I rose to my feet, using the side of the wooden cart for balance. The owner had stopped and was glancing back and forth as nervously as we were.

"Maybe that GI doesn't like onions," I said.

"That's it," Ernie said, laughing. "His mom forced him to eat too many shallots, and now he's taking it out on every greengrocer he sees."

"You think it was the bank robbers?" I said, dusting myself off.

"Probably," Ernie said. "Who else hates us that much? Other than a few female acquaintances, I mean." He placed his hands on his hips and paced in a small circle, calming himself. Finally, he looked up and said, "But how the hell'd they find us?"

"I don't know. I'm working on that."

We could've called the Korean cops or marched back to the compound and reported this incident to the MPs. We decided against it because that would take too much time, and we didn't see what good it would do. Besides, I could always slip a description of what happened into our own report, if I decided to. What we did instead was search for the spent bullet. After a few minutes, we found it. It had rebounded across the pedestrian alleyway and rolled next to a loose brick. Ernie picked it up with a snack bar napkin he had in his pocket and tucked it away for later analysis.

Keeping a wary eye out for more jeeps, we walked to the main road.

"These guys aren't playing," Ernie said.

"No. You saw what they did to the bank guard, and to that teller."

"With her they were shooting to frighten everybody, and the ricochet got her. This time, they were shooting directly at us."

"If it was them."

"Who else would be after us?" Ernie paused, thinking about it, arms folded.

"Nobody," I admitted.

"And how in the hell did they find us?" he asked again, the question still bothering him.

We waved down a cab and climbed in the back. The little sedans were a tight fit, but we managed. The driver pulled the front passenger seat forward, giving me more legroom. I told him we wanted to go to the Bando Hotel, and he flipped the metal flag atop the meter, and we took off.

For the first few minutes, Ernie and I were quiet, reflecting on what had happened, still trying to slow our heart rates. Outside, a guy on a sturdy Korean-made bicycle pedaled near us, cardboard pallets of fresh eggs tied with twine to the metal platform atop his rear tire. They were balanced to a height a full two feet above his head.

"If he falls," Ernie said, "that'll make one hell of an omelet."

I imagined a bullet tearing through my cranium and the similar mess it would've made.

Pedestrians carried briefcases or lugged too-large loads on A-frames strapped to their backs or pushed carts laden with more weight than they were designed to carry. Everyone was working hard. Straining. Nobody strolled along aimlessly. They had a mission to accomplish, and they went about it as if their lives depended on it. Which it often did.

I thought about the bank robbers. Wherever they were stationed, they must've somehow spotted a copy of this week's *Overseas Observer*. Which confirmed, in my mind, that they were GIs. Everybody in uniform in-country was buzzing about the hookers being transported north toward the DMZ by order of the I Corps commander. So if these criminals were on or anywhere near a military base, they almost certainly would've heard about the latest *Overseas Observer* newsflash. They would've read the salacious headlines on the front page and thumbed through the paper, stopping at page three and studying the picture of me and Ernie in front of the Kukmin Bank. Reading the article, probably, from start to finish. Thanks to Katie Byrd Worthington, it was easy for them. They knew now what we looked like, that we were CID agents in Seoul, and that we were coming after them. What better plan than to take us out, and immediately?

What did they know about us? Had they done enough research to know we were the only CID agents capable of operating off base? The only ones with a direct line to the Chief Homicide Inspector of the Korean National Police? Had they done their homework? Or were they working the odds, figuring that if we had enough gumption to go after them by canvassing the shops in Itaewon, if they pushed us out of the picture, the investigators who replaced us wouldn't be as motivated? Our hypothetical replacements would, understandably, fear for their lives. Maybe they'd hesitate before pushing the case forward, or at least be a hell of a lot more reserved than me and Ernie were being.

I explained my thinking to Ernie.

"Makes sense," he said. "Still, though, how would they have found us so fast?"

"Pretty obvious they have access to a jeep. They drive to Seoul—"

"Or they're already stationed here."

"Yeah. Could be. Either way, they check the CID office and see it's closed. So they start cruising around Yongsan Compound—past the parade field, past the bowling alley, maybe they park their jeep in the PX parking lot for a while."

"Send somebody inside to see if we're there."

"Yeah," I agreed. "Maybe. Anyway, somewhere along the line they spot us. Maybe at the snack bar, maybe near the *Stars and Stripes* office."

"Why not take us out then?"

"Too many eyes on compound," I said. "Trained eyes, people who would recognize the sound of gunfire coming from an M16. People who would immediately check the unit designation of a fleeing jeep."

"And on compound, they can't tape up their bumper."

"No. An MP patrol would pull them over in seconds. But off base, the Korean civilians ignore US military vehicles. In Samgakji, army vehicles driving through are so common they're practically invisible. And whether the unit designation is taped over or not is of no concern. Not to civilians."

"Right. So the bank robbers get lucky. They've spotted us walking down the road and they follow us off base, watch us as we go down the side streets of Samgakji."

"But they don't want to be seen following us on foot carrying a freaking assault rifle. So they park the jeep, tape over the unit designation, and sit and wait, patiently, like hunters in a duck blind."

"And take their potshot," Ernie said, "when the two dumb *freaking* mallards emerge back out into the sunlight."

"A plan that would've worked, too, if it hadn't been for that guy with the onion cart. He saved our bacon. We should've tipped him."

"God, Sueño. You're the only guy in the world who wants to tip a clumsy old man pushing a produce cart."

"So after attempting to kill us," I said, "they drive off."

"Why didn't they take a second shot?" Ernie asked. "Or come after us while we were rolling around in the dirt?"

"For all they know," I replied, "we're packing. Carrying our .45s under our jackets. They're afraid we'll start shooting back."

"And a shootout would alert even the half-asleep gate guards back on the compound."

"Yeah. So they drive off, making their getaway. Then turn north toward Seoul Station, the same direction we're traveling now. There are KNP checkpoints up ahead so they have to stop somewhere and rip that masking tape off their bumper."

As we talked, I'd been keeping an eye out for just such a place. So far, I hadn't seen one.

"Actually, in this traffic," I continued, "they could get out of their jeep at a red light, run around back and rip off the tape. All these impatient drivers probably wouldn't notice or wouldn't care. GIs do crazy things. It's none of their business."

"Yeah," Ernie agreed. "Could be."

The cab approached the front entranceway to the Bando. A man wearing a brimmed cap and a coat with epaulettes blew his whistle and waved us in. Under the enormous cement overhang, the little kimchi cab rolled to a stop, but before anyone could open the doors for us, Ernie and I popped out. I paid the driver, then we pushed through the rotating glass door and entered the lobby.

It was as if we'd wandered into the past. The tattered carpet on the floor reeked of mildew. The scarred mahogany of the check-in counter gleamed with layers of polish that I imagined had originally been applied when Japanese and Nazi diplomats used the Bando Hotel to plan the overthrow of legitimately elected governments. A heavy stone pot sat in the center of the floor, holding a jagged rose bush which seemed to be committing suicide by refusing water. Ancient celadon vases sat perched atop curved-leg tables in front of flower-papered walls.

Ernie inhaled deeply. “Smells like nobody’s aired this place out since fleas were invented.” He nodded toward the head clerk. “That guy looks like he’s about to foreclose on a mausoleum.”

The head clerk was indeed a bony old man with dried skin hanging over a skull that had long since fossilized. I stepped in front of him and pulled out my identification.

“Katie Worthington,” I said. “She’s expecting us.”

The old skeleton made a show of pulling on the sleeves of his wool coat, opening the ledger hidden on a platform just out of sight, and checking it carefully. After staring long enough for his moist eyes to glaze over, he raised his head and said, “We have no guest by that name.”

“She’s a reporter,” I said. “For the *Overseas Observer*.”

His eyes studied me unwaveringly, as if I’d spoken ancient Greek.

“Try Katie *Byrd* Worthington,” I told him.

He tugged on his sleeves again and reopened the ledger. A bony finger ran down a long list and he finally looked back up at me. "I'll see if she's in."

He turned and grabbed a black telephone on the back counter. I tried to catch what room number he dialed, but he anticipated that and shuffled right and then left to block my view.

"Crusty old son of a bitch," Ernie said.

The clerk spoke in muffled tones, not just for a few seconds but for almost a minute. He hung up the phone and turned back to us. "She's not in," he said.

"You just talked to her," Ernie said, pointing at the phone.

Again, the old clerk stared impassively, not responding.

Ernie was about to do what I assumed he would, but instead of stopping him, I decided to help him out. I moved to my left and slammed my hand on the counter, then leaned forward and reached down, grasping for a pen. Startled, the old clerk rushed toward me, and as he did so, Ernie leapt across the counter like a dolphin sliding out of a pool and, balancing on his stomach, reached down and grabbed the leather-bound ledger. He pulled it up and out and sped off, racing with it to a seat against the far wall.

The clerk panicked. He was screaming something in Korean that I didn't quite catch, but it must've had something to do with calling security, because before his voice faded into blessed silence, three men in black suits appeared, as if by magic, from a door behind the central stairwell.

Ernie handed the ledger to me, stood, pulled the pair of brass knuckles he always carried from his pocket, and charged the three security guards.

Apparently he didn't slug anybody right away, but grappled with them to slow them down. Which gave me time to open the ledger and frantically flip the pages until I found an entry in *hangul* that, when you sounded it out, came to something like *Kei-ti Bu-duh Wo-ting-ton.* Korean usually skips over "r" sounds before consonants and doesn't have "th" sound at all. I checked the room number.

While Ernie shouted at the security guards and they shouted back at him, I slipped past the shoving mass and tossed the ledger back onto the check-in counter, then sprinted for the stairway that led upstairs to the seventh floor.

I was winded by the time I got there. Not much, but enough to want to slow my breathing before knocking on the door of room 703. Unfortunately, I didn't have time. So with my chest still heaving, I pounded on the door and waited to see darkness behind the peephole.

There wasn't any. Nobody looking out. I pounded again. Still no shadow. I tried the knob. Locked. She must've gone out, probably immediately after the desk clerk had called to notify her that someone was here to see her. What in the hell was she so nervous about? If she just left, that meant that I must've missed her. Maybe by seconds. She hadn't come down the stairwell, or I would've bumped into her. And it seemed unlikely that she would've taken the elevator, since she would've been trapped and would've been seen by whoever was in the lobby. So where had she gone? How would she get downstairs?

And then I spotted it down the hallway. A red sign that said PISANG-GU, emergency exit.

The sign was wrinkled and yellowed and seemed to have been pasted there back before the end of the Chosun dynasty. It sat above an open window. I ran toward it and poked my head outside and saw a rickety metal contraption that might've once passed as a fire escape, although I doubted it would hold my weight. Down below, at the bottom of the spindly steps, a figure seemed to be hanging by her hands like a trapeze artist, clinging for dear life to the last rung of the ladder. Katie Byrd Worthington, I presumed. But she was hesitating, as if she'd reached the limits of her gymnastic abilities.

She looked up and saw me peering down at her. We made eye contact. Apparently, that was the catalyst. She let go of her handhold and plummeted the last few feet to the ground, hitting hard, and falling on her butt as the melon attached to her body snapped backward and slammed into the dirty blacktop below. Except it wasn't a melon, it was her skull. Even from up here, I could hear the *thwunk.*

Apparently, she had a hard head. Maybe a requirement of her position at the *Overseas Observer*. She pushed herself up to a seated position, rubbed the back of her cranium, and slowly rose to her feet. Some sort of equipment bag had landed near her. She picked it up, reached inside, and pulled out a camera on a long leather strap. She swung it in a looping arc over her shoulder. Thus outfitted, she took a few uncertain steps and, as if remembering something, stopped and looked up at me. She was a blonde woman with short bobbed hair. Skinny, almost spindly, wearing khaki pants and a multi-pocketed matching safari jacket over a blue blouse. Once we made eye contact again, she flipped me the bird. Apparently satisfied, she retracted her finger, grinned, turned, and trotted off.

-10-

When the elevator doors opened, I burst into the lobby.

Ernie was still in a shoving match with the security guards, his right fist cocked and covered with the cold brass of his store-bought knuckles. I shouted at him as I ran past. "She's getting away!"

I shoved through the rotating door and felt it shudder as Ernie slammed into the door behind me. We ran past the liv-eried doormen and halted when we hit the street. I pointed west. "That way," I said. "She just flipped me the bird."

"How rude," Ernie said.

"Check the cars going past," I said, "especially the taxis."

Ernie and I ran alongside the flow, peering into the back of every kimchi cab we saw, startling the drivers and the passengers. Like a herd of angry cattle jostling one another, traffic was stopped at a red light in front of a major intersection, no one paying any attention to the designated lanes. But as Ernie and I darted between the cars, the light changed to green. Suddenly, like parched buffalo heading toward a watering hole, the cars began their inexorable stampede. We kept darting between them, holding up our open palms and shouting at them to stop, but gradually had to make our way back to the safety of the sidewalk.

Finally out of harm's way, we stood side by side. Ernie ran his hand through his short hair. "Nothing. How'd she get away from you?"

"Down the fire escape. Freaking Harry Houdini wouldn't have followed her. If she didn't grab a kimchi cab, what'd she do?"

"A bus," Ernie said.

We glanced down the road, past the Bando and beyond to where I'd seen her turn and flip me the bird.

"She must've gone east," Ernie said. "There's a bus stop down there."

"Right," I said.

And then we were running.

One long block past the Bando, a bus was pulling away from the curb. Ernie pulled his badge, waved it in the air and ran straight at the front of the bus, ordering it to halt. But the driver pulled farther out into traffic and swerved around us, even as Ernie cursed and waved his arms. I almost made it to the side door, which was still open. A bus maid in her full uniform of blue skirt and red vest and red beanie was holding on for dear life, spread-eagled in front of the opening, making sure that no one in the packed jumble of humanity behind her popped out onto the pavement. But the bus was moving too fast now for me to hop on, and besides, every step was filled with human feet. Even if I'd been crazy enough to make the leap onto the moving bus, I would have been unable to find a toehold.

As the internal combustion leviathan glided past, I searched the faces staring out the steam-smeared windows. One was familiar. A narrow Caucasian face amidst a sea of Asians, with a pointed nose, sunken cheeks, and big round eyes blinking in surprise. Katie Byrd Worthington. She held her right hand atop her head. For two reasons, I imagined. One was to give her more space amongst the human sardines packed into Seoul's city conveyance. And two, she must've been nursing an ugly bump from the beating her head had taken when she'd dropped from the fire escape.

Once again, we made eye contact. The right side of her mouth twisted into a broad smirk. She was enjoying herself. But at least this time, she didn't flip me the bird. Probably because she couldn't get her hand free.

At KNP Headquarters, Inspector Kill seemed relieved to see us.

"You're working Sunday," he remarked.

Ernie shrugged. "Can't dance."

Mr. Kill puzzled over that statement, trying to work out

its meaning. Of course, it didn't make sense to anyone else either, but that didn't stop it from being widely used. Mr. Kill motioned for us to take a seat on the vinyl-covered benches on either side of the long coffee table in front of his desk. Normally, we would've received tea or coffee, but by way of explanation he said, "I ordered Officer Oh to take the day off. If I don't, she shows up. No matter what."

"Sort of like those bank robbers," Ernie told him.

Mr. Kill studied him. "What do you mean?"

Ernie reached into his pocket, pulled out the wadded napkin, and laid it on the coffee table. Wrinkled tissue unfolded like a spring flower, revealing the smashed bullet inside. He nodded toward me, and I explained what had happened in Samgakji. Mr. Kill spent a moment processing the narrative. Finally, he said, "So these aren't your average GIs."

"They're clever," I said. "They figured out how to find us. And they're thorough, wanting to close off loose ends."

"Meaning us," Ernie added.

Mr. Kill nodded. "Yes. Clever. Very thorough." He reached for the bullet, lifted it carefully by its paper wrapping and turned, placing it behind him on his desk. "I'll have our lab take a look at this."

Eighth Army didn't have a forensics lab. According to the honchos, there wasn't enough crime to warrant putting US taxpayers to such an expense. Which was true, in a way. If you refuse to see things, you can pretend they don't exist. As a result, we had to package up all crime evidence, like spent bullets and blood samples, and ship them to Camp Zama in Japan. Exactly how high a priority the techs at Zama put on the evidence we shipped to them, I couldn't be sure. But we seldom received results in less than two weeks.

Having the Korean National Police crime lab, located right in this building, process the evidence was much faster. Besides, they already had the fatal bullet from the latest bank robbery and would be able to compare the two.

Mr. Kill turned back to us. "I have bad news. The price of poker is going up."

"Where'd you learn that?" Ernie asked. "'The price of poker.'"

"At counterinsurgency school."

"They have poker games there?"

"Pretty much constantly."

"Did you win?"

I elbowed Ernie to shut up. "What happened?" I asked.

Mr. Kill paused and said, "The story about the bank robberies is about to break in the Associated Press."

If the story made international news, even the *Stars and Stripes* would be forced to pick it up. And 8th Army wouldn't be able to deny the involvement of American soldiers any longer, which I expected would elevate their anger from a middling pissed off to absolutely enraged.

"*Damn*," I said.

"They'll blame us for this getting out," Ernie added.

"If it makes you feel any better," Mr. Kill responded, "my government is blaming me, too."

"Shit rolls downhill," Ernie said.

"The only good thing," Kill said, "is that this allegation against your First Corps commander is demanding even more headlines. A little thing like a killing during a bank robbery is easy to ignore. But sex trafficking on the DMZ . . ."

He shook his head without finishing the thought.

"There's no contest," Ernie said, "when mere murder has to go up against blonde hookers."

"Well, in the meantime, the best thing we can do is catch these GIs who shot at you this morning."

"I agree," I said. "The question is how."

Mr. Kill slid a KNP police report toward me. It was typed in *hangul.* I studied it and picked out a few words and phrases, but to decipher it accurately, I'd have to sit down with my Korean-English dictionary and pull the sentences apart one by one. Mr. Kill realized this and began to explain.

"Are you familiar with Paju-gun?"

I told him I was. It was an administrative district north of Seoul, similar to an American county but smaller, wherein many of the US Army combat units in the Western Corridor were deployed. Ernie and I had been there on more than one case. Unfortunately, all of it was under the military jurisdiction of the 2nd Infantry Division, which meant that "rear-echelon

MFs" like Ernie and me were about as welcome as cats at a sardine convention.

"Illegal money changers," he continued. "Our KNP office in Bopwon-ni monitors them."

"They don't bust them?" Ernie asked.

"No point. We close them down, they set up shop somewhere else. Better to tolerate them and make sure no one gets too far out of line."

The money changers filled a need. GIs who made money on the black market or in other illegal activities needed to change their ill-gotten Korean *won* into US dollars. At the authorized credit union on base, changing *won* to US dollars was prohibited. The brass figured that if an American soldier had somehow amassed a large amount of Korean money, he must be up to no good. They were usually right. But the GIs could get what they wanted, with a favorable exchange rate, by dealing with the illicit Korean money changers. Once they had US dollars, they could go on base to the APO, the Army Post Office, buy money orders and send their profits home. But they had to be careful with how much they sent. That, too, was monitored by the Command. Anything substantially above the amount they received according to their rank and pay grade would be reported to military law enforcement.

So the KNPs allowed the illegal money changers to continue doing business, keeping a close eye on them. I also suspected the local cops took a cut of the profits in exchange for their silence. But I wouldn't be so gauche as to say that out loud in front of Inspector Kill.

"There's been suspicious activity near Bopwon-ni," he continued. "Both times immediately after the bank robberies. The money changer in question had to hustle to scrounge up more than two thousand US dollars."

"For one transaction?" Ernie asked.

Kill nodded.

Ernie slid to the edge of his seat. "Which GI made the buy?"

"We aren't sure. GIs don't use names when they go to money changers. At least, not real ones. According to the KNP report, he was in civilian clothes. The money changer was vague about physical description. Just a GI, he said. They all look alike to him."

"Is the money changer aware that we might be interested in this GI?"

"No. This came to light during casual conversation. Our officer was merely monitoring the money changer's profits. Something he does routinely. And he was careful not to push for a more precise description and tip his hand."

That was also, I imagined, when the cop took his cut of the money changer's profits, passing the lion's share on up the line to his superiors.

"Is this GI a regular customer of the money changer?" Ernie asked.

"Sporadic. He's seen him a few times. But only for fairly small amounts. A couple hundred dollars at most. The money changer assumed it was from the usual black marketeering or selling American government property, like C-rations or copper wire—or both. Apparently, this GI had made a big score."

Ernie looked at me. "We ain't there yet?"

"We would recommend a cautious approach," Mr. Kill said. "We don't want to scare him away."

"Caution is our byword," Ernie said.

Coming from him, it was a very odd thing to say.

Mr. Kill gave us the name of the Korean cop in Bopwon-ni and told us he'd make arrangements for a meeting the next night, Monday. I wrote down the information, unsure of how to spell the cop's name in *hangul*, when Mr. Kill generously offered his help, taking my pen and my notebook and jotting it down in an easy hand. I read what he'd written, admiring the practiced calligraphy.

"Hey-kyong. That's a woman's name, isn't it?"

"Yes," he said.

"A female cop," Ernie said, "working a GI village?"

"Not just any woman," Kill replied. "She's almost as tall as you, with a third degree black belt in taekwondo. Tough. And with a mind set on overcoming adversity."

"How do you know?"

"Because when she was twelve years old, she escaped from North Korea."

Ernie whistled. "You're hooking us up with a Commie?"

"To broaden your perspective," Mr. Kill said.

The next morning when we arrived at the CID Admin office, Staff Sergeant Riley and Miss Kim were both on the phone, and Colonel Walter P. Brace, Provost Marshal of the 8th United States Army, stood in the center of the room, hands on his hips, staring back and forth between the two of them. When he heard us enter, he swiveled and said, "There you are." Without another word, he thrust a copy of the *Stars and Stripes* into my hand.

There it was, on the front page: GIS ACCUSED OF BANK ROBBERY. And below that, KOREAN BANK TELLER FATALLY INJURED.

The article was bylined by an Associated Press reporter, not a *Stripes* reporter. Now that it was international news, they were obligated to carry the story, but since the subject matter was sensitive, the editorial staff wasn't about to do their own write-up or in any way leave their fingerprints on this mess.

Riley was speaking to someone at the personnel records section about providing us a list of all GIs in 8th Army who had been allowed to enlist despite prior criminal convictions. Apparently, it would be an enormous list, and he was receiving a lot of flak about how much time and effort it would take.

"Top priority," Riley kept saying. "By order of the Provost Marshal."

Miss Kim was speaking in Korean to someone who seemed to be questioning her about how much the family of the murdered woman would receive in compensation. She was trying to refer them to either the 8th Army Claims Officer or Judge Advocate General, but the person on the other end of the line wasn't having it. Miss Kim was trying to appease them, but I could tell she was getting nowhere. She was too nice and too honest for our way of doing things in military law enforcement. Riley would've just hung up on them.

"I've put Burrows and Slabem back on the case," Colonel Brace said. "We need all hands on deck."

Ernie said, "Mr. Kill doesn't want Burrows and Slabem on this case."

Wrong answer. Blood rushed to Colonel Brace's face. "Mr. Kill doesn't run the *goddamn* Eighth Army Provost Marshal's office," he said. "I have Burrows and Slabem down at Personnel now, putting together a list of soldiers in the command who were granted waivers for their civilian criminal behavior prior to enlistment. Kill can't control that."

Ernie'd been behaving pretty well lately, refraining from pissing off the brass, but I guess I couldn't have expected it to last forever.

"That could help, sir," I said, trying to divert his attention, "especially if the information they gather intersects with the leads we're developing."

"What leads are those?"

"Still working on them," I said, "but apparently, we struck a nerve."

"How so?"

I told him about the shooting.

"Oh, that," he said. "Yes, I saw that on this morning's blotter. Gunfire reported in Samgakji. That was directed at you?"

"Both of us," I replied. "So we believe."

"Oh. Maybe you did strike a nerve." As an afterthought, he said, "Either of you hurt?"

"No, sir," Ernie said. "Caught the bullet between my teeth."

Colonel Brace shot him a furious look. "Always the wiseass, huh, Bascom?"

Ernie didn't reply, and Colonel Brace didn't continue his inquiry on our physical welfare. Instead, he repeatedly jammed his fingertip onto the edge of Miss Kim's desk as he said, "I expect a full written report on all your activities on this bank robbery each and every morning, starting with this morning. Is that clear?"

"Clear, sir."

Actually, since we'd been released to work with Mr. Kill, Colonel Brace was temporarily not our boss. But I knew better—even Ernie did—than to piss him off over some damn report.

He took a deep breath to calm himself and said, "So, what did this Katie Byrd Worthington have to say?"

"Well, sir," I replied, "I'm afraid she didn't want to cooperate."

"Didn't *want* to? Did you tell her we could pull her Eighth Army press credentials?"

It was a threat that our previous conversation had made clear we weren't supposed to make, but, once again, I didn't argue.

"Actually, sir, we were unable to talk to her at all. When we located her at the Bando Hotel, she avoided us by climbing down the fire escape."

"The fire escape?"

We both nodded.

"What's wrong with this woman?"

Neither of us tried to answer that one.

"Well, find her, goddamn it. And get me a full report on this bank robbery investigation. *Now*!" Then he seemed to remember something. "Come with me, both of you."

We followed him down the hallway and I expected him to lead us to his office but halfway there, he turned and stared at us.

"You're under pressure," he said. "I understand that. But we can't let up now. There's a lot on the line for the Command"—he paused for dramatic effect—"and for you."

I supposed he wanted us to ask what he meant, but neither of us did. He cleared his throat and spoke again. "This ROK Army Third Corps business, these ridiculous accusations against General Crabtree." The I Corp Commander. "It's been decided that we want you to look into them."

"Along with the bank robbery investigation?" Ernie asked.

"Yes. Along with that. And we want you to look into these accusations *pronto*. I've called the Second Division commander and told him to expect you to be operating in his area."

"Bet he wasn't happy about that," Ernie said.

"Damnit, Bascom, I don't care if he's happy. This is coming straight from the head shed. They want to know the truth behind these accusations."

"So if we find out," Ernie said, prodding him, "that General Crabtree did in fact ship hookers up north with an MP escort for indecent purposes, should we arrest him?"

"*No!*" Colonel Brace seemed shocked. "Just report back to me. We'll take it from there."

"We" being him and the 8th Army power structure.

"We'll be stretched sort of thin," Ernie said. "Any chance of an increase in our expense allowance?"

Colonel Brace nodded and waved his hand dismissively, as if this was too petty for him to waste time on. "Tell Riley I said to double it. And report back to me immediately when you know something." He pointed a knobby forefinger at me. "And I mean *immediately*. You got that, Sueño?"

"Yes, sir."

With that, he turned and strode toward his office.

We made an about-face and walked the other way. "*Double*," Ernie whispered to me, proud of his coup. We'd now receive a hundred dollars a month each for miscellaneous expenses instead of fifty.

"We're in the money," he said, smiling. "Thanks to me."

I wasn't so sure that an extra half-a-yard was going to cover the grief we were about to be subjected to at the ROK Army III Corps headquarters. But Ernie didn't seem worried about it. So I decided not to worry either.

11

In the Military Police Arms Room, the weapons checkout form attached to a battered clipboard had multiple columns, one of them headed PURPOSE. Before Ernie received his .45, he wrote down, *To stop people who are trying to kill me.*

The new guy in charge of the Arms Room was Specialist 4 Elgin. He was of average height and weight, with a slight potbelly. His hair was combed much in the way Adolph Hitler once combed his hair, but instead of a Charlie Chaplin mustache, the main thing one remembered about Specialist Elgin were the red acne spots covering a face as pale as a West Texas desert. He was from Oklahoma and talked slowly, considering every word, which was probably a good thing. And pretty unusual in the US Army. He stared at Ernie's entry, then looked up and said, "Who's trying to kill you?"

"If I knew that," Ernie said, "I would've arrested them already."

Elgin pondered the answer, nodded, and said, "You want a protective vest?"

"How heavy are they?"

Elgin grabbed one from a wooden crate and hoisted it onto the counter with a *clunk*. The thick contraption was covered with olive drab canvas material. Slide-in metal plates kept the front and back stiff. Ernie slipped it on and buckled it, and it fit fine.

"How do I look?" he asked me, holding his arms out to the side.

"Smashing."

"Nah," Ernie told Elgin, slipping the vest off and slapping it back on the counter. "That wouldn't be sporting. The bad guys haven't worn any protective vests so far, so I won't wear one either."

"There's more than one guy trying to kill you?" Elgin asked.

"We think so."

"Damn," Elgin said, shaking his head. "I didn't know Korea had gunfighters."

"Yeah," Ernie said. "Frozen Chosun's becoming a regular OK Corral."

Elgin issued me my .45 along with the accompanying shoulder holster. I signed for it and under the PURPOSE column, I wrote: *Mayhem*.

He stared at the entry and paused, and I almost expected him to say something. In the end, he didn't. He looked at me and blinked. I didn't think he was a hundred percent sure what mayhem meant.

I wasn't sure what it meant to us right now either. But as we got deeper into these cases, it seemed to be chasing us, evolving into something more dangerous by the minute.

Ernie fueled up the jeep at the POL point before we went to the barracks and changed into our running-the-ville outfits: blue jeans, sneakers, sports shirts with a collar, and nylon jackets with writhing dragons embroidered on the backs. We stopped at the 8th Army Snack Bar just as noon chow was ending. Strange sat at his usual table, an empty mug in front of him.

"He's been waiting for us," Ernie said.

I nodded. That was why he hadn't replenished his mug of hot chocolate. He expected us to do it. We joined Strange at his table.

"Had any *strange* lately?" he asked, studying us through his opaque shades.

"More than even *I* can handle," Ernie said. "What's the latest at the head shed?"

For once, Strange didn't demand up-front quid pro quo. Instead, he leaned forward and said, "You're toast."

"Sourdough or English muffin?"

"Knock off the bullshit, Bascom," Strange said. "I'm serious."

"Okay, you're serious," Ernie replied patiently, waiting for him to spill.

Strange glanced at the empty tables at our sides as if he were about to cross the Hollywood Freeway. Satisfied that no Commie spies were lurking near the short-order line, he leaned forward again and told us what he'd learned from a classified transcript of this morning's 8th Army Command briefing.

"The First Corps Commander, Lieutenant General Crabtree, is having a nervous breakdown. A local MD up there at First Corp headquarters recommended he be airlifted back to the One-Two-One for further evaluation." The army's 121st Evacuation Hospital in Seoul.

"Okay," Ernie said. "With the kind of publicity he's getting from the *Overseas Observer* about him pimping hookers using the MPs, it figures he'd be a little out of sorts."

"But that's nothing a laxative can't cure," Strange said. "According to Second ID reports, he was seen wandering around headquarters at night in only his skivvies, shouting at the moon, yelling orders for a DMZ-wide move-out alert."

"Did anybody follow the order?" I asked.

"No. It got rescinded before it became official."

"By who?"

Ernie and I both knew that when a Corps Commander issued an order in this man's army, it was usually followed.

"By his Command Sergeant Major. A guy named Screech Owl Tapia."

"Screech Owl?" Ernie said.

"Yeah. He's an Apache or something. With a combat record as long as your arm. He policed up General Crabtree and took him back to his quarters, then tucked him in his bunk and ordered the Staff Duty Officer not to mention the outburst in his log."

"That's not kosher."

"No. And that's not the only thing Command Sergeant Major Screech Owl is up to."

"Like what?"

Strange paused, staring at us cagily. "You're going up there, aren't you?"

"What's it to ya?" Ernie said.

"You'll be gone a while." He glanced at his empty mug and frowned. I took the hint.

"You want a refill?"

"Yes. Only one marshmallow this time." He patted his belly. "I'm watching my weight."

"Watching it expand like a helium balloon," Ernie said.

"You mind your manners," Strange replied.

As they bickered, I rose from my chair, grabbed the mug, and proceeded to the serving line. I was in no hurry because I knew Ernie was probably telling Strange a story about the "strange" he'd received in the last few days. The stories were most often figments of Ernie's imagination—or exaggerations of the truth—and neither of us felt good about such a sleazy way of doing business, but Strange's information had yet to be proven wrong. It was pure, unlike him, straight from eyes-only documents and the most highly classified briefings 8th Army had to offer. I often wondered what would happen if the three of us were ever caught in violation of the regulations on the passing of classified information.

If the JAG office was turned loose on us, we really would be toast. Low-ranking enlisted men were made examples of. High-ranking officers had excuses made for them by the Command and were allowed to retire with full benefits to Florida golf courses. But so far, we hadn't been caught. And after all, the information we received was used for only one thing: to put away bad guys. As long as that was the case, I'd keep buying Strange mugs of hot chocolate with as many marshmallows as his greedy heart desired.

At the end of the serving line, I slapped a quarter in front of the middle-aged Korean woman operating the cash register and said, "*Anyonghaseiyo*?" Are you at peace?

She nodded wearily but didn't answer as she rang up my quarter and slid the receipt to me across stainless steel. I grabbed the short slip of paper but didn't bother her any further. She'd been on her feet since the snack bar opened at six this morning.

When I returned to the table, I placed the steaming cup in front of Strange.

"Where's my spoon?" he asked.

Without a word, I got up and pulled a teaspoon from the

stainless-steel rack alongside the serving line, returned to the table, and handed it to Sergeant First Class Harvey, NCO in charge of the 8th Army Headquarters Classified Documents Center.

He frowned at the spoon, grabbed a napkin, and wiped it until it shone. Satisfied at last, he stirred his hot cocoa, looked around surreptitiously, and continued to preach. For the moment, he told us, the 8th Army honchos had decided to disregard the doctor's orders to have Crabtree transported to the One-Two-One.

"Too embarrassing to the Command," Strange explained. "It would make them look like idiots for appointing him as I Corps Commander in the first place."

"Aren't they?" Ernie asked.

"Aren't they what?"

"Idiots."

"No. They believe Crabtree will get over it. Besides, he has too many allies back at the Pentagon."

"Those nephews."

"Right. And old friends. So they're giving him another chance. Hoping he'll straighten up and fly right."

"But if he doesn't," I said, "and this Sergeant Major Screech Owl can't keep him in line, he could start another war on the peninsula."

Strange shrugged. "Then make sure Screech Owl keeps him in line."

"Thanks. And if we don't?"

"Millions of people will die."

"The Eighth Army honchos are really taking that chance?" Ernie said. "Leaving him up there when there's so much at stake?"

Strange shrugged again. "Hey, look on the bright side."

"Which is?"

"If another war breaks out, it'd be good for promotion."

"You'd make master sergeant."

Strange grinned.

"You said we were toast," I told him. "What'd you mean?"

"You're being set up. You and this *Oversexed Observer* broad, you're going to be blamed for the whole hookers-transported-north business. For leaking it to the press. A phony story, Eighth Army will claim. And if General Crabtree doesn't straighten up and fly right, they'll blame Command Sergeant Screech Owl for not taking him in for observation early enough."

"Which is why they're sending us up there," Ernie said. "So we'll be involved, and they can pin the other half of the blame on us if something goes wrong."

"Right. The deeper you sink into a tub of shit, the harder it is to climb out."

We stared at him—both of us, I think, pondering his revolting imagery.

Strange lifted his cocoa, drained the final dregs, and set the empty cup down with a *plop*. "Thank you, gentlemen," he told us. "Enjoy your day."

With that, he rose from the table and shuffled off.

On the drive north to Bopwon-ni, Ernie and I reviewed our two cases.

The bank robbers were nervous as hell. Even though we had no idea who or where they were, they couldn't be sure how much we'd found, and as such, were reacting with a violence seldom seen in 8th Army. Sure, soldiers killed fellow soldiers. Sometimes they went nuts, or sometimes they acted on a grudge or extreme jealousy. But seldom did we see groups of GIs act in concert to commit serious felonies, then once again to eliminate the law enforcement officers assigned to their cases who were simply doing their job. It was a level of malice aforethought that could legitimately be called organized crime. And they were paying careful attention to the news, now that their exploits had hit what passed for the mainstream media here in the ROK. They were monitoring the *Overseas Observer*, and presumably the *Pacific Stars and Stripes* as well.

"We know next to nothing about these guys," Ernie complained.

"Yeah," I agreed. "We need a solid lead. Something to sink our teeth into."

"You think they'll strike a third time?"

"They've already done the worst, which is kill for money. With all the law enforcement attention, maybe they'll lay off for a while."

Ernie shook his head. "I don't think so."

"Why not?"

"Whoever's in charge of this group," he said, "and there's always someone in charge, he'll realize that he has a tightly knit, disciplined assault squad. He'll also realize that in the Army, no group stays together too long. People get transferred out—they leave, they have a change of heart. So now's the time to strike, while he's got this well-oiled machine at his command."

"But the KNPs are on alert, from the DMZ down to Pusan."

"Sure. But greed knows no bounds. Besides, you know how many banks there are? Even the KNPs can't cover them all. And these guys are feeling invincible. That's why they came after us. And they have plenty of firepower."

"They've shown a willingness to use it," I said.

"That they have."

We passed a sign that read SEOUL CITY LIMITS and kept cruising north past acres of fallow rice paddies. Ernie's fingers caressed the steering wheel. He was in a talkative mood, almost buoyant. Nothing like chaos to get him revved up.

"This lead up in Bopwon-ni is probably the best we've gotten so far." Ernie thought about it and then corrected himself. "The *only* lead we've gotten. The crooks have to either spend the Korean *won* here in-country or change it into dollars and send it home."

"Or they could save it until DEROS," I said. Date of Estimated Return from Overseas. "And exchange it once they're safely back in the States."

"Is that legal?"

"I believe so. As long as when you land, you declare anything worth more than $10,000 on your customs form."

"They haven't exceeded that yet."

"Not yet."

"And if they do exceed it but they don't declare it to customs, what happens then?"

"Nothing, as long as they're not caught."

We left the outskirts of Seoul and were cruising north on the newly built Tong-il Lo, Reunification Road, past rice paddies on the left side of the road and tree-spotted hills on the right, some with huge white placards that said DENG SAN KUM JI. Don't Climb the Mountain. The signs were there because, although twenty years had passed, many of the hills in South Korea had yet to be cleared of landmines and other explosive ordnance left over from the Korean War.

Around a bend, we reached the first 2nd Infantry Division checkpoint. A ROK Army MP waved for us to reduce our speed. Beyond him, two American MPs wearing combat fatigues and protective vests with M16 assault rifles crooked in their elbows motioned for us to stop.

"Destination?" one of them asked.

"Bopwon-ni," I said.

"Where?"

"The biggest town in Paju County," Ernie said, a sneer in his voice. Then he shook his head and added, "Moron."

The MP shifted his rifle from the crook of his arm and held it with two hands. "Who you calling a moron?"

Ernie swiveled his head back and forth, pretending to search the area. "You see a big crowd around here?"

"Stuff it, wise guy."

The other MP approached the opposite side of the jeep and motioned for our dispatch. I handed it to him. He studied the paperwork. "Eighth Army," he said. "Emergency Dispatch. Well, *la di da*."

"He can read," Ernie told me.

"Don't sweat it, Franks," the guy said to his gun-happy fellow MP. "These guys ain't nothing but rear-echelon pukes."

He tossed the dispatch back. I caught the clipboard on the fly.

"What brings a couple of CID assholes up here to Division?" Franks asked.

"Your mom," Ernie replied. "Didn't you see the line?"

Franks seemed like he was about to slug Ernie, but the other MP, the one with an additional stripe, warned him off. "Go on," he said, waving us forward. "Get the hell out of here."

We started to roll forward. Another ROK Army MP dragged a four-foot-high contraption made of crossed steel bars out of the roadway. They were easy to transport, and when strewn together, effective at stopping vehicular traffic. Ernie wound through the maze, and soon we were back on the road heading toward the turnoff that led to Bopwon-ni.

"Did you *have* to mess with them?" I asked.

He shrugged. "Why wait? They'll mess with us sooner or later. I like to get a jump on the festivities."

"Those guys are already on the radio letting their MP commander know we've entered their area of operations."

"That'll give him time to set up the brass band."

I turned and gazed back at the checkpoint. From this distance, the MPs looked like toy soldiers standing amidst a maze of giant jacks. All they needed to complete the image was a six-foot-high red rubber ball.

After turning off the main road, we were in a belt of natural green composed of small trees and shrubs on gently rolling hills with rice paddies and cabbage patches layering the valleys. Most of the farmhouses had tile roofs and TV antennae, but a few still had the traditional roofs of bundled straw thatch that had been used for centuries.

"It's pretty idyllic out here," I told Ernie.

"Unless you're the one who has to transplant those rice shoots."

He'd seen it done so often in Vietnam that he knew how backbreaking the work was. The road curved north, now paralleling Tong-il Lo, but about five kilometers farther inland, almost thirty *klicks* from the edge of the Yellow Sea.

"So Bopwon-ni was the county seat once upon a time," Ernie said.

"Still is. Bopwon translates to 'law hall.' We'd call it a court."

"Where the hanging judge presides."

"I think they used to garrote people back in those days. With silk ropes."

"How civilized," Ernie said.

The first large building we saw in Bopwon-ni was an old grain storage shed with walls of rotted wood. Beyond that were more homes, then businesses, mostly catering to agricultural supply, and finally a modern wood frame building with metal siding that, if I was reading the sign correctly, was where the agricultural bounty of this valley was available for purchase by dealers from Seoul. Now, in midafternoon, it was locked and deserted, since that was the type of business that was conducted at oh-dark-thirty, so the fresh produce could be transported before dawn south toward the big city.

Finally, we reached an intersection in the main part of town. There were clothing stores and noodle shops and tea houses and a movie theater and a large bus stop with a sign that said, SEOUL EXPRESS. And a lone taxi stand with one driver sitting in his cab, snoozing.

"Any nightclubs?" Ernie asked.

"A couple," I said. "But their signs are in Korean, not English." Which meant they didn't welcome GIs.

"My favorite," he said.

I spotted the Korean national flag, a yin-yang symbol of eternal harmony surrounded by four trigrams representing heaven, earth, fire, and water, all on a white background symbolizing the purity of the Korean people. It fluttered above a whitewashed-cement-block building, the type mass-produced by the South Korean government and placed strategically in every city, town, and hamlet in the country.

"There it is," I said. Ernie hung a right and stopped in a narrow, gravel parking area and switched off the jeep's engine. Something shuddered, coughed, and sputtered reluctantly to a halt.

"Damn," Ernie said. "Needs a tune-up."

"That'll cost you another bottle of Johnny Walker Black," I told him.

"Unless I can sweet-talk the dispatcher."

"Good luck. That old buzzard only understands money."

At the 8th Army motor pool in Seoul, which dispatched all vehicles for the headquarters complex, it could take a week or longer to get a vehicle back after turning it in for maintenance, even for something as simple as a tune-up. But whenever Ernie slipped a bottle of scotch to the head honcho—liquor that could easily be sold on the sly at over twice its purchase price—his jeep was returned the same day in tip-top shape, along with a thorough wash, vacuuming, and tire rotation.

We climbed out of the jeep and pushed through the big double doors of the Bopwon-ni police station.

"Anybody home?" Ernie yelled cheerily.

A tired cop looked up from a stack of pulp and glared at Ernie as if he was about to reach for the garrote he'd kept handy since the end of the Chosun Dynasty. I stepped in front of Ernie, bowed to the officer, and spoke in Korean using honorifics. After a few sentences, he nodded and set down his pen.

The woman we were looking for, Police Sergeant Kang Hey-kyong, was in her office. The desk officer led us down a hallway and motioned us through a large, open doorway that led to the arms room. Sitting on a straight-backed wooden chair was a husky woman with strong, masculine bone structure wearing the KNP khaki uniform. Behind her loomed a metal-reinforced cage which held neat rows of rifles and other weaponry on pegs against the wall. She held a revolver in her hand and idly twirled the cylinder, gazing at it, her lips partly open, like a Buddhist monk fondling a prayer wheel, deep in the throes of meditation.

She looked up at us and said, "*Wasso*?" You've arrived?

I started to say something, but she clicked shut the cylinder, turned halfway in her chair, pointed the revolver at me, and pulled the trigger.

-12-

That evening, we sat in a chophouse in the GI village of Yongju-gol, glancing out the steam-smeared front window. I picked listlessly with my wooden chopsticks, poking a spread-eagled crab that lay atop my bowl of lukewarm buckwheat noodles and trying to decide whether or not it was still alive.

"I've heard of buckwheat pancakes," Ernie said, "but never buckwheat noodles."

"You've had them pretty often," I told him. "You just didn't know it."

"Only the translucent type." He hoisted a clump of noodles above his bowl and let them dangle like tangled hair, twisting them in the overhead fluorescent light. "These are more like mouse gray."

"Yeah," I said.

"Tasty, though." He bit into a clump. After chewing, he said, "You about shit a brick when she aimed that revolver at you."

"I don't like it," I said, still smarting from the confrontation.

"It's not good policy to point a weapon at another human being unless you intend to kill them."

"Well, lucky for you, that's not what she intended."

What she'd done was twist her wrist at the last moment and aim the revolver at a tilted bucket of sand that police officers used to clear their weapons. After checking the cylinder, they would aim the weapon into the sand and pull the trigger as a final safety check. If a bullet was fired, it slammed harmlessly into the large bucket and no one was hurt.

"It was a dirty trick," I said, trying to sound indignant rather than petulant.

I'd berated her for pointing the gun at me, but she'd proceeded to explain in Korean that she was only trying to startle us into the awareness that the boys up here in the Western Corridor didn't play nice. There were about a dozen US Army compounds, all manned by combat units—tanks, artillery, long-range reconnaissance patrols—and probably forty or fifty ROK Army units, in fortified defensive positions, scattered across the nearby hills. Each and every soldier was firing armaments pretty much every day. Pistols, rifles, howitzers, anti-aircraft guns, you name it. And off duty, they were almost as violent as they were on duty. Although usually, in the bars and brothels, they only used broken beer bottles, pool cues, fists, and the occasional bayonet that they managed to smuggle off base.

"*Dongmul i-ji*," Sergeant Kang said. They're animals.

After we'd gotten to talk to her, I'd realized she was competent and maybe even friendly. Still, I treated her with a wariness that I usually reserved for violent drunks. She was unpredictable. Maybe good for a cop in a tough neighborhood, but dangerous for those new to working with her. I'd stared into her black eyes, which reminded me of a shark's, as we'd gone over our plans for the evening's work.

Three hours later we were here, poking at our food, wasting time in this dingy little chophouse. There were about thirty bars and nightclubs in the three or four acres that comprised the tightly packed village, the main roads of which were aflame with flashing neon. We weren't all that hungry since we'd both loaded up on hamburgers and fries at the 8th Army Snack Bar before leaving Yongsan Compound. Besides, we were trying to make our food last since this vantage point gave us a good view of the opposite side of the street and the mouth of an alley down which one of the most notorious money changers in the GI village of Yongju-gol operated. At least, according to Korean National Police Officer Kang Hey-kyong, the woman who'd startled me so badly that I probably wouldn't need laxatives for the rest of my overseas tour.

The money changer known to GIs as Old Hwang had a little shop right here in the heart of the GI bar district, and any American soldier who dabbled in the Korean black market, which most did, soon learned that Old Hwang would treat them right. It was even reputed that he gave out payday loans, which I found surprising, since GIs who were about to leave the country could stiff him pretty easily. But maybe his profit margin was high enough to cover the losses.

"There she is," Ernie said.

Across the street, standing beneath the glow of a yellow streetlamp, stood Officer Kang. She was no longer in uniform and wore a long beige cotton coat to protect herself from the chill fall evening. Our prearranged signal was that when she spotted something important and wanted us outside, she'd reach up to adjust the bun on the back of her head.

"There's our cue," Ernie said, tossing down his chopsticks.

We slipped on our nylon jackets and were out the door in about ten seconds. Officer Kang had already turned away and was stepping into the gloom of the dark alleyway. Glancing both ways, Ernie and I crossed the main drag of Yongju-gol, gazing longingly at the bars and nightclubs and sparkling neon. But instead of exploring them, we followed this certifiably mad Korean female police officer into the endless night.

Officer Kang Hey-Kyong was waiting at an intersection of two narrow pedestrian passageways. A red bulb above a locked wooden door illuminated her face. Her prominent square jaw stood out in the lowlight, and her eyes were more focused now than they had been when she'd been fiddling with her revolver in the arms room, planning to scare the crap out of us. She looked up at Ernie, then at me, and spoke in Korean.

"Old Hwang sent a boy," she told us, "to signal me that the GI who tried to exchange the two thousand dollars is back, as he told Old Hwang he would be."

"To collect the rest of his money?"

"Yes. At their first meeting, Old Hwang had only fifteen hundred dollars on hand. They made the exchange and the GI asked Hwang when he would be able to get more US cash. The GI said he might have as much as another two thousand dollars' worth of *won*. They settled on this evening."

She let me translate for Ernie. Then she said, "He won't be in there long. You must act quickly."

We had already determined that Ernie and I would make the arrest. That way, we wouldn't have to go through the hassle of having the ROK authorities charge him with a crime and have to do the paperwork to turn him over to the US Army. We'd have him directly. No middleman.

"Be careful," she said.

"You think we haven't busted GIs before?" Ernie said.

She reached up and slapped him lightly on the cheek. "Wake up," she said in English, then switched back to Korean. "Don't let your pride lull you into a trance. Stick with what we planned. Exactly. Danger is a ruby-eyed goddess with a thousand faces."

I didn't bother to translate for Ernie. I wondered if Kang Hey-kyong might've been a Buddhist nun before becoming a cop. She seemed to view the potential of violence as some sort of cosmic lesson, one she'd tried to teach us when we'd first met her. A lesson I wasn't too anxious to learn. Ernie and I proceeded down the narrow passageway to arrest a GI who we perversely hoped had shattered a bank guard's jaw and shot a bank teller who was a wife and a mother of three.

"He ain't getting away this time," Ernie muttered.

A glow emanated from the dirt-smudged plate glass window of Old Hwang's shop. Ostensibly, he sold used clothing and farm equipment, although everyone knew that the bulk of his income came from changing money for GIs and those Korean businessmen who ended up with US dollars—of which there were many in Yongju-gol.

A GI stood at the wooden counter. He was wearing civilian clothes. Blue jeans and sneakers. Broad shoulders were crammed into a light-blue windbreaker; bristly black hair was combed tightly backward along his skull.

"A bodybuilder," I said. "Fits the description given by the bank employees."

"Musclebound," Ernie replied. "That's good. Clumsy. Easy to take down."

I liked his attitude, though the guy looked pretty strong to me.

Voices were raised. The GI and Old Hwang were arguing. Hwang was jabbing his finger into the air, demanding something from the GI. I stepped slightly to my left and realized that the GI had just stuffed a wad of what looked like greenbacks into his jacket pocket. Maybe he hadn't given Hwang the stolen *won* yet in exchange. Hwang's face was turning red. He reached beneath the counter and pulled out a *naht*, the short-handled sickle with a wickedly curved iron blade used by Korean farmers for centuries to harvest backbreaking acres of rice and other types of grain. Old Hwang waved it at the GI's face, swinging it back and forth expertly.

The GI recoiled, and when Hwang swung again, the GI surprised both me and Ernie by leaping forward like a cat charging a bird. With one hand, he grabbed Hwang by the neck, and with the other hand he yanked the iron sickle out of his grip. Still holding on to the man, he climbed over the counter, shoved Hwang to the ground, and finally, warning the old man to stay put, searched the small shop for more money.

"*Now*," Ernie said, stepping forward.

"Wait." I grabbed him by the elbow. "Let him come out of the shop. That way the robbery is completed, no question. And we won't have to wrestle him boxed in by all those counters and shelves."

"What if he hurts Hwang?"

"Too late now. Hwang's already down."

If we'd gone in earlier, the GI could've claimed there was no robbery, that he'd just been haggling with Hwang over a transaction. Anyway, it became a moot point because the GI finished his search, apparently found nothing other than the cash he'd already pocketed. He hopped back over the counter and pushed through the narrow door out into the street.

Ernie and I walked quickly toward him, me holding my badge up and shouting, "Military Police! Hold it right there."

The guy froze for a millisecond, then darted to his right. Ernie and I veered after him, and since Ernie already had a running start, he reached the muscular GI just as he entered another narrow pedestrian passageway. Ernie hit him like a deep safety tackling a tight end. The two men went down and rolled on the ground, punching one another. I joined the melee, searching for one of the GI's wrists to grab, slap a handcuff on, and twist until the other wrist was behind his back and likewise locked in cold metal. Which was the way it usually worked. The way I expected it to.

Until two other demons ran screaming out of the darkness.

They jumped us without hesitation. Ernie and I were pushed back, and my handcuffs clattered onto the cobblestoned road. I jabbed with my left, caught one of them, then swiveled and landed a short front kick that I believe slammed into ribs. Too high. I would've preferred the groin. Ernie and I were holding our own, and the three GIs backed away from us. Within seconds, I knew they would turn and make a break for it.

I fumbled inside my jacket for my weapon, but before I could pull out the .45, somebody threw a brick and got lucky, hitting Ernie right in the forehead. He grabbed at his face and went down. I turned to check on him, but instead of taking the opportunity to run off as I'd expected, the broad-shouldered guy bulled past his cohorts and rammed headfirst into my side. He kept pushing as I staggered and tripped over Ernie's legs, and before I knew it, the world was swirling, and I slammed onto cobblestone.

Then the real nightmare started. The big guy was on top of me and reaching into my jacket for the .45 I'd checked out of the MP Arms Room. I held on for dear life, knowing that once he had the weapon, he would pop a round into my skull without hesitation, and maybe Ernie's, too, thereby putting a stop to at least this portion of 8th Army's criminal investigation.

I bit his finger. He screamed. Then a whistle shrilled. Officer Kang Hey-kyong, I hoped, with reinforcement. The burly GI stood up, backed away, and said, "Second time you've gotten away from us. Third time will be the charm."

The voice was deep, winded, raspy, loaded with frustration and angst. He seemed aggrieved, like a person who believed that life's sole purpose was to heap abuse on him, entirely unfairly. Footsteps pounded. He glanced in their direction, narrowed his eyes at me one more time, and turned and ran.

Officer Kang emerged from the darkness. Her long beige jacket had disappeared. She wore a black cocktail dress with a string of what I presumed were imitation pearls around her neck. I sat up and gawked. Why was she dressed like that? An undercover operation? Maybe she had a date later. But for the first time, I realized—incongruously considering I'd just been on the verge of being killed—that she had a knockout figure. Ernie started to rise also, glancing at his surroundings as if just waking up.

Officer Kang stood over us, straddling the alleyway, her revolver out and pointed down the walkway, a look of resolution on her face. I had no doubt that if those three GIs returned, she'd be more than happy to bust a cap in their mugs. And then it happened again.

A blinding flash of light.

I groaned and lay back down.

Ernie and I could've traveled south about five miles to the Camp Howze Dispensary. But somehow, we didn't feel like having anything more to do with GIs that night. Instead, Officer Kang had us pile into a boxy KNP truck, and we were driven over to what Koreans called the Bopwon-ni Byongwon. The Bopwon Village Hospital. In reality, it was little more than a clinic, but that turned out to be all we needed. The nurse there checked our temperature and blood pressure, and then a doctor examined us, pointing a tiny flashlight at our eyes while ordering us to follow his finger from side to side. Once he determined our heads were too hard to be damaged, he gave orders for the nurse to clean our wounds, apply disinfectant, and bandage them with fresh gauze, which she did. She also gave us a cup of water and two aspirin each, after which we stopped at the cashier's desk and paid the bill of 12,000 *won*—twenty-four bucks for the both of us—and we were discharged.

At Camp Howze, the medical care would've been free. But again, who needed the grief? We didn't feel like watching the Division medics smirk at the discomfort of two CID agents.

In the waiting room, Officer Kang sat with bare legs crossed reading a Korean celebrity magazine. She set it down when we approached. Sitting next to her was a Caucasian woman. Narrow-faced, with a pointed nose and straight blonde hair with long bangs that hung down almost to her eyes. She wore blue jeans, sneakers, and a jungle fatigue shirt with a dozen large pockets. A leather strap that sat diagonally across her chest led down to a Nikon camera with flash attachment. She was neither particularly attractive nor unattractive. Her age could've been anywhere between thirty and sixty-two.

She stood up without offering her hand. "I'm Katie Byrd Worthington." She paused for a moment. "Hope you boys weren't banged up too much."

When we didn't answer, she said, "I have a present for you."

I glanced at Officer Kang. She seemed perfectly relaxed, smiling for the first time since we'd known her.

"Why do you keep blinding us with that damn flash?" Ernie asked.

Katie's eyes widened. "Because it's nighttime. And it's

dark. How else would I get the shot?" She edged her camera slightly behind her, as if to protect it. "You want to see that present or not?"

"Why'd you run away at the Bando Hotel when we came to talk to you?"

"Why wouldn't I? How in the hell was I supposed to know what you wanted? You didn't call first or anything. For all I knew, you were up to no good."

"We just wanted to ask a couple questions, for Christ's sake." I showed her my CID badge. "We're not crooks. We're not trying to mess anyone up."

She sniffed. "Huh. Heard that one before. Like in Pleiku, when the Army helicopter pilots locked me in a room for fourteen hours so I couldn't file a story. But I broke out and had the last laugh on them. That's why they call me Bird." She crossed her thumbs and fluttered her fingers. "Free as a freaking sparrow, that's me."

I nodded toward Officer Kang. "You two know each other?"

"Me and Kyong?" Katie Byrd asked. "We're friends. What of it?"

"Nothing. Colonel Brace, the Provost Marshal, wants to talk to you."

"About what?"

"I don't know. He didn't say."

"Tell him to take a flying leap." She hoisted the canvas bag from the seat behind her, swung it over her free shoulder, and said, "Me and Kyong are going to a teahouse not too far from here. You two coming or no?"

"Will we be getting that present you promised?" Ernie asked.

"Only if you're buying."

Ernie shrugged. "Tea? Sure, why not."

-13-

The Dragon Goddess Tea House was located on the second floor of an old wooden building in the heart of downtown Bopwon-ni. The tables and chairs were made of varnished wood in a style that struck me as Parisian. We sat on an open balcony overseeing the traffic and bright lights below. The voices that drifted up to us were Korean, not American. Unlike Yongju-gol, a few miles north with all its bars and nightclubs, Bopwon-ni was no GI village. It was a fully Korean town, the type of place in which Ernie and I seldom hung out.

It had been a cool fall, and after the events of today, the chilled air seemed to invigorate all four of us. A large lace doily sat in the center of the table. The chair was rickety and groaned under my weight. The ladies, however, seemed perfectly comfortable. A waiter appeared wearing a black vest, a white shirt, and a bow tie. I expected Katie Byrd Worthington to order Black Dragon tea or something of the sort, but instead, she ordered a champagne cocktail. Officer Kang, still looking stunning in her black cocktail dress, ordered a double shot of Jinro soju.

"I thought you were here for tea," Ernie protested.

"You *assumed* we were here for tea," Katie replied. "It's never smart to assume things when you're an officer of the law."

I asked the waiter if they had OB Beer cold, not room temperature. He said yes, but only in liter bottles. I conferred with Ernie and we ordered one bottle with two glasses. We knew that these places were far more expensive than GI bars. The joints catering to Americans kept their prices low for a couple reasons. For one, if they didn't, GIs would complain, and eventually the post commander would pass those complaints on to the Korean mayor, who would lose face if he couldn't provide acceptable accommodations to the brave American servicemen who were so selflessly protecting the freedom of the Korean people. Also, the GI bars might make less profit per drink served, but they more than compensated for that with the sheer volume of booze consumed by parched American soldiers.

When the waiter departed, Katie asked, "You want your present now or when the drinks get here?"

"Everything's better with booze," Ernie said, so we waited.

"Do you speak Korean?" I asked Katie.

"Not yet. But I'm working on it." Then she rattled off a sentence in Vietnamese that I didn't understand.

"What's that supposed to mean?"

"It means you're as curious as a hungry monkey." She

turned toward Ernie. "You were in Vietnam for two tours and you didn't understand that?"

"I spent most of the time hiding in my bunker," Ernie replied.

"Stoned?"

Ernie shrugged. Then he seemed to realize something. "How'd you know I was in 'Nam?"

"Sources," she said.

"Ones with access to personnel records?"

Now it was her turn to shrug.

"We could pull your press credential," Ernie continued.

"Bull. You wouldn't even be here talking to me if that were a real possibility. Your bosses would just pull my credentials, order the Korean cops to arrest me, and have me deported back to the States. And they'd do it, too, except for a little thing called the First Amendment. Some sympathetic congressmen would raise hell, and poor old Eighth Army would never hear the end of it."

"You're pretty confident in yourself," I said.

"Always," Katie replied.

The waiter arrived with our drinks. After serving the ladies, he poured a glass for me and Ernie, bowed, and departed the table.

"Cheers," I said, raising my glass.

Officer Kang Hey-kyong said, "*Dupshida*." Let's drink.

So we drank.

"Now," Katie said, reaching into her canvas bag. "Time for your present."

She pulled out a sheet of stiff paper, which I quickly realized was a five-by-seven photograph. She slapped it onto the middle of the table, where it sat evenly framed by the lace doily.

"I had this printed while you boys were getting patched up," she said. Ernie and I leaned forward, staring at it. I moved a candle to get a better look.

"You've got to be shitting me," Ernie said. "You can't publish this."

"Says who?" Katie asked.

Ernie looked at her. "You *can't*."

"Try me," she said. "All I have to do is say the word and this photograph runs Sunday." She grinned. "In the world-renowned *Overseas Observer*. You'll both be even more famous than you were in our last issue."

Which had almost gotten us killed.

"For God's sake," Ernie said, staring at the photograph as if it was his doom.

Officer Kang studied the photograph, too, although she seemed quite pleased with the likeness.

I lifted the glass of beer to my lips, tilted it back, and drained it. Then I poured myself more.

"What'd we ever do to you?" I asked Katie.

"It's not you," she said. "It's who you represent."

"So nothing personal?"

"No. In fact, I find you two quite entertaining." She toasted me with her glass and glugged down the last of her champagne cocktail.

Ernie's lips had moistened. His face reddened, and he seemed to be choking on his own saliva. Officer Kang watched him warily. Without warning, Ernie reached out, grabbed the photograph, and held it next to the flaming candle. Before it could start to smoke, Officer Kang grabbed Ernie's wrist, twisted, and with her other hand reached behind her back, apparently going for her handcuffs. Ernie jerked backwards and they both rose to their feet, wrestling over the photograph.

I stood up. Katie backed away from the table, protecting her camera equipment. Using great force, Ernie managed to pull the now-crumpled photo to his mouth, bend down, and bite into it. Undaunted, Kang jerked his hand downward, and then the two of them were scraping their feet along the wooden floor, pushing and shoving like a demented Fred Astaire and Ginger Rogers.

The photo was now just a tiny wrinkled wad in Ernie's massive grip. He seemed to forget about it as he and Officer Kang stood with their bodies pressed together, perspiration on both of their foreheads. They were so close that they must've been able to smell each other's breath.

"Back *off*!" Katie screeched. "You're wasting your time. I've already shipped the negatives by courier to Seoul. Tomorrow they'll be airmailed to Hong Kong." She stared at the two sweaty wrestlers. "Break the clinch already," she told Ernie. "You've been checkmated."

The two combatants stood together for what seemed to be another half minute. Ernie didn't pull away. Finally, Officer

Kang did. They finished their drinks, staring at one another warily. Ernie spit bits of paper onto the floor, using the beer to rinse out his mouth and spit some more. Before we left, I noticed that Officer Kang slipped something into Ernie's palm. I didn't think it was an arrest warrant.

That night Ernie and I stayed in a *yoin-suk* in downtown Bopwon. It was a clean place, but crowded. Since we were foreigners, they gave us our own room. The larger main room was shared by about a half-dozen customers, all of whom slept on cotton-covered sleeping mats that were rolled out on the warm *ondol* floor. Ernie and I were each issued a sleeping mat, a comforter, and a bead pillow. The *byonso* was outside.

Sometime past midnight, I rose to use the porcelain pee pot. That's when I noticed Ernie was gone. At first I was worried, wondering if the GI bank robbers had somehow tracked us to this hole-in-the-wall inn. But I quickly realized that was not only unlikely, it was damn near impossible. Ernie must've left on his own recognizance. Being the top-notch detective that I was, I figured out why.

To rendezvous with the sensual, reckless Officer Kang Hey-kyong. That paper she'd slipped into his hand probably had all the information he needed.

The next morning, Ernie returned shortly after dawn.

"Get much sleep?" I asked.

"Who had the chance?"

"At least you'll have some new stories for Strange."

"He won't believe them." Ernie grabbed his back and groaned.

"Pretty rough?"

"Strongest broad I've ever known." He pressed his open palms against his lower stomach. "Demanding, too."

After using the *byonso* and the two pans of hot water provided by the proprietress for washing up, we hopped in the jeep and inched our way through narrow lanes until we reached the main road. With little traffic heading south, we arrived at KNP Headquarters in Seoul in record time. We needed to brief Inspector Kill on what we'd found. We now knew, pretty much conclusively, that these guys were GIs. They had to be. They were too young, too physically well-trained, and too close-cropped in hairstyle for them to be anything else. And they had definitely been the same guys who'd robbed the banks—the burly guy hadn't known how much he'd given up when he'd mentioned a previous attempt to kill us. In Samgakji, with that misdirected bullet. Then the second time, when we'd been the ones to hunt them down in Yongju-gol. He'd promised that the third time would be a success.

Other than that, there wasn't much to go on. We still didn't know where these men were stationed. Yongju-gol sat in the geographic center of a circle of at least six small US combat units. And the roads from all thirty or so US compounds in the Division area ran there like the spokes of an even larger wheel. Which was probably one of the reasons it had sprung up as a hub for bars and brothels and nightclubs. Easy access. Both Korean civilian buses and the free-of-charge US military bus ran right through the center of town. And cab rides were cheap, especially if three or four GIs piled into a cab and split the fare. It wasn't unusual for GIs from as far away as Camp Casey in the Eastern Corridor to commute for a change of scenery, as well as to experience the famously debauched charms of Yongju-gol. Even DACs, Department of the Army Civilians, sometimes drove up there during the day from 8th Army headquarters in Seoul to play hooky. It was a pretty good distance and, because of Seoul's traffic, a good hour's drive, but it was worth it to be away from the flagpole and prying eyes.

Since we knew that the bank robbers had wheels, they could've come to Yongju-gol from even farther away. From Camp Humphreys down in Pyongtaek or maybe even Osan, the big US Air Force base thirty miles south of Seoul.

"It would've made sense for them to travel a good distance to change their money," Ernie said.

"Right," I agreed. "They wouldn't want to stay too close to home and make it easy for us. So we're back where we started. All we know is that they're GIs, not which service they're in or where in the hell they're stationed. And we only got a good look at one of them. After jumping us, the other two were back in the alley so quickly I didn't get a chance to ID them."

"Yeah, neither did I, especially after that brick." He touched the bandaged wound on his forehead.

"We're still trying to find three needles in a fifty-thousand-man haystack."

"Don't forget the driver," I said.

"Oh, yeah. Four needles."

"But he wasn't there last night."

"Nope. Maybe he just provides the wheels and doesn't like the rough stuff."

"Smart guy."

We reported all of this to Mr. Kill. He expressed appreciation for our efforts, though he knew that despite our new bumps and bruises, we hadn't really made progress. He asked what our next move was.

"ROK Army Third Corps," I told him.

"Case of the blonde hookers?"

"Exactly," I replied. "The head shed's embarrassed, so the provost marshal wants us to go up there and establish the facts."

"Pretty obvious, aren't they?"

"What do you mean?"

"I mean the ROK Army Third Corps commander, Major General Bok Jung-nam. He's infamous."

"Infamous for what?" Ernie asked.

"For his ambition. And for thinking the rules don't apply to him."

"Isn't that dangerous for someone along the DMZ?" I asked. "And wouldn't President Park normally hammer him down?"

"Yes, normally. But this isn't your standard situation."

"What do you mean?"

"General Bok Jung-nam is married to the First Lady's cousin. It's why he was promoted so fast."

"He's young, then?"

"Very. Especially for a two-star general. Barely in his thirties, they tell me." Kill paused. "Also, he's known to have an eye for the ladies. So much so that when military nurses are assigned there, their mothers cry."

"He's *that* much of a terror?" Ernie asked.

"Maybe it's all rumor," Mr. Kill said, ever the diplomat. "But maybe not."

"Does he have other vices or weak spots?" I asked. "Besides women. Is there any way to get to him?"

"His wife," Mr. Kill said. "They say she's jealous. Checks up on him all the time."

"Which is why he stays at Third Corps," Ernie said.

"Right. Unauthorized civilians aren't allowed there."

"What about the press?" I asked.

"He loves the press," Mr. Kill replied. "As long as he controls the stories they publish."

I thought of Katie Byrd Worthington. Good luck telling her what to do.

"By the way," he said. "We received the results on that bullet from Samgakji."

"The one that barely missed my noggin," Ernie said.

"Yes. It perfectly matches the shell of the one that killed the teller at Daehan Bank."

"The same guys," I said.

"Pretty dangerous guys," Mr. Kill told us.

I rubbed the bump on the top of my skull, angry at myself for letting them get away again. But we'd find them. I wasn't sure how, but we'd find them. And soon.

Back on Yongsan Compound, we stopped at the POL point and topped off the jeep's tank. Then we drove to the barracks. I pulled my duffel bag from the back of my wall locker, shook it out, and loaded it with the field gear I might need. Ready to go, I went to meet Ernie in the parking lot and we took off.

Outside the back gate of the compound on a shaded lane in Huam-dong, Katie Byrd Worthington stood waiting for us, still in her loose, multi-pocketed fatigue shirt and, of course, carrying her trusty Nikon.

I climbed out of the passenger seat and used the up-and-forward tilt feature standard to all Army jeeps to make room for her to jump in the back. Once we were settled, Ernie took off with a roar of the engine. Katie pulled herself forward by the corners of our canvas-covered seats.

"You didn't warn anyone, did you?"

"No, ma'am," Ernie said facetiously. "We followed your instructions to the letter. Nobody knows you're riding with us."

"Good boy." She patted his shoulder. "Stick with me and you'll make military history."

"That's what I'm afraid of," Ernie said.

"Look, Katie," I said. "We're not in this for the recognition."

"Then what in the hell are you in it for?"

"We don't like to see people abused."

"Or murdered," Ernie added.

She sat back, crossing her arms. "Very noble. But you're also here because you don't want me publishing a picture of a Korean female police officer in a tight cocktail dress saving your asses."

"She didn't *save* us," Ernie said indignantly.

"Pictures don't lie," Katie replied.

"This one does."

"Huh. Wanna try explaining that for the rest of your life?"

Ernie and I were quiet, refusing to acknowledge our very real fear at the prospect of that photograph appearing in the *Overseas Observer*. It was of me and Ernie flat on our backs, a scantily-clad Korean woman standing over us pointing her revolver into the night: our protector. Not only would we never live it down, but there was no way the 8th Army honchos would ever accept such humiliation for two of their law enforcement officers. We'd be canned as CID agents. Probably sent to push paper somewhere in the vast bureaucracy of the 8th United States Army. Maybe in the Arms Room. Maybe even working for Strange.

The possibilities were horrifying. So Katie Byrd Worthington had the upper hand, at least for now. Quid pro quo for putting the kibosh on the photograph was us procuring her an interview with Lieutenant General Abner Jennings Crabtree, I Corps Commander—the man who'd ostensibly arranged for those blonde hookers to be transported by the MPs up to ROK Army III Corps headquarters. And since that was what she wanted, we'd help her get it. Of course, most military officers saw the reporters from the *Overseas Observer* as their enemy, so whether or not Crabtree would consent to the interview remained to be seen.

"But first," Katie said, "I want to talk to Screech Owl Tapia."

"Okay, okay," Ernie said. "Whatever you say."

Ernie was even more terrified of the photograph falling into the public eye than I was. His carefully crafted macho image was at stake.

I turned and looked at Katie. She leaned back in her seat, completely relaxed.

"Do you always use blackmail and coercion," I asked, "to get what you want?"

"Whenever the opportunity presents itself," she replied. "If I didn't, you boys wouldn't tell me *nothin'*."

She was probably right.

-14-

I found him at Camp Red Cloud on the outskirts of Uijongbu, sitting alone at a table at the NCO Club with a shot glass half full of what looked like bourbon. He lifted the glass and sipped slowly, staring straight ahead at the go-go dancer gyrating on an elevated platform. He was the only one watching the girl perform. It was early, just after the close-of-business cannon had gone off. Except for a few guys in the dining room, the place was deserted.

"Sergeant Major," I said, walking up to him and pulling out a chair to sit. He turned slowly, his craggy face pocked by what must've been smallpox in his youth. Weary brown eyes studied me.

"*Command* Sergeant Major," he said.

"Yes. Command Sergeant Major Tapia." I pulled out my badge. "I'm Agent Sueño. Eighth Army CID."

His lips twisted slightly at the edges. Almost a smile, but not quite. "I didn't black-market *nothing*," he said.

"No. I didn't think you did. It's not about that."

He stared at me, waiting.

"It's about Lieutenant General Crabtree," I said. "The Provost Marshal sent us, me and my partner Agent Bascom. He's outside."

"The Provost Marshal is outside?"

"No. Agent Bascom."

"Okay." He set down his glass of bourbon. "What about General Crabtree?"

"We understand he's been acting a little erratically lately. Running outside at night, ordering alerts. Stuff like that."

Tapia shrugged. "Just blowing off steam."

"Seems like a little more than that. Didn't you have to escort him back to his quarters and cancel the alert order?"

"Like I said, he's just blowing off steam. This is a high-pressure job. He's a good man, General Crabtree."

"I don't doubt it. But we need to report back. Especially after this incident with the women being transported north to ROK Army Third Corps."

"Huh." Sergeant Major Tapia chortled, leaned forward, and lifted his shot glass to his mouth. He tilted it backward and drained it. Like magic, a Korean waitress, padding silently on soft-soled shoes, appeared at our side.

"*Ddo hana*?" she asked, lifting the empty glass. Another?

Tapia shook his head. "*Ani.*" No.

He rose to his feet. A tall man, six-two, I figured, with legs that seemed somewhat spindly for his size, but a chest that barreled out right where the ribcage should be. His fatigue uniform fit perfectly, as if he'd had it tailored.

"What was your name again?"

"Sueño," I said.

"A dream," he said.

"That's right."

"Us Apaches learned some Spanish, mostly from the Catholic priests who were sent to the res to keep us in line."

I nodded, unsure how to respond.

"So what do you want me to do?" he asked. "Have Crabtree talk to a shrink? Ruin his chances for another star?"

"No. Me and my partner want to talk to him. Get his side of the story and report back to the Provost Marshal."

"You believe that shit in the *Oversexed Observer*?"

"No, not necessarily. But we need to get the facts."

He studied me, coming to a decision. Finally he said, "Do you know where the Grand Hotel is?"

"In downtown Uijongbu?"

"The same."

"Sure." It was the only tourist-class hotel in the city. That is, the only one with Western-style accommodations, including indoor toilets, tiled showers, and beds that weren't sleeping mats on the floor.

"The old man and I are going there tonight. Downstairs in the ballroom. He's receiving an award by the mayor at nineteen-hundred hours. Afterward, if you want, I'll try to convince him to have a word with you."

"Okay," I said. "Where do you want to meet? In the coffee shop there or what?"

"He doesn't like those fancy places. General Crabtree is a field soldier, like me. He only goes to the Grand Hotel when he has to. Can you track down a place called Chonwon Bulkalbi?"

"Country Village Barbecue Ribs," I said.

"Yes." He nodded approvingly.

"Is it within walking distance of the Grand?"

"About two blocks."

"I'll find it."

"Okay, then. Nineteen-hundred." He offered his hand. I shook it. "By the way," he said, "tonight, you can call me Screech Owl. We'll drop all this formal bullshit."

"Okay," I said.

He walked out of the NCO club. I wondered if the offer to use his first name was an attempt to be friendly, or if he meant to break military decorum and throw me off balance. I supposed I'd find out soon enough.

Looking exhausted, the go-go girl climbed down from her platform. I glanced at the jukebox. She watched me warily. I grinned and waved my hand to indicate I wasn't about to pop in a quarter and force her to dance to an empty room. She had it hard enough.

She sat at an empty table, placed her cheek in her open palm, and closed her eyes.

"A drunk Indian," Ernie said.

"God, Ernie. Don't talk that way when you meet Sergeant Major Tapia."

"I thought I was supposed to call him Screech Owl."

"You are, but you can show a little respect."

How we were going to work this out, I wasn't quite sure. Katie Byrd was waiting off base again. Even though she had a press credential that allowed her access to every US military compound in Korea—aside from top-secret restricted areas—she preferred, whenever possible, to remain off base.

When we asked her why, she said, "Once an MP spots my credentials at the main gate, the first thing he does is get on the horn and notify the head honcho and God and everybody else. Before you know it, a directive is issued, and everyone on base is under orders to zip it."

"SOL," Ernie said.

"You got that right. Shit out of luck."

Ernie studied her. "You've been working with the Army too long."

"What do you mean?"

"You talk like a GI. And a foul-mouthed one, at that."

"Up yours," Katie said.

Once I mentioned our meeting with General Crabtree and Screech Owl Tapia, Katie said she wanted in.

"You can't," I told her.

"Why the hell not?"

"Because this is part of our official investigation, not a news conference."

"An official investigation where you decide on the lies you'll tell the rest of the world?"

"No, you're twisting my words."

"You'll get over it. All I want to do is sit down, talk to Crabtree. He's a big boy—he can answer or not as he sees fit. And when we're done, we can all drive up to ROK Army Third Corps and get their side of the story."

"You don't ask for much, huh?" Ernie said.

"Only the truth," Katie Byrd said.

Ernie and I were trying to mollify Katie and stop the photograph from being published, and at the same time avoid being skinned alive by 8th Army for aiding the enemy. In this case, "the enemy" being an *Overseas Observer* reporter by the name of Katie Byrd Worthington, who couldn't leave this story alone. It was a delicate balance. All we could do was take one precarious step at a time, clinging to a very slippery cliff, and repeatedly telling ourselves not to look down.

That evening at eighteen-forty-five hours, we tracked down the barbecue spot Chonwon Bulkalbi almost by mouthwatering

scent alone. It was a rustic little place catering mainly to tired Korean office workers who wanted to loosen their ties, roll up their sleeves, and relax with good cheap food and maybe a few shots of *soju* with a co-worker or two. There weren't any Americans here and no hints that any ever patronized the place. The menu, brief and to the point, was written in *hangul* on a whiteboard on the side wall. In addition to *bulkalbi,* it listed *bulkogi,* marinated beef, and one of my favorites, *dengsim gu-i,* sliced flank steak. We took a table near the front window.

"I'll wait outside," Katie told us.

I figured she was going for a last smoke. But through the signage on the front window, we spotted her trotting off into the night.

"She's headed toward the Grand Hotel."

"With her camera," I said, groaning.

"Who knows what that broad has in mind?"

"We're up against it, Ernie. She's pushing us around. Treating us like a couple of punks."

"You just noticed?"

"Maybe we should call her bluff. Tell her to stuff it."

"And let her publish that photo in the *Overseas Observer*? What are you, nuts? Two military law enforcement officers flat on their backs and a local dame dressed up in an evening gown saving them from the bad guys with a gun leveled."

"It's not an evening gown," I said. "It's a cocktail dress."

"Who are you, Coco Chanel? Who gives a damn what kind of dress it is? The point is, it's a dress, and she's a woman and we're supposed to be men."

"We are," I said. "Officer Kang helping us out a little doesn't change that."

"Oh, yeah? You tell that to Riley and Strange and Colonel Brace and the Eighth Army Chief of Staff. See if a single one believes it. Or any one of the ten-thousand GIs who will see that photograph in the *Oversexed Observer* and turn us into laughingstocks. And what will those same GIs do when they see us show up for an investigation? Probably ask us where the broad is who's supposed to save our asses."

A middle-aged Korean woman with a white apron and a matching bandana atop her head approached our table and asked, "*Muol duhshi-keissoyo*?" What'll you have?

I told her we were waiting for a couple of friends, and that we'd just take barley tea for now. She slapped two handle-less earthen cups in front of us and poured warm tea from a brass pot. After she waddled away, Ernie said, "We *have* to play ball with Katie Byrd Worthington. We've got no choice."

I could tell how wrapped up Ernie's ego was in that photo's potential publication. While mine was, too, I figured I could weather the storm better than he could. If the picture did come out and someone said something to me about it, I'd consider the source—usually a GI who hadn't read a book since his first-grade teacher read Dr. Seuss to him and the whole class.

As for Ernie, I had no doubt how he'd react—with violence. He couldn't beat up every GI who read the *Overseas Observer*, but he would try. And long before he reached that goal, he'd be in the psych ward.

"It's like in those old British movies," I said.

"What do you mean?"

"You know how they say that thing when they're in a tight spot? Katie Byrd Worthington has us by the short and curlies."

"Speaking of which," Ernie said.

Lieutenant General Abner Jennings Crabtree and Command Sergeant Major Screech Owl Tapia walked into the glow of the floodlight out front, both in civilian suits, looking like a couple of bankers rather than military men. Inside, the portly proprietress scurried out from behind her work counter, smiling broadly, and bowed deeply as they entered. They spotted us, and General Crabtree frowned and whispered something to Sergeant Major Tapia.

Tapia nodded and walked toward us. "Let's sit in back," he said. "Old habit from Vietnam."

"Fragging," Ernie said.

The Sergeant Major looked at him and said, "So you've been there."

Within seconds, the proprietress had taken Crabtree's coat, and he'd loosened his tie, unbuttoned his collar, and rolled up the sleeves of his white shirt. Sitting there with his hairy arms resting on the round wooden table, he now looked like an off-duty plumber ready to chow down at his favorite diner. He held up his hand and said, "Don't salute. I've had enough of that crap today."

Instead, we shook hands and pulled up stools to sit. The proprietress buzzed around us and General Crabtree ordered for the table in Korean: four plates of sliced short ribs. Everything else—the rice, various types of kimchi, *panchan* side dishes, lettuce leaves, *deinjang* bean paste, and the plates of fresh garlic cloves—came gratis with the meal. The general looked at Ernie and me and said, "You through drinking that barley tea crap?"

We told him we were, and he ordered four liters of cold OB Beer and two bottles of Jinro soju.

Before she hurried away, the proprietress lit the gas burner beneath the barbecue plate in the center of the table. When the beer arrived, General Crabtree employed the two handed etiquette used in polite Korean society to pour beer into our glasses, which we held out in turn. Then he allowed Sergeant Major Tapia to fill his glass to the brim with the frothing liquid. Once everyone was served, Crabtree raised his glass in a toast and said, "To the ROK Army Third Corps."

We all raised our glasses and drank, then went through the ritual again.

Using shears, the proprietress sliced the short rib meat from its bones and laid the resulting strips flat on the barbecue grill, where it began to sizzle. Crabtree popped a few cloves of garlic onto the hot metal, and after the proprietress left, used his wooden chopsticks to flip the meat.

I was surprised that he spoke Korean so well, and that he was so attuned to Korean custom. But I was most surprised by the way he treated me and Ernie as equals despite our difference in rank.

"Okay, Screech Owl," he said. "You wanna tell me why these two cops are up here hounding me?"

"They say they want to know about that picture that appeared in Sunday's issue of the *Overseas Observer*."

"Total bull," General Crabtree said, staring at Ernie and then me. "The photograph's real, but the circumstances described in the story are a complete fabrication."

We poured shots of *soju* all around, and Crabtree said to Tapia, "You want to do the honors?"

He did. The I Corps Command Sergeant Major raised the thimble-sized glass of fiery rice liquor, and said, "To all lying bitch reporters. May they rot in *hell*."

We started to drink when footsteps approached from behind. "I heard that!" Katie Byrd Worthington said as she snapped a photograph of the four of us enjoying a traditional Korean feast.

Enraged, Screech Owl rose from the table and reached his giant mitts toward the fragile neck of Katie Byrd Worthington. But before he could touch her, she hopped forward and snapped a kick to his balls. To my surprise, her small boot landed right on target.

The Sergeant Major stood up straighter, apparently experiencing a momentary state of shock, and then keeled forward, writhing in agony. Katie Byrd's bulb flashed and she took another picture, this one of him clutching himself and grimacing. While he struggled to regain control, she snapped a third. Crabtree was on his feet now, not furious, as I expected, but apparently amused by the entire scene. Instead of ordering Ernie and me to take Katie Byrd into custody, he stood relaxed with his hands on his hips, his creased face assessing the situation before breaking out into a wide grin.

Ernie and I tried to help the Sergeant Major, but there was nothing we could do other than stop him from falling. I expected Katie Byrd to scamper away—in fact, I was hoping she would, and never come back. Instead, she remained, shuffling from side to side and testing angles while occasionally snapping another photograph of Crabtree.

Though solicitous of Sergeant Major Tapia, Crabtree could barely hide his laughter. Once the Sergeant Major sat back down on his stool, still clutching his groin and leaning forward and groaning, Crabtree motioned toward Katie Byrd and said, "Will you stop kicking my men in the balls, please?"

"I'll take it under consideration," Katie Byrd replied.

He turned toward the Sergeant Major, placed his hand on his shoulder, and said, "A tough old street fighter like you? I wouldn't have believed it if I hadn't seen it."

"That was cheating on her part," Screech Owl said. "Girls aren't supposed to kick."

Crabtree turned toward Katie and said, "Why don't you pull up a seat?"

Surprised, Katie glanced around, spotted an empty stool, and dragged it toward the table between Ernie and me, opposite the still-moaning Sergeant Major Tapia. Ernie and I sidled away from her, not wanting to be associated with this madwoman from the tabloid most despised by the 8th United States Army.

Once she sat, Katie adjusted the strap of her Nikon and shoved it toward her back, then reached forward and grabbed an earthen cup of barley tea. She poured the cold tea on the floor and refilled the cup with beer from one of the brown OB bottles.

She grabbed an extra set of chopsticks, broke the wood apart, and started helping herself to generous portions of the roasting short rib flesh and blackened cloves of fresh garlic. Without permission, she palmed my bowl of rice and shoved a generous dollop of steaming carbs into her mouth. With a bulge in the side of her cheek, she chewed lustily, finally swallowing enough to say to General Crabtree. "So why'd you take those hookers up to Third Corps?"

He laughed uproariously.

The Sergeant Major had started to return to form and was sitting up straighter with his hands on his knees. Other than looking like he was about to hurl, he seemed almost normal. General Crabtree poured some beer for his Command Sergeant Major and bade him drink. He did, swallowing a timid sip.

"Who in the hell told you *I* was running those girls up to Third Corps?" General Crabtree asked.

"I don't reveal my sources," Katie replied.

"Well, whoever it was, they're feeding you a load of bull. That photo you ran showed a truck full of women crossing Freedom Bridge, that's true, but they weren't going up to Third Corps. They were coming back."

Katie shrugged. "A good pimp escorts his girls home after a night's work."

"There's no such thing as a good pimp," Crabtree said.

He sipped some more beer and, realizing we were almost out, shouted across the room, "*Ajumma, meikju juo, nei byong.*" It was a minor detail, but "*nei byong*" was the precise wording for four bottles, whereas most foreigners would've said "*nei gei,*" which was more general and translated loosely as "four pieces." Crabtree knew his Korean.

When the old woman arrived with four bottles, she didn't bring Katie an extra glass, instead allowing her to continue to use the earthen cup. Her way, I imagined, of showing her disapproval of this newcomer kicking a grown man and a good paying customer in the crotch.

After we refreshed our glasses, General Crabtree toasted again. We drank and set the glassware down. He leaned toward Katie and said, "I was helping those women, Ms. Worthington, not pimping them."

This surprised Katie. She set down her chopsticks and pulled out a steno pad and a pen. Poised to write, she said, "Tell me."

General Crabtree did.

While the tang of burnt meat drifted through Chonwon Bulkalbi, General Crabtree said he would authorize us to travel north to the ROK Army III Corps. He wanted us to interview the South Korean commander there, Major General Bok Jung-nam, and ask around for ourselves, for us to corroborate the story he was about to tell me and Katie and Ernie.

-15-

According to General Crabtree, he and Sergeant Major Tapia had traveled far and wide along the five ROK divisions protecting the DMZ. Not only by helicopter or jeep, but often on foot. They'd hiked rugged mountain trails, taking a personal look at the defensive fortifications and examining the fields of fire. They even spoke to many of the ROK Army troops who manned those lonely outposts, facing across the wire at the North Korean soldiers who were sometimes no more than a literal stone's throw away. These forays into the wilds of the DMZ were detested by Korean Army brass. They were afraid of any problems the Americans might uncover. Ones that might embarrass the local commander and cause him or his superior to be overlooked on the next promotion list, or worse, be relieved of command.

"They spied on us every step of the way," General Crabtree said, reaching with his chopsticks for another thick slice of *peichu* kimchi, "sweating the reports we turned into Eighth Army. They tried to compromise us more than once."

"How so?" Katie asked, interrupting.

Crabtree shrugged. "The usual way."

"With women?"

"Sure. In local villages, they'd send some low-ranking officer to meet us, find us a room at a country inn, and feed us a spread like this." He waved his chopsticks to indicate the entire table of food. "Then hostesses would come in, and if we wanted to take them back to our rooms, we could."

"Did you?"

"I didn't."

We all looked at Sergeant Major Tapia. He stared straight ahead impassively, not answering, not moving a muscle on his face, still livid at Katie Byrd Worthington's earlier breach of etiquette.

None of it seemed to bother Katie. "So what about the Third Corps?" she asked.

"A nice headquarters," General Crabtree said. "Excellent Commo and Intel Shop, rapid execution of command directives, and a terrific direct observation point for a vast expanse of the DMZ."

"So they're on a mountain?"

General Crabtree nodded. "And General Bok Jung-nam is a sharp cookie. Knows his business."

"But you're saying you *didn't* take girls up there for him?"

"They were already there."

"Already there?"

"You got it."

Katie scribbled in her notebook, then she placed the tip of her pen to her lower lip, thinking. She asked, "Blondes?"

Crabtree shrugged. "Mostly. But a couple of brunettes."

"Were all these women reserved for General Bok?"

"I didn't ask."

"But they were brought out when you and the Sergeant Major arrived. Along with a couple of bottles of Johnnie Walker Black, I'd guess." The Korean party drink of status.

"I don't drink scotch," General Crabtree said. "Too rough on the body. A little beer, a little *soju*, plus some food—these are natural. The next morning, I'm always ready to run six miles—or hike twenty." He turned to Sergeant Major Tapia. "Right, Screech Owl?"

The Sergeant Major, eyes half-closed, mouth tight, nodded his head slowly. I imagined he was wishing he was somewhere else, far removed from anything having to do with Katie Byrd Worthington.

"So were these women being paid for their services," Katie asked, "or what?"

"I suppose. Most didn't speak English. European, I think. Maybe Greek, maybe Turkish? But one did speak for the group. According to her, they'd been recruited at various dives in Seoul. For the most part, they didn't know each other, since many of them were from different countries, but foreign women—in the same line of work—were targets of resentment here in Korea, so they had to stick together. Eventually, they were driven up to ROK Army Third Corps voluntarily, thinking they'd be serving a party of Korean Army officers for a long weekend. Instead, they'd been up there for almost a month. When they asked to be taken back to Seoul, they'd been told that no vehicles were available. After pestering and pestering, one of them finally had a chance to speak to General Bok. He told the woman they'd be returned to Seoul when it was convenient for him and not sooner. When she persisted, she received a black eye."

"From General Bok?"

Crabtree shrugged again. "I didn't ask."

"Was the black eye still visible?"

"Barely."

"So what'd you do?"

"At first I didn't believe them. But after thinking about it, I spoke to General Bok. He was embarrassed. Said it was strictly a transportation problem, that they'd had some heavy rains lately and some of the roads had been washed out, so it had taken his combat engineers longer than expected to make repairs."

"What about a chopper?"

"Up there, choppers aren't always a good idea. The updrafts and other wind turbulence can be treacherous. Even on a calm day, it'll surprise you. Sudden squalls. Wind shear. Also, I figured flying those women onto a military airfield wasn't exactly a good idea in terms of avoiding unwanted attention."

"I'll say," Katie replied. "Like the *Bob Hope Christmas Show*."

"So Sergeant Major Tapia called back down to Camp Red Cloud and ordered the MPs to send a three-quarter-ton truck, along with an armed escort, up to the ROK Army Third Corps Headquarters. When they arrived, we loaded up the women and had them taken back to Uijongbu, where they were released." He knocked back the last of the soju. "End of story."

"How innocent," Katie said.

"Yep."

"Like a fairy tale." She stood up, slipped her steno pad into her pocket, and said, "Not what my firsthand sources told me."

"Then they lied."

"Maybe," Katie Byrd said. "Maybe not." She leaned forward, bracing herself on the edge of the table. "General Crabtree, do you know the difference between a fairy tale and a war story?"

"Do tell."

"A fairy tale begins with 'Once upon a time,' and a war story begins with 'This is no bullshit.'"

With that, she turned and walked out of the chophouse. Sergeant Major Screech Owl's lifeless eyes followed her every step of the way.

■ ■ ■

Later that evening, I called Officer Kang Hey-kyong just to check in, and I was glad I did. The Bopwon-ni cops, working with those stationed in Yongju-gol, had been canvassing the area near Old Hwang's money-changing shop, asking if anyone had noticed anything out of the ordinary or maybe spotted the three GIs who'd assaulted Old Hwang, not to mention Ernie and me. They'd found nothing until one of the paralegals in the area spilled about a claim he was filing on behalf of a local businessman against the US Army.

"A jeep," Officer Kang told me in Korean. "It was parked in front of a *kagei*." An open-fronted convenience store. "One GI sat behind the wheel, and when three more GIs ran up to it and climbed in, the driver backed up, hitting the cooler filled with Chilsung Cider that the proprietor kept on the edge of the sidewalk." Korea's most popular soft drink. "He smashed it with his rear bumper," she told me, "while turning around. Fifty-thousand *won* worth of damage." A hundred bucks. Which was maybe an exaggeration, but the complainant had to cover the extra fee the paralegal would be charging. The description the store owner provided was vague. "*Potong Mikun*," he'd said. Average American soldiers. In civilian clothes, probably blue jeans.

I thanked her, thinking these might be our guys because the timing matched up. But I didn't see how it offered us much new information, other than the driver had in fact been present, and they'd probably used the same jeep from the two bank robberies. And that that jeep might now have a dent in it, which didn't exactly make it unique amongst 8th Army vehicles.

I was about to hang up when Officer Kang said, "One more thing." Paper shuffled as she presumably thumbed through notes. "The owner of the *kagei* said he spotted writing on the rear bumper."

My heart leapt.

The bumper wasn't covered with tape, which made sense. First of all, they weren't robbing a bank, only a small money changer. More importantly, Yongju-gol and the entire Division area crawled with GI convoys and military vehicles and practically constant MP patrols by both the US and Korean armies. Tape on a bumper would attract attention, whereas the actual unit designation would probably be glanced at and immediately forgotten.

"What'd he see?" I asked, trying to keep the excitement from my voice.

"He doesn't read English," she told me, "so to him, all the American letters were just lines and squiggles."

My heart fell.

"But he can read numbers."

Of course. Although Koreans had a writing system with its own form of expression for numbers, they still relied on Arabic numerals. After all, those were what was used internationally in higher mathematics, a field much loved in this education-focused country.

"What'd he see?" I asked again.

"Nineteen," she told me.

"Nineteen?"

"Yes."

"That's it?"

"Yes. The number nineteen."

"Were there any other numbers?"

"No. Just two numbers. He was sure of it. Nineteen, that's it, and then gibberish."

"Okay," I told her. "Thank you. We'll be looking into it."

"How's Katie?" she asked.

"As ornery as usual. Maybe more so," I said in English. When she said "What?" I translated it into Korean. Or tried to. What I ended up saying was that she was still mean.

"Yes," Officer Kang agreed. "That's her." Hesitating, she tried another gambit. "And Sergeant Bascom?"

I was standing at a Korean public phone booth, Ernie nearby. I motioned to him and pointed to the receiver. He puckered like he was sucking on a lemon and shook his head. "He's fine," I said.

"Is he there?"

"No," I lied. "Not right now."

"Tell him I said hello."

"I will."

We said our goodbyes and I hung up.

"She ask about me?" Ernie said.

"Yes. Why weren't you at least polite enough to talk to her?"

"Afraid."

"Afraid?"

"Yeah, she's way too rough for me."

"You're getting soft."

He grabbed his spine and leaned backward. "Lumbago," he said.

The next morning, Katie Byrd Worthington was waiting for us in front of the Camp Red Cloud main gate. She climbed in the back of the jeep and we drove south toward Seoul. After winding through the vicious Seoul morning traffic for the better part of an hour, we dropped Katie off in front of the Bando Hotel.

She climbed out and waggled her forefinger at us. "Don't get any funny ideas about leaving for the ROK Army Third Corps without me. I still have plenty of time to call Hong Kong and tell our editorial staff to publish that photo."

I told her I'd call her as soon as we ran down the bank robbery lead.

"And keep me posted on that, too," she said.

As we drove to 8th Army's Yongsan Compound, Ernie let out a whoosh of relief. "It's nice having that witch off our backs."

"For now," I reminded him.

He pursed his lips as if he were swallowing something sour.

On compound, Ernie parked the jeep in the narrow lot behind the 8th Army Snack Bar. We entered through the big double glass doors, and the first thing we spotted was Strange sitting alone at his usual table. After grabbing some chow at the serving line, we joined him, but he didn't ask if we'd had any *strange* lately. Even for him, it was too early for debauchery. I sipped on hot coffee and Ernie wolfed down a bologna and egg sandwich.

"What've you got for us?" I asked Strange.

"Nothing. Everybody's waiting for your report on General Crabtree."

"He's a good man," I said.

"Gimme the real skinny."

"Can't yet," I told him. "What do you know about a general named Bok Jung-nam?"

Strange sat up, shoving his almost-empty mug away.

"Bold dude. They're talking about him being the eventual replacement for Park Chung-hee himself."

Ernie glanced up from his sandwich. "President Park's going somewhere?"

"No. But the North Koreans tried to kill him a few years ago." In fact, they'd sent thirty-one commandos into Seoul to accomplish the task. And they'd almost succeeded, coming within sight of the Blue House, the presidential palace, before they were neutralized as a fighting force with two captured and the rest killed.

"Okay, so the US needs a backup South Korean president, if it comes to that. Who's been talking to General Bok, grooming him for the job?"

Strange shook his head. "Too highly classified."

"That means the CIA," Ernie said.

Strange kept his eyes averted and sipped on the dregs of his lukewarm chocolate.

"Find out for us," I said. "We need to know who's talking to General Bok and what they're talking about."

"That won't be easy," Strange said.

"If anyone can do it," Ernie said, "you can." Which was bull, but Strange preened, basking in the praise.

"What are you going to do with the information?" Strange asked. "If, that is, I manage to get it."

"Probably nothing," I told him. "Just for background."

Neither of us told Strange that as soon as we followed up on that lucky number nineteen lead, we'd be traveling north to the ROK Army III Corps. Not a trip I was looking forward to. Wandering far from the 8th Army flagpole was something Ernie and I usually considered a relief. We were free, avoiding unwanted scrutiny. But being that far away and out in the middle of the Taebaek Mountains, which bordered the North Korean Communist regime, wouldn't exactly be a vacation. This was an area of jurisdiction without any Korean civilian oversight to check the whims of the ROK Army III Corps commander.

Last night, during our meal at Chonwon Bulkalbi, Sergeant Major Tapia had assured us he'd been there many times. And then he'd said, "You two go. Not her." Tilting his head at Katie Byrd Worthington.

"You don't think I'd miss *this* story, do you?" she'd asked. "Not on your life."

Sergeant Major Tapia had protested again, insisting the ROK Army III Corps was no place for a woman. Before Katie could jab a chopstick into his eyeball, General Crabtree had intervened and said she could go.

That had placated Katie.

Sergeant Major Tapia had sat glumly for the rest of the evening, arms crossed, apparently lost in thought. I might've been mistaken, but it almost seemed like there was a certain sense of satisfaction lurking in his grim expression.

I rose from our table in the 8th Army Snack Bar, went to the serving line, and purchased Strange another cup of hot chocolate. As I set it in front of him, with only one marshmallow since he was on a diet, I said, "Go find out who in the US government is sponsoring this Major General Bok and what their plans are for him, if any."

"I got it, I got it. You don't ask much, do you?"

"Remember those blondes in the *Oversexed Observer*?" Ernie asked.

"Do I?"

"I might have a story for you. Not yet, but soon."

"You better. I'll be sticking my neck out. Info on CIA operations is like kryptonite at the head shed."

Then it *was* the CIA.

The night before, when Katie's instincts had told her General Crabtree was giving her a line of bull about III Corps and his role in rescuing those women from General Bok, she might've been right. There was more going on here than a military-sponsored sex party. The American CIA was involved. What was their endgame?

We left Strange sipping on his steaming cup of cocoa and returned to the jeep.

-16-

"Where in the hell you guys *been*?" Sergeant Riley shouted.

"Nice to see you, too," Ernie said, waving as he brushed past the CID Admin Sergeant, heading straight for the stainless steel coffee urn in the back.

Riley turned and glowered at me, eyebrows raised.

"Working on the First Corps report," I told him.

"What'd you get?"

"You'll see it once I type it up."

"We need that report *now*." He jammed his forefinger into the center of his government-issue desk blotter.

"No coffee first?" I asked.

"Fine. But make it snappy."

That was him. Staff Sergeant Riley loved nothing more than giving orders, even though most of the time he was ordering us to do things we already knew we had to.

After I pulled a cup of hot coffee from the urn, I walked over to a chart on the wall with the bold-print title of 8th

United States Army Organization Chart. The way the numerical designation of military units worked had always been somewhat obscure to me, and to other people in the Army as far as I could tell. Units were created, units went away, then for some alchemical reason that no one quite understood, they were sometimes brought back to life. Each unit had not only a number, but also a nickname and usually its own coat of arms. To keep track of it all, the Pentagon had a department called the Institute of Heraldry. I didn't believe I'd have to go so far as to consult them to figure out what the number 19 on that jeep bumper meant.

In general, the smaller the number, the higher the headquarters. For instance, 1st Army, which covered the eastern United States. The place we all worked, 8th Army, was responsible for the Korean Peninsula. The main subordinate unit of 8th Army was the 2nd Infantry Division. Again, only one number. Farther down the line were units with three numbers, like the 501st Military Intelligence Battalion or even lower, the fictional 4077th MASH unit, made famous by Hollywood. So a unit identified by the number 19 would be pretty high up on the organizational chart. And there it was. Right toward the top. The 19th Support Group, providing maintenance and supply to the entire US military endeavor on the Korean Peninsula. Their headquarters was at Camp Henry in Taegu, over a hundred miles south of Seoul. But they had outlying support units scattered all over the peninsula. If the Korean *kagei* owner with the smashed soda cooler had been able to read English letters, his information probably would've pinpointed the exact compound the jeep had come from. Though he hadn't been able to, I knew from a previous case that about two thousand GIs were assigned to the 19th Support Group, so we'd just dropped our odds of finding them from over fifty thousand American servicemen and women stationed in-country to a group a fraction of that size.

Progress.

I grabbed one of the 8th Army Telephone Directories, sat down at a rickety field table, smiled, and started dialing.

I discovered that the elements of the 19th Support Group operated out of thirty-five different compounds throughout the country, stretching from the port of Pusan at the southern end to as far north as Camp Edwards in the Western Corridor, just south of where Freedom Bridge crossed the Imjin River. Twenty of those outposts were either in Seoul or within easy driving distance of 8th Army Headquarters here on Yongsan Compound.

The question now was how to narrow my search further without alerting the robbers. I had no idea where they worked. I might arrive in a 19th Support Group Orderly Room, ask a few questions, and later find out that I was talking to one of the miscreants himself, maybe the driver, maybe one of the two guys we'd caught a glimpse of during the fight in Yongju-gol.

We could also go through the mugshot-like photos in the personnel records and find the body builder.

We'd gotten a fairly good look at him in the dim lighting of Old Hwang's money-changing shop, but it would take time, a few hours at least. Worth the time, but there was a catch: the 8th Army personnel shop was itself a 19th Support Group function. Just by the act of two CID agents walking in to look at records, it was possible, even likely, that the GIs we were looking for would be alerted. Even if no one was present while we did our research, GIs were notorious gossips. Our arrival would spread throughout the enlisted barracks and officers' quarters like wildfire. *CID is combing through the 19th Support Group personnel files.* Who else could we be looking for but the bank robbers in the case we'd been assigned? And once the perpetrators were alerted, what might they do? We knew they weren't afraid to arm themselves and take action, lethal and otherwise. Being reckless with our investigation could cost lives, and not just our own. Better if we could sneak up on the crooks without risking prior notification and take them down before they knew what had hit them.

While I was pondering these matters, Miss Kim's phone rang. She politely asked the person to hold, covered the receiver, turned to me, and said, "Do you know someone named Katie Byrd?"

I took the call.

■ ■ ■

The blonde bouffant hairdo looked out of place not only in this smoke-filled cocktail lounge but in this country at large, where the standard to conform to was straight black hair.

She took a final drag on her cigarette, held it in for a moment, and exhaled toward the ceiling. I recognized this woman as one of the six in the photograph in the most recent issue of the *Overseas Observer*. If General Abner Jennings Crabtree wasn't pulling our leg, she'd been one of the women transported from ROK III Corps headquarters back to civilization thanks to himself, Sergeant Major Tapia, and the special MP detachment. Katie Byrd Worthington had tracked this woman down somehow through her contacts. When I asked her about it, she shot me a look that translated to: *Mind your own freaking business.*

The woman flicked her cigarette atop the edge of a crystal ashtray. Her stubby white fingers were covered with rings of all shapes and sizes. Gold, silver, cheap gems—no real diamonds there, as far as I could tell.

"You talk," she told me in a thick European accent. "I no like speak English. Make me tired."

Katie Byrd Worthington patted her solicitously on her bare forearm. "You're doing fine, Sofia."

We sat in a place called the Top Hat Scotch Corner in the northeastern Susaek-dong area of Seoul. It was a small cocktail lounge sitting pretty much by itself amidst a few square blocks of textile factories. Three Korean businessmen in cheap suits sat at the bar, smoking and discussing labor costs. Also, I thought based on my eavesdropping, how to find short-term loans to cover those labor costs. An electric piano and a couple of horned instruments sat on a dark stage, waiting for the musicians to come along and breathe life into them. We were early.

"Who paid you to go into the mountains to the army base?" Katie asked.

"I told you already," Sofia said.

"He needs to know, too."

Sofia studied me. "He's cop. Cop always trouble." When neither of us responded, she said, "What Sofia get? Who pay me this time? I talk, no get money. Only get trouble."

"You'll get justice," I said.

Her eyes widened, puzzled. "What's that," she said, "justice?"

For a moment, I thought she was asking a philosophical question. Then I realized that the word fell outside of her vocabulary.

"It means," Katie Byrd told her, "that those men at Three Corps will be punished."

"Go to jail?"

"Yes," Katie replied. "Jail."

Sofia puffed on her cigarette. "That be good," she said.

"So tell us what happened."

She did. Painfully and slowly, using the limited English she had, not knowing enough Korean to switch to that instead. Katie, I realized, could've been a trauma counselor or a father confessor. She patiently pulled every last drop of information out of the troubled woman. A woman alone and adrift in the world, stranded in a country she didn't understand amongst people who didn't value her aside from her body.

Finally, it came out. What General Bok and his subordinates had done to her and the other girls. How they'd been kept up there for weeks against their will. And that none of them had ever received the money they'd been promised.

A juicy story, I knew, for the *Overseas Observer*. Still, I wondered if Katie would publish it. It criticized representatives of the Korean government, a regime that didn't have a First Amendment and wasn't planning on establishing one any time soon. Katie Byrd and anyone else associated with the *Oversexed Observer* could be kicked out of the country for good—if they weren't charged with sedition and thrown in jail.

"Who convinced you to go up there?" Katie asked. "General Crabtree?"

"No. He very nice. And that dark man, mean face."

"Sergeant Major Tapia?" I said.

"Yes, him. He nice, too."

I sensed Katie start to lose interest in the story. No way to hammer the US Army. But then Sofia mentioned something that neither of us had considered.

"General Crabtree, he really like Estella."

"Estella?"

"Yes. I think General Bok, he no like. How you say?"

I had no idea what Sofia was talking about. Katie was the one who came up with the word. "Jealous?" she asked.

"Yes. Jealous."

Katie's nose for news began to quiver. "So did General Crabtree bring Estella back personally? Is he taking care of her now?"

Sofia studied Katie, puzzling out what she'd said. "Estella now with General Crabtree?"

"She is?" Katie started to write.

"No." Sofia shook her head. "Not with General Crabtree."

Katie let her notebook rest back on her knee. "Then where is she?"

"With General Bok."

"Here in Seoul?"

"No. Up there."

"In Third Corps?"

"Yes. He no let her leave. Estella must stay."

"Why?"

Sofia shook her head. The heavily teased hair rustled like dried straw. "General Bok want her to stay. General Bok no let her go."

"She's a captive?"

Sofia shook her head again. For a moment, I thought she

didn't understand the word "captive." Then I realized she did understand it but didn't think it was the right word. "She, how you say . . ."

Katie and I waited.

Finally, light came to Sofia's eyes. "Estella, she *hostage*."

"Hostage? Why?"

Sofia shrugged. "I don't know. General Bok, he want General Crabtree to do something. What he want him to do, I don't know. So don't ask me. I'm tired."

She pulled out a fresh cigarette and lit up.

Katie gently tried to question her a little more, but to no avail.

Before we left, I insisted Sofia take 10,000 *won*. Twenty bucks. Which she did, slipping it quickly into a loose pocket in her skirt without thanking me. She lit another cigarette and puffed madly, glancing at the preoccupied businessmen. Not getting their attention, she turned back to her lonely table next to the wall. She didn't say goodbye to either of us as we walked out.

So Major General Bok was using Estella to coerce General Crabtree into doing something for him. But what?

Ernie made a list of the 19th Support Group compounds within a reasonable driving distance of Seoul. Right after evening chow, we started our search, wearing civilian clothes since it was after duty hours. We knew for sure what one of the bank robbers looked like, the burly guy who'd tried to rob Old Hwang in Yongju-gol. The one who'd been described by witnesses in the robberies as a bodybuilder type. He was strong—that I could vouch for.

"You think he's Mexican?" Ernie asked.

"No," I answered, shaking my head. "No way. He wasn't Mexican."

"Then what was he?"

"Something we don't see much of in the army. Middle Eastern, maybe."

"Five o'clock shadow, dark hair, heavy eyebrows."

"Yeah. Somewhere in the Levant."

Ernie didn't know what the Levant was. I told him: the countries bordering the eastern shore of the Mediterranean Sea.

"How'd you learn a word like that?"

"Eric Ambler," I said.

"Who?"

"Eric Ambler. He's an author. Writes thrillers about exotic places."

Ernie swerved through a gyrating thread of speeding kimchi cabs. "*You* oughta write about exotic places," he said.

"Me? Exotic places? Like where?"

"Like here."

The reek of garlic hit us as Ernie surged past a three-wheeled produce truck piled high with a small mountain of cloves.

"Here?" I asked. "What's exotic about here?"

"Yeah, I guess you're right. Just another day in the R-O-K."

"Another night," I corrected.

"That, too."

"How about the other two guys?" I asked. "Besides the dark-haired one. Did you get a look at them?"

He shook his head. "Negative."

Neither of us was sure about them. They'd appeared out of the dark alley and attacked so quickly that I knew I wouldn't be able to make a positive ID. Unfortunately, they could certainly identify me and Ernie. So we had to be circumspect. The two we couldn't recognize could spot us and attack without us even being aware that we were in danger. We decided to focus on locating the jeep first.

We started at the 21st Transportation Company motor pool in Seoul, and after threatening the night dispatcher with our CID badges, he told us that none of the jeeps in their inventory had been reported with a dented right rear bumper. Just to be sure, we walked down three long rows of parked jeeps, checking the bumpers with our flashlight beams, not finding any that had been recently damaged.

Then we drove to Camp Coiner and the Far East Compound in downtown Seoul, and then out to ASCOM, the Army Support Command, in Bupyong. Shortly before midnight, we arrived at Camp Mercer in the city of Bucheon. And it was there that we walked through the dark and silent motor pool, inspecting each vehicle with the beam of our flashlights, and finally found a right rear fender, dinged and with a slash of white paint on it.

"Maybe," Ernie said, bending down, examining the dent closely.

We checked the jeep, not finding anything inside except for the routine roadside emergency gear. I jotted down the unit designation: HHC, RR&I, 19SG.

"What in the hell's that mean?" Ernie asked.

HHC stood for Headquarters and Headquarters Company. 19SG meant the 19th Support Group. But what RR&I was, neither of us knew. We walked over to the Staff Duty Office at the Camp Mercer Headquarters building. A Sergeant First Class named Homer was leaning back in a swivel chair, combat boots up on the desk, watching a small television set tuned to the American Forces Korea Network.

"What you watchin'?" I asked.

He jerked forward, tilted to his side, and almost fell out of his chair. "Nothing," he said, standing up and switching off the TV.

"Looks like *Gunsmoke* to me," Ernie said.

"Had to be," I said, turning toward Ernie. "I'd recognize Matt Dillon anywhere."

AFKN was famous for reruns. Oldies but moldies.

"I wasn't watching anything," Sergeant Homer said. "Just getting ready to do my hourly inspection."

"Good. Maybe you can show us where RR&I is."

"Why should I?" he asked warily.

"So we don't turn you in for watching television on duty," Ernie replied.

He thought about it and said, "RR&I is the third building down on the right."

"That old warehouse?" I asked.

He nodded.

"Do they have a duty officer?"

"No. Locked up at night."

"And their barracks?"

"They're billeted with the rest of Headquarters Company. In the three buildings behind warehouse row." He motioned toward the eastern wall of the compound.

"Thanks." We started to walk out.

At the door, Ernie turned and asked, "What the hell does RR&I stand for, anyway?"

"Refrigeration Repair and Inspection."

"What kind of refrigeration?" I asked.

"Like big freezers at transshipment facilities. Or walk-ins at mess halls."

"Food storage."

"Yeah."

We turned and started to walk out. Behind us, the SDO yelled, "Who the hell are you guys, anyway?"

"Just lookin' for a friend," I told him.

He sat back down heavily in his chair. When we were ten yards out, we heard the sounds of gunfire. Apparently, Marshal Dillon was busy dispensing frontier justice.

The RR&I facility was closed and locked up tight.

Lights were on in the three barracks behind the warehouses, but they were mostly deserted. Through the bare windows, only a couple guys were visible. One sat on his bunk reading, and the other fiddled with a towel and shaving kit, preparing to head to the latrine. We recognized neither.

"Should we question them?" Ernie asked.

"No," I said. "Better if we come back tomorrow during duty hours when it's more likely the guys we're looking for will be here."

"Yeah," Ernie said. "With backup."

We both knew that with criminals as trigger-happy as these, overwhelming force and the element of surprise would be critical to a clean arrest. One with no bloodshed.

Before dawn the next morning, we were on our way to the Snack Bar when we heard something that sounded like a large lizard.

"*Pssst*," somebody said.

Ernie and I turned. Lurking in the darkness on the edge of the Quonset hut was Strange, his sunglasses and cigarette holder peeking around the gray metal.

"*Pssst*," he said again.

"We heard you," Ernie told him. "Quit imitating an overweight iguana."

We followed him around the edge of the building and then across the street to some single-story brick buildings, where he finally stopped out of the line of sight of anyone who might pass by on the main road. The only illumination was from caged red bulbs above the entranceways.

"What the hell is it, Strange?" Ernie asked.

"The name's Harvey."

"Right, Sergeant Harvey. What is it?"

"That's Sergeant First Class Harvey to you."

I suspected Ernie had pissed him off with the overweight reptile remark.

"What've you got for us, Sarge?" I asked.

"Two things." He looked around warily. These were supply buildings, dark and locked from the outside. No prying eyes. "First, confirmed that it's our CIA talking to Major General Bok. There's a lot of unhappiness in the country with Park Chung-hee. You know, all those Commies and sweet young university dollies waving signs and protesting in the streets."

Koreans called these protests *demos*. Most took place either on college campuses or in the heart of downtown Seoul, demanding free elections and the cessation of the arrests and disappearances of President Park's political opponents. Some of these demonstrations had consisted of hundreds of thousands of people and had brought Seoul to a grinding halt.

Even worse was the resulting violence—sometimes starting with the more radical protesters, sometimes with the riot police—which was broadcast on televisions all over the world, embarrassing not only to the Park Chung-hee regime, but also to its most stalwart ally, the United States of America.

"So our CIA wants President Park gone?" I said.

"Maybe, maybe not. But they want another option in case that becomes a yes."

"Okay. So the CIA's talking to General Bok," Ernie said, "setting him up for the big time. That explains why he figures he can kidnap a bunch of foreign hookers and nobody will say shit. What else you got?"

"Isn't that good enough?" Strange asked.

"You said you had two things."

"I *do*."

"Well, spill."

"I will. But a guy deserves a little appreciation first."

"I don't have time to come up with bullshit stories for you, Strange," Ernie said, stepping toward him.

"Come up with *bullshit* stories?"

"You know what I mean," Ernie said, realizing he'd stepped in it.

"No. What *do* you mean?" Strange asked.

"I just mean bullshit as in shooting the breeze too long. I'm getting plenty of strange. More than I can handle, in fact, which is why I pass it along."

Strange adjusted his shades. "Okay," he said, somewhat mollified. He turned toward me. I nodded.

"The second thing," Strange continued, "is that General Crabtree has been going off script. That's why he was ranting and raving in his skivvies the other night—because he was so damn mad that Eighth Army told him to cooperate with General Bok and to stop sending up so many critical reports."

"Critical reports about what?"

"About Third Corps' defensive posture. And their readiness. Crabtree doesn't think Bok is a qualified commander. Says a North Korean invasion would run right over him. And that he only landed his position by virtue of being related to the First Lady."

This flew in the face of what General Crabtree had told us at the chophouse, describing Bok as a competent commander.

I paused, thinking it over. We didn't have much time; the supply functions around us would be coming to life soon. "Why is sending up reports critical of General Bok's expertise considered to be going off script?"

"Isn't that obvious? Because the American CIA likes Bok. He's a committed anti-Communist."

"So is Park Chung-hee."

Strange's cigarette holder tilted upward. "Have you ever seen Park Chung-hee on television? He's a disaster. Looks like the guy in the torture chamber tying your grandmother onto the rack. This is the celebrity age. Bok offers glamour."

"The CIA would tear down a government just for that?"

"No. But it looks as if the South Korean people are about to make the change for them. Better to get out ahead of the power shifts."

"Plan B," I said.

"Exactly."

"What else you got?" Ernie demanded.

"That's not enough? Don't I get some hot chocolate?"

"One marshmallow," Ernie said.

"No, I want two this time."

"You off your diet?"

"Yeah," Strange said, slapping his sizeable stomach. "Finally hit my fighting weight."

Ernie glanced down. "Doesn't look like it to me."

Strange looked up, aggrieved, but out here in the darkness, he didn't have the nerve to say "up yours" in response.

The three of us walked toward the bright lights of the 8th Army Snack Bar.

I kept wondering why the Army wouldn't take General Crabtree's reports seriously concerning the III Corps' deficiencies. Wasn't that vital? What was more important than defending the Republic of Korea from a North Korean attack, which was why we were here?

And then I thought of the bigger picture of the Cold War. The precarious standoff called mutually assured destruction that kept a nervous peace between the United

States and our enemies: the Soviet Union, Red China, and North Korea.

What kind of pawns were we being played as, and by whom? Of what international consequence was one European prostitute? None, I imagined, other than good copy for Katie Byrd Worthington.

We grabbed some chow to go and hurried to the CID office. We had a military-style assault to organize.

-17-

The group was locked and loaded and ready to move out at zero-eight-hundred hours. I showed everyone a sketch map of the Camp Mercer compound. Using a pointer to indicate the front gate, I told Staff Sergeant Palinki and Corporal Muencher to stay there with a jeep, keeping the gate locked and making sure no one escaped. Two other MPs I assigned to the rear gate, and the rest of us—six MPs plus me and Ernie—would search Headquarters Company barracks, the Refrigeration Repair and Inspection warehouse, and any other associated 19th Support Group functions. We were searching for the GIs we suspected of robbing two banks, assaulting a security guard, killing a teller, and attacking a money changer by the name of Old Hwang in Yongju-gol. Not to mention attacking me and Ernie.

"Brotha," said Palinki, who was from Hawaii, "we stopping a *crime* wave."

Everyone laughed.

With Ernie leading the way, our convoy of four jeeps took about a half hour to reach Camp Mercer in Bucheon. As instructed, Palinki and Muencher secured the front gate while Ernie and I barged into the Headquarters Company Orderly Room and served the unit commander with the Provost Marshal's signed order permitting us to search the premises and detain any and all 19th Support Group Personnel we considered to be suspects. While the CO sputtered after reading the order, Ernie led the armed posse to the RR&I warehouse, rounded up all GIs there, then went outside to the associated supply offices and the barracks. Within ten minutes, we had a ragtag formation of GIs standing in the small central parade field, all of them bitching about being away from the comfort of their diesel space heaters, some of them smoking despite the MPs' barked orders to put 'em out.

"What are you gonna do?" one of the GIs asked. "Shoot me?"

I studied the face of each GI, not seeing the dark-haired man who'd knocked me down in Yongju-gol. Ernie checked with the Motor Pool NCO and determined that a guy named Poulson, Corporal Wilford R., had been the dispatched driver of the vehicle yesterday—and for a number of days before that.

"Where's Poulson now?" I asked one of the senior NCOs.

"You just missed him. He left right after morning formation, about twenty minutes ago."

"Alone?"

"No. With the same three guys who usually travel with him. Gottfried, Wells, and Sarkosian."

"What's their duty?"

"They're refrigeration inspectors. Check the ration storage facilities and the mess halls to make sure the refrigeration equipment is maintained and functioning and that perishable foodstuffs, especially meat, are transported and stored at the correct temperatures."

"Sounds like a get-over," I said. "On their own, wandering around the countryside from compound to compound?"

The sergeant shrugged. "They have a regular route to follow. And inspection and maintenance check sheets that have to be reviewed and signed off on by the mess sergeants and officers in charge of the storage facilities. If the job's done right, there's plenty of work to keep them busy."

"And if it's not?"

He shrugged again. "Then we all die from food poisoning."

"Who's in charge of this detail?"

"Sarkosian, Spec Five." A Specialist 5, the same pay grade as a buck sergeant. "His first name's Karim, which is what everybody calls him."

Based on the way he said it, I thought the name was pronounced *care-em*, rhyming with "harem." But I knew that probably wasn't right, so I checked the official records in the Orderly Room and eventually found that it was Karim—said as *car-EEM*—a fairly common Middle Eastern name. The butchering of the original pronunciation wasn't surprising, based on the creative Army interpretations of my own last name.

Once we were sure the guys we were looking for were no longer on compound, the formation was dismissed. GIs wandered back to their work stations, kicking dirt and cussing.

In the Headquarters Company Orderly Room, I asked the CO if anybody had a photograph of Sarkosian or the three guys traveling with him. It turned out that the Company clerk was a shutterbug. He showed me and Ernie some black and-white-snapshots he'd taken a few months ago at the unit's summer picnic.

"There's Gottfried and Wells," he said pointing to two guys playing volleyball. "And there's Karim."

He was a muscular guy with a scowl and close-cropped bristly black hair. Ernie and I glanced at one another and nodded. Definitely the guy we'd tangled with in the alley in Yongju-gol. The one we'd almost slapped handcuffs on before his two pals jumped us.

I asked if I could keep the photos. When the clerk hesitated, I told him to write down his name and address so I could mail them back to him as soon as we no longer needed them. He agreed and addressed the front of a large pulp envelope with a felt marker, then handed it to me.

"Where were these three guys headed this morning?" I asked.

He phoned the RR&I unit, spoke to someone for a minute, hung up, and said, "They're on their way to Camp Humphreys."

Down in Pyongtaek, about forty miles southeast of our current position.

"A long trip," Ernie told me.

"But worth it if we can corner them there."

We decided to leave two reliable MPs here, Palinki and Muencher, in case Sarkosian and his crew doubled back at any point.

Usually, Ernie and I operated alone without bothering to keep the 8th Army CID office apprised of our whereabouts, which drove Staff Sergeant Riley nuts—which also happened to be the fun of it. But with this many MPs traveling with us, I thought it was best to check in. Using the Company clerk's phone, I called our office, expecting to hear Miss Kim's lovely voice. My plan was to leave a brief message with her and hang up. I'd only spoken a couple of words when Riley snatched up the phone.

"Where in the hell *are* you guys?" he said.

"You know where we are. Camp Mercer."

"Still? You better get off your lazy butts and get over to Suwon."

"Suwon?"

"Yeah. Where in the hell else would you go?"

Suwon was about twenty miles southeast of Seoul. It was

known for its ancient Hwaseong Fortress and the beauty of its reconstructed palaces and temples, plus the relaxed atmosphere of its scenic countryside. It also wasn't too far out of the way for someone traveling from, say, Camp Mercer to Camp Humphreys.

"What happened in Suwon?" I asked.

"Seriously? A goddamn bank robbery, that's what. Except this time, the guys with the M16s weren't as nice as they were before."

"How many bodies?"

"The KNPs are still counting. All I know for sure is that there's a hell of a lot of blood and they haven't even sorted it out yet. The Provost Marshal is about to shit a brick."

"We're on our way," I said and hung up.

Suwon was small enough that our little convoy entering the outskirts attracted quite a bit of attention from the locals. We weren't met with pleasant smiles, which did sometimes happen with Koreans who liked the American effort to help defend their country, but rather with worried looks and furtive steps back into doorways. At a KNP roadblock, I showed the officer our 8th Army dispatch. The heading was, of course, printed in English, but with *hangul* type beneath that. He handed the dispatch back to me and shook his open palm in a gesture that meant no. "No go," he said in English. "You no go."

I answered him in Korean, telling him we were military police. Relieved to be able to communicate, he explained that there'd been a bank robbery which had resulted in a number of casualties, and he and the other five armed cops at the roadblock were under orders not to allow anyone to proceed into or out of Suwon. I explained that we were working for Chief Homicide Inspector Gil Kwon-up. This received the startled reaction I expected it to, and I challenged him to use his radio to confirm that we should be allowed in to view the crime scene. I also flashed him my badge.

The mention of Mr. Kill, as it often did, changed his attitude. After a brief radio conversation, the KNP nodded, saying, "*Yeh, yeh, yeh,*" then turned and waved us through.

The Kukchei Import-Export Bank sat about thirty yards from the main gate of the stone-walled Hwaseong Fortress, on the edge of a traffic circle that surrounded a green-tile-roofed pagoda with a giant brass bell in the center.

"What's that bell for?" Ernie asked.

"Buddhist monks ring it in the morning to call people to prayer or meditation," I said, "and in the evening to put them to sleep. It has a calming effect."

Van-sized Korean ambulances and blue police Hyundai sedans, red lights flashing, jammed the entryway to the cement edifice that fronted the bank. Bodies were still being wheeled out on gurneys, and what appeared to be fresh blood stained the front stone steps. People stood scattered, hugging one another, and crying.

"Holy hell," Ernie said, his voice filled with awe.

We parked our three jeeps where we could. It looked like we were the first Americans on scene since the perpetrators of these murders. I told the uniformed MPs to wait in their jeeps. The nervous gazes of the KNP technicians processing the crime scene turned to us as Ernie and I strode forward. We stopped at the yellow tape strung in front of the bank. Up close, I saw there was more blood on the steps than I had thought. Its smell was metallic and frightening.

After the first surprised glance, everyone quietly returned to their work, ignoring us. We stood there for a couple of minutes before Ernie said, "Fuck this," and ducked beneath the tape. I followed. We stepped gingerly into the bank, and this time Korean cops in white shirts with rolled-up sleeves, hands in plastic gloves, turned to look at us. The bank was enormous, more like a high-windowed cathedral. Apparently the Kukchei Import-Export Bank was one of the more prosperous businesses in the city of Suwon. A couple of teller windows had been shattered by gunfire. Behind the counter was most of the activity, everyone focused on things on the floor that we couldn't see.

A uniformed cop, right hand on the hilt of his pistol, hurried toward us.

"No," he said, waving his palm. "No can."

We flashed our badges, and I told him we were looking for Inspector Gil Kwon-up. Per usual, this gave pause. The chief homicide inspector of the Korean National Police was well known to every cop in Korea. "Wait," he said. He rushed off and conferred with a gray-haired man in a suit. Next to him stood a female cop holding a pen and clipboard. After receiving some sort of instructions, the uniformed cop bowed to the gray-haired man and returned to us.

"Wait by the tape," he told me in Korean. "Inspector Ahn will speak to you soon."

"How many are dead?" I asked.

"Three, so far. Others," he said, shaking his head, "we don't know."

"They're in the hospital?"

He nodded and insisted once again that we return to the tape.

We did.

"See?" Ernie told me, pulling out a stick of ginseng gum and popping it into his mouth. "If you play by the rules, like you do all the time, nothing gets done."

"Rules are good," I said.

"Huh," Ernie said dismissively. "What'd they ever get you?"

"This job," I said.

Ernie chomped loudly on his gum. "See what I mean?"

For me, serving in the Army as an agent of the Criminal Investigation Division was a step up in life. My mother had died when I was very young, and for reasons I still hadn't figured out, my father ran off to Mexico, his home country. I'd grown up in foster homes at the sufferance of the Supervisors of the County of Los Angeles. Some of my foster parents were okay, some not so much, but as soon as I turned seventeen, I joined the army. A line I once heard in basic training had always stuck with me. "Three hots and a cot. I've never had it so good."

Of course, the guy saying it was doing so sarcastically. But for me, it was true. I had a job, clean clothes, three regular meals a day if I wanted them, plus a paycheck at the end of the month. More importantly, I *was* somebody. I had a name and rank and fit firmly into a hierarchy. The Army had become home for me. And when I was transferred to South Korea, I was mesmerized by the beauty and mystery of the country's traditions. Ever since, I'd been studying as hard as I could to understand its culture. The more I learned the more I understood how little I really knew.

"Wake up," Ernie said, elbowing me. "Here comes the head honcho."

The gray-haired cop in the sharp suit approached us with a blue-clad female officer tagging closely at his heels. He reached out his hand and we shook. I bowed as he told us in English his name was Inspector Ahn.

Ernie stopped chomping quite so loudly on his ginseng gum—which was his way of being polite—and let me do the talking. I showed Inspector Ahn my badge and explained who we were and that we'd been working with Mr. Kill on the string of GI robberies. I felt a wave of guilt as I said it, wondering if we might've prevented this by arriving a half-hour earlier at the 19th Support Group.

His eyes narrowed as he studied me. Eventually, he said, "Come."

He turned, and Ernie and I ducked under the tape and followed. The four of us stepped gingerly around the edge of the bank of teller windows and the half-dozen desks that had been pushed out of the way from the center of the floor. One of them had been turned on its side, as if being used as a barricade. Behind the desk lay two bodies. Both Americans. One of them with part of his skull blown off, blood and brain matter spattered everywhere. The other seemed to have taken a shot to the gut. He was curled into a fetal position, his hands by his stomach, as if trying to hold in the gray intestines that had partially spilled out onto the granite floor.

Ernie and I breathed in and out heavily, trying to maintain our cool in the face of this carnage. Both GIs wore standard-issue fatigues and combat boots. I knelt to get a better look. Their faces were slathered in camo stick, and it took me a minute to look past the purposeful concealment and discern the contours of their eyes and mouths. Reaching into my side pocket, I pulled out one of the photographs we'd been given by the company clerk back at Camp Mercer. I looked closer at the two young men leaping for a volleyball, then back at these death masks.

"Gottfried and Wells," I said to Ernie, handing him the photo. He knelt and compared the corpses to the picture.

"Right," he said, handing the print back to me. I stood and stuffed it back into my pocket.

I turned to Inspector Ahn. "Any others?" I asked.

He walked me through the large room, pointing to his right and left. One corpse after another, huddled against walls and booths.

"Christ," Ernie whispered.

At the big door leading deeper into the bank, we stopped and I asked Inspector Ahn, "How many total?"

"Korean employees," he said. "Five dead now, seven more in hospital."

He turned right and led us to the end of a hallway. Ernie stepped closer to me and said, disbelief in his voice, "They waged a freaking *war*."

Halfway down a long passageway stood what appeared to be a large cashier's cage embedded into the side wall. The barred, steel-reinforced window had been completely blown out with an explosive. The hallway continued straight ahead and eventually led outside to a green garden area with magpies and robins flitting around.

"What did they use?" I asked Inspector Ahn, pointing to the bent metal and shattered glass.

"Hand grenade," he said. "We think."

He warned us against touching anything. We retraced our steps back down the hallway, past the small foyer leading into the catacombs of the massive bank, through the desk-strewn work area, to the other side of the teller windows, and finally across the entrance hall and out the front door.

Gazes followed us as we passed. Cops and forensic techs, their eyes betraying a less-than-professional hatred.

"Okay," Ernie said sotto voce, "maybe I *won't* get a date in Suwon tonight."

Outside, Inspector Ahn paused to explain. "Because of the bank robberies in Seoul, we worried that soon these men come to Suwon. We were right. So every bank in Suwon have two police officers with rifles." He mimicked aiming a rifle. "They hide in office, behind tellers. When American GIs come inside through front door, start yelling, tell everybody get down, our Korean police officers come out. Shoot."

"And the GIs shot back?"

"Yes. They have better weapons." The Korean cops were armed only with old-fashioned M1 rifles. "GIs get all the way to cashier's cage, use hand grenade to get inside."

And so, about two dozen employees and a handful of customers suddenly found themselves in the middle of a firefight. I wasn't sure this was the technique police departments would have used in the States, but in Park Chung-hee's South Korea, they didn't play around.

After finishing his explanation, Ahn led us off the stone steps to a cement curb on the side of the bank, and we followed him as he spryly hopped down onto a neatly tended garden area. At the side of the stone building, the shattered window we'd seen from inside loomed about ten feet above us. Below, as if he'd fallen head first, lay another GI on his back, mouth open, staring at the sky. I didn't have a photograph to compare him against, but the nametag on the front of his fatigue shirt was plain: Poulson. Rank insignia, corporal.

"The driver," Ernie said. "The one who dispatched the jeep." Ernie knelt and felt for a pulse, then stood back up, shaking his head.

"By the way," I asked Inspector Ahn. "Did you find a US Army jeep?"

"Over here."

He led us around the bank. "There was a fourth. Big man," he said, rounding his forearms at his sides to indicate someone huskier. "We think jeep here." He pointed to the side street behind the bank. "He climb in, drive away."

"All this gunfire," Ernie said, remembering the bullet holes we'd seen in the tellers' stations and the desks and the walls inside the bank. "And nobody popped him?"

Inspector Ahn paused, trying to figure out what Ernie meant.

"Nobody shot him?" I repeated.

"No. No shoot," Inspector Ahn said. "Too afraid after grenade. But one very brave man try."

Near a clump of bushes more yellow tape was strewn, and two technicians in gray overalls stooped behind a clump of thick shrubbery. Inspector Ahn gave an order and they stood up and backed away, each man grabbing a handful of brush. They pulled the branches apart. Lying on the ground was a blue-uniformed Korean cop. His white gloves and the whistle hanging around his neck indicated that he was part of traffic control. And standard procedure dictated that Korean traffic cops weren't armed. Inspector Ahn explained that this cop had heard the gunfire, run over to see if he could help, and confronted the last GI as he sprinted toward the jeep.

He was a young man, baby-faced, barely in his twenties. Thin, maybe not much more than one-ten or one-twenty. Black-rimmed glasses lay twisted next to his lifeless face, his expression now peaceful and childlike. The worst part was that this innocent-seeming man who'd charged a criminal twice his size, unarmed, had his head tilted at a brutal angle, his neck twisted far past the point of breaking like a snapped wooden chopstick.

"*Christ*," Ernie said softly.

He'd suddenly become religious.

So had I.

For some damn reason, low and somber, the brass bell sounded.

-18-

"Sarkosian is Armenian," I told Ernie as we sped along in the jeep heading back to Camp Mercer.

"From the Levant?" he asked.

Maybe I was talking just to talk, to show off what I'd read. Or maybe the shock of the crime scene at the Kukchei Import-Export Bank required movement of the mouth, expelling hot air from lungs, noise to counter the sounds reverberating from the little jeep, nodding heads, more questions—all to keep my battered mind preoccupied. So as Ernie drove, I spoke. "They were," I said. "At one time. Centuries ago, Armenia stretched from the Caspian Sea all the way to the Mediterranean."

"Is that a lot of ground?"

"Yes," I replied. "Especially in the Middle East."

"Good on them. How are they doing nowadays?"

"They've been swallowed whole by the Soviet Union."

"*Ugh*," Ernie said. "So how'd this guy Sarkosian wind up in the US Army?"

"Because of the diaspora."

"I thought that term was only for Jews."

"Before the Holocaust, the Armenians were persecuted by the Ottoman Empire. So they've been fleeing their homeland for over a century. A lot of them ended up in the US."

Ernie shook his head. "Christ, Sueño. Why do you bother filling your head with all this useless information?"

"Why do you memorize baseball stats?"

"They're important," he said.

"What's important," I said, "is that we find this holy terror and lock his ass up."

"Yeah," Ernie said. "I concur wholeheartedly, Professor."

As it turned out, Sarkosian never returned to Camp Mercer. The jeep was found abandoned late that afternoon near the main bus station in downtown Seoul. The KNPs interviewed every ticket seller who'd worked that day, and a few remembered foreigners buying tickets, but because of the thick plastic windows that hid the tellers from the public, no one could identify the foreigners or recall whether any of the Caucasian men purchasing tickets had been wearing a military uniform. The KNPs also checked the Seoul Train Station about a mile away, but no leads there either. At least we knew he hadn't left the country—other than military conveyance, there were only two legal ways to depart South Korea. Either through the Kimpo International Airport outside of Seoul or the ferry to Japan that left from the Port of Pusan. The customs

officials at both locations had been fully alerted and would be waiting to arrest Sarkosian if he turned up.

But for now, he had disappeared. Inspector Ahn determined that he'd been the bag man at the Suwon caper and had gotten away with at least 600,000 *won*, about twelve hundred dollars. So he had walking-around money, and maybe more if he'd stashed the previously ill-gotten loot somewhere other than Camp Mercer.

His wall and foot lockers on base were inventoried by his CO and First Sergeant—along with me and Ernie—and nothing of value was found. His traveling bag—which GIs call an "AWOL bag"—was missing, along with a few changes of civilian clothes, as confirmed by his houseboy. Had Sarkosian had a backup plan? We couldn't be sure. But he was gone, *karra chogi*, somewhere in-country with a bag full of money and a change of underwear and we had no freaking idea where in the world he was.

While at Camp Mercer, we checked the wall lockers of Sarkosian's three late confederates as well. Again, no cash or expensive items. In the arms room, we determined that only three rifles had been checked out—none by Poulson, the driver—and by comparing serial numbers, we discovered that all three rifles had been used at the shootout at the Kukchei Import-Export Bank in Suwon. They were still in Inspector Ahn's possession. As far as we could tell, Sarkosian was no longer armed since the meticulous records required by army regulation showed that all previous weapons checked out had been fully accounted for and checked back in.

The armorer who'd allowed all this unauthorized checking in and out of weapons was now in a world of hurt. He told us he'd been intimidated by Sarkosian and his boys, afraid to tell them no, and thought they were using the weapons and the ammo for target practice. He was small-fry, not worth our time. His fate would be decided by the charges his unit commander was already typing up.

The other GIs in the unit who knew the four bank robbers were tight-lipped, but they seemed to agree that no one had any idea what they'd been up to. The four had always stuck together, tight as thieves, and seldom associated with others.

An all-points bulletin was put out for Specialist 5 Karim Sarkosian, not only by the Korean National Police, but also by the Provost Marshal of the 8th United States Army. Every law enforcement agency in-country would soon have a copy of his photo and be on the lookout for him.

"He's trapped," Ernie said.

"He might have a good time hiding from us for a while, but eventually his money will run out. Then he'll have to turn himself in."

"Unless he uses his money to buy a gun," Ernie said, "and comes back shooting."

"So let's find him," I said.

"Right," Ernie replied. "But how?"

"I'm working on it."

Early the next morning, we picked up Katie Byrd Worthington at the Bando Hotel. Wearing her usual jungle fatigue shirt, blue jeans, and sneakers, she hopped into the back seat of the jeep. As Ernie pulled out into traffic, she looked back and forth between us.

"What's with you two?" she asked. "Why so glum?"

We told her about the bank robbery in Suwon and the resulting deaths, plus the GI who'd gotten away.

"Yeah, I heard about that. We're running a story on it, mostly based on the Associated Press reports, but you guys could add some color." She raised an eyebrow at us and pulled out her notebook. When neither of us spoke, she said, "Okay. I get it. You want a trade."

We still didn't answer so she leaned forward and said in her husky voice, "Sarkosian."

I swiveled my head. Ernie almost plowed the jeep into the kimchi cab in front of us.

"How'd you know that?" I asked. The names of the GIs hadn't been released by 8th Army, pending notification of next-of-kin for the three dead GIs, and because we didn't want to tip off Sarkosian as to how much we knew or didn't know.

"I have my sources." She smirked and leaned back in her

seat. "Now that I have your attention, I can tell you he called me last night."

Ernie slammed on the brakes, tires screeching, and somehow managed to avoid the honking traffic behind us. He pulled over to the side of the road and swiveled in his seat.

"Sarkosian?"

"I don't remember stuttering," she said primly.

"What? He called you at the Bando?"

"Where else? The Ritz was all booked up."

"What'd he say?" Ernie asked.

"Uh uh *uh*." She waggled her forefinger at us. "First, a little color about that bank robbery so the *Overseas Observer* doesn't seem as bland as the AP and UPI."

"And in return, you tell us everything Sarkosian said. Word for word."

She waved her narrow notebook in the air. "I have it right here." She flipped it open and showed me the page.

In the dim light I squinted. "What's that?"

"Shorthand," she said. "You really oughta take the time to learn."

"That's for broads," Ernie said.

"Yeah. Along with short skirts and crossed legs. And more brains than you poor testosterone-addled Neanderthals will ever have."

Ernie grunted. "You kicked some serious testosterone out of Sergeant Major Screech Owl."

"And I'll kick more out of you if you don't mind your p's and q's."

"*Hold it!*" I said, waving my arms like a referee. "Enough with the bickering. Listen, Sarkosian's a seriously bad dude." I pictured the young man whose neck he'd snapped. "I need to know what he said to you and how he got your number."

Katie adjusted herself on the canvas seat and crossed her legs to steady her notebook. "First, the bank in Suwon. Tell me."

So I did. Ernie started the jeep again, pulled out into traffic, and wound us through the downtown area. He finally hit the road leading east toward the Walker Hill resort area. By the time we'd reached the Han River and crossed at the eastern extreme of Seoul Dukbyol-Si, or Seoul Special City, Katie was through leaching information from me about the horrific scene at the Kukchei Import-Export Bank.

"This will help," she said. "Make that AP stringer look like the lazy slob he is."

"Now," I reminded her, "the phone call."

"Oh, yeah." Katie flipped back a couple of pages in her notebook. "I was asleep," she began. "And at about twenty-two-hundred hours, the phone rang. 'They fucked me up,'" she said, reading from her notes. "He kept repeating that. 'They fucked me up.' Like that justified his actions and might protect him somehow."

He must be seriously disturbed, I thought, to imagine that

after yesterday, he'd ever be able to escape the wrath of the KNPs and 8th United States Army.

"At first, I didn't know who was talking," Katie continued. "His voice was deep and gravelly, like he was really tired. There was some background noise, horns honking, so I figured he was in the middle of a big city. Probably Seoul."

"He could've been across the street from you," Ernie said.

Katie hugged herself. "Thanks for sharing. But I don't think so. He has no interest in me for anything other than publicity."

"And are you going to give that to him?"

"Are you kidding? A GI robs three banks, murders God knows how many people, watches his accomplices slain by Korean police, and now he's on the lam with every cop in the country, both military and civilian, looking for him, and you think the *Overseas Observer* isn't going to run *that*?"

"No sex," Ernie said.

"We'll *find* some," Katie replied.

Ernie sensed I was impatient at the interruption, so he swallowed his retort, which would've been good, I could tell.

I turned in my seat. "Tell me what Sarkosian said. From the beginning."

Katie looked down at her notes.

"The main thing he wanted me to relay is that he's going to kill you."

"Me?" I asked.

"Both of you. He saw that photo in last Sunday's edition

with you two standing in front of the Kukmin Bank in Itaewon. And he knows it was you who tracked him down to that money changer, Old Hwang, in Yongju-gol. For some reason, he figures that if he kills you two, he's home free."

"What'd you tell him?" I asked.

"Not my job to tell him anything," she said. "I'm just a reporter."

"A reporter who's sicced a killer on us."

"And how have I done that?"

"By publishing that photograph without asking us."

"Oh, phooey," she said. "You ever heard of something called the First Amendment?"

"How about blackmail?" Ernie continued. "I can't believe you're still holding that photo of us flat on our backs in Yongju-gol over our heads."

She giggled. "Being saved by a girl, don't forget."

"I haven't," Ernie said. "That's the only reason we're taking you back to Third Corps."

"How else is a girl supposed to get around? You guys have the vehicle with the emergency dispatch, the Eighth Army CID badges, permission from the First Corps Commander to talk to Major General Bok. And what do I have? Nothing but a damn press pass. The army doesn't give a hoot about that, especially the Korean army. So I have to rely on a little help from my friends."

"You're using 'friends' pretty liberally," Ernie said.

I tried to steer the conversation back to Sarkosian.

"Did he give you any hint of where he is right now, or where he might be going?"

"All he said was that he'd find you."

"That's really it? That's all he wanted to tell you? That he plans to kill us?"

"Yeah. He sounded pretty decided. He said, 'They fucked me up.'"

"He thinks it's *our* fault that the KNPs ambushed him in Suwon?" Ernie asked.

"Apparently. I mean, he's gotta blame somebody." She glanced back at her notes. "He also said that all he was ever trying to do was get enough money together to go into business when he got back to the States. Buy a little store or something. He never intended to hurt anyone. The ricochet bullet that killed the teller at the Daehan Bank was an accident. Nothing more. In Suwon, according to him, the Korean cops fired first. All he and his pals did was try to defend themselves. He was almost in tears when he described how his friends were gunned down in cold blood by what he called the 'fascist Korean police.' He claims that if they hadn't been attacked by the cops, everything would've been fine. Nobody would've gotten hurt. With the money he pulled down in Suwon, he would've had five thousand dollars, which was his original goal. Enough for a down payment on a plot of commercial real estate he'd already checked out."

"Five thousand would be around the total take for all three robberies. What about his fellow bank robbers? Weren't they supposed to get a share?"

Katie snapped her fingers. "Damn. I didn't think to ask him." Sheepishly, she said, "I was still pretty groggy."

"He still has the money, doesn't he?"

"Yeah, but because of your investigation, he can never walk free in the States again or go into business like he'd hoped. That's why he blames you two."

"It's all our fault," Ernie said wearily.

"You know criminals," Katie replied. "They always blame everybody and anybody except themselves."

"Since Sarkosian's life is ruined," I said, "his only goal is to find and kill us so he won't go down alone?"

"That's what the man says."

"Why'd he call *you*?" Ernie asked. "And tip us off to his intentions?"

"He wants to be in the *Overseas Observer*. He wants his story told."

"Are you going to put it in? The part about his hopes and dreams, how he's just an ambitious young fellow messed up by evil cops?"

"We're thinking about it."

"*We?*" I asked.

"That's the editorial *we*."

"You and your main office in Hong Kong."

"Right."

"So," I said, "a guy with a sack full of money and no future who's already murdered multiple bank tellers, a traffic cop, and maybe more civilians is searching for me and my partner, and his only objective is to kill us before he's arrested or killed himself."

"That's the long and the short of it," Katie said. "Great copy."

"But you don't have a photograph," Ernie said.

"No. We could do a posed one of you two, but that's pretty boring."

"Thanks."

"What I really want is an action shot."

"Of me and Sueño being gunned down?"

"Would you mind?"

"Not in the least," Ernie said. "Once I'm dead, I probably won't mind much at all."

"There's one thing, though," Katie said.

"What?"

"If I put your photo in this Sunday's edition of the *Overseas Observer*, it'll put Sarkosian in a jealous rage."

"How so?"

"He wants his photo in there."

"Did he mention that when you talked to him?"

"Not exactly. But I can tell he's concerned about how he's portrayed in anything we might run. Which is why he called me in the first place."

"Do you think he'll call you back?"

She thought about it. "No. Not unless we run a story about you two. With a photograph. About how you're bravely hunting down a murderous bank robber."

"That's what we're doing, aren't we?" Ernie asked.

"Not at the moment."

"Not our decision. But we'll be back to tracking him as soon as we get this Third Corps crap out of the way."

"Watch your language," Katie said.

"*My* language?" Ernie asked.

"Pull over here," Katie said, pointing to a flat area overlooking a beautiful panorama of the mountains.

"What for?"

"Just do it."

Ernie did. Then we climbed out of the jeep, and Katie had us pull out our .45s and pose like a couple of lawmen about to gun down Jesse James. After she clicked off a half-dozen shots, she popped the lens cover back onto her camera and said, "That ought to frost his butt."

By now, we'd climbed about two thousand feet into the Taebaek Mountains and were nearing the outskirts of the city of Chuncheon. After passing the downtown area, Ernie turned into the main gate of Camp Page for a rest stop. Katie had to show her press credentials, and we flashed our CID badges. The MP gave us directions to the POL Point, and after wandering around the compound for a while, Ernie found it and gassed up the jeep.

Katie took advantage of this break to use the latrine, as did I.

As we were driving back toward the main gate, she pointed to the headquarters Quonset hut of the 38th Air Defense Artillery Brigade. "Stop here," she said.

"What the hell for?"

"I need to use their phone," she said, tapping her notebook, "to file this story."

"You're going to call all the way to Hong Kong?"

"Why not?"

"They won't let you use their phone for long-distance," Ernie said. "Those are for official use only."

"All they need to do is log me in under an AUTOVON number." AUTOVON was the long-distance telephone network the military used, with each call receiving an authorization number issued by the local commander. The AUTOVON operator would record the number and then patch you through. "Once I have the number, I can talk to our editorial office for as long as I want."

"Not official business," Ernie said. "They wouldn't approve it."

"Sure they will," she said, holding her Nikon camera in front of her. "What do you think I have this for?"

"What do you mean?"

"I mean I go in, take a couple of photos of the Battalion

Sergeant Major, and ask if I can take a picture of the CO, too. After that, while they're making me promise to send them copies, I ask really sweetly if I can use their phone to call my editor. They always say yes."

"So you manipulate people," Ernie said.

"Who doesn't?"

Ernie pulled over into the gravel lot, and Katie Byrd Worthington, smiling and waving, bounced into the battalion headquarters.

"What'd you think about what she said about Sarkosian?" Ernie asked.

"I think he's more resourceful than we've given him credit for. Somehow, he found Katie. And fast. And now it looks like he might eventually have his side of the story published in the *Overseas Observer* after all."

"In the morning he's involved in a shootout with Korean cops," Ernie said. "He watches as his partners are shot down at close range and escapes by blasting his way out of a side window. To top off his day's work, he murders a traffic cop with his bare hands and almost immediately starts the publicity side of his legal defense."

"What a guy," I said.

Ernie nodded. "If he'd gone straight, he could've been one of those bankers or professors you're always talking about."

"Instead, he's a wanted man. Whose last wish is to murder *us*."

"About half the women I ever went out with will be rooting for him."

"But they're justified," I said.

"Yeah," Ernie said, leaning back in his seat and resting his hands behind his head. "They are."

Twenty minutes later, Katie Byrd Worthington emerged from the main door to the Quonset hut. Three GIs, including one with Sergeant Major stripes, followed her out, smiling and waving. At the jeep, she threw them a big kiss and climbed back in.

Ernie said, "You're shameless."

"You bet your sweet ass I am," she replied. "But I got my story filed."

Ernie backed out of the parking area, gunned the engine, and headed toward the main gate.

"Do those guys think they're going to appear in the next issue of the *Overseas Observer*?" I asked.

"I told them they wouldn't. Not unless they found a beautiful blonde mistress with a direct line to the Kremlin."

"Up here in Chuncheon?" Ernie said.

"Okay, it's not likely."

"But you're going to send them copies of those photos?"

"Sure," she replied. "Posthaste."

After we passed through the main gate, she opened her camera and showed me the empty film compartment, grinning. "The main thing is, they were happy in the moment," she said.

"That counts for something," Ernie said.

"Sure does," she agreed.

Before we left town, Katie had us stop at Chuncheon's one and only Korean post office. Inside, she scribbled some notes onto a sheet of paper and had the film with the photos of me and Ernie stuffed into a thick envelope and special-delivered to her office in Seoul. "From there, they'll ship it on to Hong Kong," she told us, "so it makes the next edition."

"You think Sarkosian will take the bait?"

"Of course he will. All he's got left is his pride."

"It's a pretty messed up sense of pride," I said.

"The only kind he's ever had," Katie answered.

We climbed back into the jeep and returned to the road leading into the Taebaek Mountains, heading toward the ROK Army III Corps, the personal fiefdom of Major General Bok Jung-nam.

-19-

A suspicious *hon-byong*, or Korean army MP, studied our dispatch, keeping his semi-automatic rifle balanced in the crook of his arm. Three other MPs surrounded our jeep, all with grim faces, living up to the sign behind them that said HUANYONG! Welcome!

The lead MP kept our dispatch, walked back into the wooden guard shack, and spoke to someone on his field radio. We waited ten minutes. When he returned he handed us back the dispatch, and without a word, waved us through. Another MP raised the metal barrier, and Ernie's wheels spun on gravel until we hit the dirt pathway winding farther into the mountains. In the distance, atop various peaks, sandbagged gun emplacements surrounded reinforced concrete bunkers painted shades of black, green, and brown.

"Sweet," Katie said. "Just like the French Alps."

"Yep. The skiing must be great here when it snows," Ernie said.

"*Huh*," Katie said. "You wouldn't know a slalom from a switchback."

Offended, Ernie said, "Not true. I went to a skating rink once."

"Let me guess. With the City of Detroit's Endangered Youth Program?"

He almost turned around. "How'd you know?"

"I'm a reporter, remember?"

"You've been snooping around in our personnel records again," I said.

"Somebody's gotta do it," Katie replied.

The reach of this woman was astounding. All the safeguards the military put in place to protect their fancy communications equipment, official-use-only personnel records, and even the occasional classified document—all of that went out the window when a personable, good-looking woman smiled and flattered and snapped photographs you could send home to your loved ones. And in return she asked for only a teensy little favor.

Soviet spies could learn from Katie Byrd Worthington.

A dirt-spattered soldier waved us to a stop. ROK Army combat engineers were expanding and repaving the road. As we waited for a tractor to finish shoveling a pile of dirt off a cliff, I asked one of the soldiers what was being built. Pleased to be addressed in Korean, he smiled a big, white-toothed smile that contrasted against his dirt-smudged face and told me they were just about finished with the project. They were expanding the road for easier, more rapid movement of tanks and other armored vehicles.

"Couldn't the tanks pass before?" I asked.

"Yes. But it was a slow drive. Lots of curves and narrow passageways. That made them vulnerable to enemy artillery or air attack. And sometimes mudslides knocked the road out completely, but we've put in support revetments this time. Now the tanks will have more space to maneuver, and it will be much faster to relocate a tank battalion to the forward area."

Improving fortifications along the DMZ was a job that had been taking place since the end of the Korean War twenty years ago, and as far as I could tell, it was one that would continue until the ceasefire was violated so egregiously that another war broke out.

Once we were allowed to pass the construction site, we reached smooth blacktop, already repaved and widened. Ernie sped up. After a couple miles, we rounded a curve and the road dropped downhill, leveling off in a valley covered with tank units, many churning up mud on narrow pathways that intersected across the landscape like a tightly woven fisherman's net. At the far end of the valley was a rise, and atop that sat a long cement-block building fronted by massive embankments of reinforced concrete. Steel bars protruded from the edifice like spears pointing at charging cavalry, and the entire wall was carefully swathed in coiled concertina wire.

A sign at the entranceway said in both Korean and English, WELCOME TO THE ROK ARMY III CORPS. HOME OF FIRE AND FURY!

By the standards of what I imagined one could find in the French Alps, the general officers' mess was Spartan. But that was luxurious compared to the utilitarian ROK Army chow halls I'd visited before. A thin carpet lay on the cement floor, and a half-dozen tables were set up in front of a row of plate glass windows.

"The DMZ," General Bok said, gazing out the window. After a steep descent, the valley below was demarcated by a long triple line of chain-link fences that split the landscape in two. "And those over there," he said, pointing about a mile away on the other side of the divide, "are the North Korean guard posts. Boxy little things. Not much protection for their soldiers."

They indeed looked like matchboxes on stilts. Occasionally, a dark figure could be seen moving within. Attached to the outer walls were large metal speakers for broadcasting propaganda.

"Why don't the North Koreans reinforce those guard posts?" Katie asked.

"Because if we attack, up on that far ridge is where they would make their stand. On the high ground."

"So these troops are just the tripwire?"

"Yes, exactly. You might call them the staked goat waiting for the tiger."

General Bok was a dapper little man. Not very tall, but broad-shouldered and thin-waisted, and in his immaculately pressed fatigue uniform, he looked ready for a Madison Avenue photo shoot. His English was very good. I was tempted to ask about his education, but I figured I'd better stick to what I was sent up here to do, which was make sure he wasn't doing anything that would compromise 8th Army. And, if we could find her, talk to Estella.

The Korean Army and Koreans in general were more relaxed than many Americans about life's natural functions, like sex. Our background was Puritan; the 8th Army honchos, in their high-collared dress uniforms, looked like nothing if not a hysterical bevy of Salem witch hunt deacons. Behind the scenes, they were every bit as debauched as the next guy. But they still wanted to make sure that if something incriminating was going on in the ROK Army III Corps, it was stopped or at least covered up before any of it seeped out into the media. Especially when millions in US military funding was at stake. If Congress was humiliated back home, they could cut 8th Army's flow of money or even eliminate it.

And our bringing Katie Byrd Worthington here flew right in the face of our task. The 8th Army honchos would have a heart attack if they knew. Sure, she'd coerced us into it with that photo, but I was starting to worry that I might live to regret the decision.

After we were seated, a waiter served us roast beef and mashed potatoes with gravy, along with cut green beans that looked like they'd come straight out of an army-issue #10 can. To my surprise, another waiter appeared with a bottle of chilled rosé wine. After General Bok approved the wine, Katie was served first. She quaffed it down. Once the waiter finished pouring for the rest of us, Katie waved her empty glass to the waiter, who refilled it.

"You like your wine," General Bok said, smiling.

"When I can get it."

She glugged down about half her glass, then dug into the roast beef.

I was considering how to phrase my inquiry when Katie, her mouth full of roast beef and mashed potatoes, said, "Where's Estella?"

Bok dropped his fork and looked up from his plate, shocked.

"Who?" he said.

"Estella," Katie replied matter-of-factly. "Your girlfriend. The one you made stay behind when the others left."

General Bok stared at her intently. I held my breath. Even Ernie sat frozen in his seat. We were surrounded by soldiers whose only reason for being there was to execute orders from this man swiftly and without question. To them, this general was practically a god. In the Korean army, discipline wasn't something that was ever ignored—as it occasionally was in the American Army—or something that could be adjudicated in a court-martial. It was absolute. It was instantaneous. After all, President Park had once been a general himself, and he demanded total obedience from his government, his military, and everyone else in the country. More than one South Korean soldier had been executed for not following orders, or for perceived insubordination. Maybe General Bok wouldn't kill us because we were Americans and that would bring too much unwanted attention, but he could certainly cause us grief.

Katie sipped more wine, set the glass down, and said, "You know who I'm talking about. Estella. Your girlfriend. Bring her out. Don't be bashful. We want to talk to her."

His face turned red. "You're referring to those six women who were sent south by General Crabtree."

"Yes."

"They were just visiting," Bok said. "Tourists. Curious about our operation and the landscape we work in."

"Yeah," Katie said, "I met one of your *tourists*. At the Top Hat Scotch Corner. So how long were they here?"

"Just a few days."

"You had a party?"

"We always entertain our guests."

"And those six women, they entertained you, too?"

General Bok's stare had turned icy. "I found them quite amusing, yes."

"So amusing you didn't want to let them go."

Suddenly, his fist pounded the table. Plates rattled. "You *liar*!" he said. "I saw your article in that trashy tabloid."

"The *Overseas Observer*," Katie corrected.

"Yes. That. You implied that those women were kept here against their will. That's not true. General Crabtree was kind enough to escort them back to Seoul. For that, I'm grateful to him, but they were *not* kept here against their will."

"I talked to one of them," Katie said, pulling out her notebook. "She says you wouldn't let them go. Not until Crabtree and his assistant, Screech Owl, surprised you with an unannounced visit."

Katie seemed calm, but I realized she was nervous, forgetting both men's military rank and calling Tapia Screech Owl.

"Who fed you this lie?" he asked.

Katie waved her free hand. "Not important. Only your answers matter here. So you didn't keep them long? How many days?"

"Two," he said. "Maybe three."

"She says almost a week."

"She's lying."

Katie nodded. "And Estella, how does she feel about staying up here?"

"She feels—" General Bok cut himself off. He sat back

in his chair, unclenched his fist, and took a long sip of rosé. Immediately, the waiter appeared to refill his glass, and Katie called him over. The waiter stood and bent forward, waiting for General Bok's instruction. He nodded, and the waiter hurried to Katie and refilled her glass as well. Not to be forgotten, Ernie had the waiter top him off, too.

Finally, General Bok said, "So you're concerned about Estella." It was a statement, not a question.

"Yes," Katie replied.

"Then you can talk to her." He snapped his fingers, and this time a man in uniform appeared. Whispering, General Bok said something to the man, who bowed and hurried away.

After we finished our food, Bok escorted us out onto a wooden deck overlooking the fortifications and the DMZ. They were still visible in the lowering sunlight. Like any tourist site in the States, a telescope was mounted on a swivel near the edge, except this one didn't require a dime to operate. He showed Katie how to look through it and turned it for her, pointing out the North Korean communications facility and the defensive trenches they'd built behind an open field riddled with landmines.

"Sweet," she said. "Do you guys send patrols over there?"

General Bok grinned. "You're asking for classified information."

"I'll take that as a yes," she said, scribbling in her notebook.

"Take it as a 'no comment,'" he said.

"Oh, I love 'no comment,'" Katie said. "In print, it makes you look *so* guilty."

Bok's face hardened. "You don't do things the same way as other reporters."

"God, I hope not."

He turned to us. "Do you have what you need?"

I cleared my throat. "General Bok, we were sent here by Eighth Army to make sure there are no women still here, or anything else that might prove scandalous in the newspapers."

"No more women," he said. "Other than Estella. And as I said, you can talk to her. After that, I must ask you to leave. We have important maneuvers launching soon."

"Yes, sir, I understand."

I'd done what I'd been sent here to do. General Bok was now on notice from the 8th US Army to not embarrass them further. He'd also told us that it wouldn't happen again. But was Estella an exception that he wouldn't let go of? The sooner we interviewed her, the better.

General Bok nodded to Katie, performed a smart about-face, and marched out of the room.

Estella insisted on talking only to Katie. Not us. One of the young officers guided Katie away, and after a while, we spotted the two women about a hundred yards off, standing alone on a berm overlooking the minefield below, moonlight shining on the North Korean observation huts. Dark figures moved silently behind gun emplacements.

Ernie and I waited on the wooden deck, breathing the night air in deeply. "No pollution," he said.

"No factories for miles," I replied. "And not too many internal combustion engines."

"Except for a couple of battalions of M48 Patton tanks."

"There's that. But it's surprising how quickly the exhaust dissipates when there aren't tens of thousands of kimchi cabs adding to the mess."

Ernie nodded toward Katie and Estella. "I wonder what they're talking about."

"Girl stuff," I said.

"Like 'Why am I being held hostage?'"

"Yeah, stuff like that."

"Is she Eastern European?" Ernie asked.

"I don't think so. When they passed under the light earlier, she looked olive-skinned. Maybe Mediterranean or Hispanic?"

"Maybe Bok gets off on foreign women."

"Who knows what he gets off on?"

Katie and Estella strolled away from the berm and approached a structure I hadn't noticed before. Made of wood, it was about ten feet tall and illuminated by dim paper lanterns.

"A Buddha statue," Ernie said.

"Yeah. All the way up here. Illuminated at night so the North Korean soldiers on the other side can see it."

"They don't allow religion in North Korea, do they?" Ernie asked.

"Not on your life."

"So this little temple, it's sort of rubbing their noses in it."

"Precisely its purpose."

The two women stood in front of the shrine and talked for another half hour. They hugged, and Estella walked away toward a clump of squat cement-block buildings to the left of Bok's headquarters. Katie trudged uphill toward us. She entered the building below and joined us on the deck a few minutes later.

"What'd she say?" Ernie asked.

"None of your beeswax," Katie said.

"What do you mean, 'none of your beeswax?' We brought you up here, for Christ's sake. Does Estella want us to take her out of here or what?"

Katie shook her head. "No. She wants to stay."

"Of her own free will?" I asked.

Katie looked up at me. "Of her own free will."

"Then let's get the hell out of here," Ernie said. "This place creeps me out."

Within seconds, we were ready to leave. One of General Bok's assistants watched us climb into the jeep but did nothing to notify his boss. That was okay with us. All three of us, for once, agreed on the same thing: it was time to un-ass the area.

As we drove away from the headquarters of the ROK Army III Corps, Katie Byrd Worthington sat quietly in the back of the jeep, jotting notes on the conversation she'd had with Estella. Every now and then, she lifted her notebook in front of her face, twisted it to catch the available light, and continued scribbling.

"Shit," Ernie said, slamming on the brakes. Ahead of us was a slow-moving convoy of army-issue five-ton trucks. Wooden signs painted white with red lettering swung from their rear bumpers. UIHOM. POKPAL-MUL. Danger. High Explosives.

Ernie flashed his high beams to pass. That's when I noticed that the rear of the truck in front of us was jammed with long wooden crates of ammunition, like coffins after a war.

"Strange," I said as Ernie gunned the engine, down shifted, and passed the trucks.

"What's strange?"

"That they'd be transporting ammunition *away* from the DMZ."

"Maybe peace broke out."

"Don't you wish?"

"No, I don't," Ernie replied. "I'd be out of a job. So would you."

"Don't worry," I replied as we sped past the long convoy. "We have plenty of job security."

When we made it around the convoy, Ernie drove quickly, since traffic in those mountains was almost nonexistent at night. Eventually, we passed the city of Chuncheon without stopping and made good time toward the outskirts of Seoul. Only when we hit the city limits did we finally encounter cruising kimchi cabs, but Ernie navigated them easily, and about an hour before the midnight-to-four curfew, we pulled up in front of the Bando Hotel.

Katie started to climb out.

"You didn't tell us what Estella said."

"It's a long story."

"We have time."

"Oh, that's right. Your emergency dispatch lets you travel after midnight."

I nodded. She thought about it.

"Okay, then." She canted her head. "Buy a girl a drink?"

"Can do," I said.

Ernie parked the jeep, and the three of us entered the almost deserted bar of the Bando Hotel. Ernie and I thought we were ready for anything—and maybe we were, except for what Katie had to tell us.

-20-

"She's Basque," she said.

"What the hell's that?" Ernie asked.

"A part of Spain," Katie told him.

"What's she doing in Korea?"

"That's what I asked her."

"And what'd she say?"

"She said I'm in danger."

"*You*?" Ernie asked. "A reporter who never pokes her nose into other people's business or publishes anything unflattering? Why would *you* be in danger?"

"Don't be a wiseass," Katie replied. "You're in danger, too."

"We already knew that."

"Not just from Sarkosian. It's General Bok."

"He's after us for outing him for bringing whores up to his headquarters?"

"Not that."

"Then what?"

In a move that reminded me of Strange, Katie glanced around the almost empty Bando Hotel barroom. When she was satisfied that no one was listening, she leaned toward us.

"Estella isn't what she seems."

"I don't even know what she *seems* in the first place," I said.

"She seems like a mistress who's living with a rich man."

"On his own personal army base," Ernie said.

"Hey," Katie replied. "I told you, don't be a wiseass. There are millions of women in this world who do what they have to do in order to survive. You men have it easy. Pick up a rifle, aim it at somebody, and you have a job. Women have to bear the brunt of all your killing."

"Okay," I said, holding up my hand to appease her. "You're right. We have work, we have benefits, we have what we need to survive in the army. It's easy for us to talk."

"You're *damn* right," Katie said, still angry.

Ernie leaned back in the narrow booth, signaling that he'd keep his mouth shut.

"Okay, so Estella's in a tough situation," I said. "Is she trying to get out of it, or is she okay being stuck there?"

"She's not stuck," Katie said. "That's the thing that surprised me most. She's there because she wants to be."

"She actually thinks she has a future with this General Bok?"

"Not that. She's there because she has a job to do."

We waited.

"She threatened me."

"Threatened you? Why?"

"She not only threatened me, but the whole *Overseas Observer*. Says we'll be shut down. If not through legal channels, then through extra-legal channels." Katie sipped the last of her beer. "She says they'll blow up our printing press in Hong Kong if they have to. And then the next one and the next one, until we give up."

Ernie was unable to keep his mouth shut. "Who's *they*?"

Katie glanced at him with withering disdain. "Let him ask the questions," she said, nodding to me.

"Okay," I said, "who's *they*?"

"Who the fuck do you think they are?" Katie asked.

Ernie came up with the answer first. "For Christ's sake," he said. "It's brilliant."

I glanced between the two of them. For once, Katie didn't protest him speaking, but lowered her head in weary acknowledgement. A grin spread across Ernie's lips.

"What in the hell are you two talking about?" I asked.

"You still don't get it?" Ernie asked. "Estella is a honey trap. She's there to make sure he follows the game plan."

"Whose game plan?"

"Think about what Strange told us. The military higher-ups who are promoting Bok so he'll be able to step in if and when Park Chung-hee goes down."

It finally dawned on me. "So Estella isn't a whore."

"Don't use that word," Katie snapped.

"Sorry," I said, holding up my hands in surrender. "Estella isn't General Bok's mistress. She's an agent."

None of us wanted to say it out loud, even though no one was listening. Estella was part of the US Central Intelligence Agency. The CIA. It figured that they'd have their claws deep into General Bok's hide. I wondered if anyone else around him was in on it.

"Are you sure?" I asked. "Did Estella admit that explicitly?"

"In the world of espionage," Katie said, "nothing is ever said explicitly."

"So you're just surmising?"

"Yep. Surmising my sweet ass off," Katie said. She rose from the table.

"One more question," Ernie said. "If Estella's CIA, and you hate the CIA, why'd you hug her when you finished talking?"

"Who says I hate the CIA?" Katie asked. "They're good copy. Besides, Estella's a woman trying to do a big job in a tough situation."

"Like you," I said.

"Don't try to butter me up, Sueño. There's still time to get that photograph in Sunday's issue." She smiled at both of us in turn. "Sweet dreams."

She turned and walked toward the old cement staircase.

The next morning as we were walking toward the 8th Army Snack Bar, I was still wondering how Sarkosian had managed to locate Katie. She herself had no idea. I asked Ernie about it.

"Maybe he's psychic," he said.

"And maybe not. I've been thinking."

"About time."

"Maybe Sarkosian found Katie the same way we did."

Ernie glanced at me. "By checking with the *Stars and Stripes*?"

"Yeah. Maybe he went to their office and asked them where he could find her."

"But the MPs have been notified to be on the lookout for him."

"When a GI in uniform walks through the front gate, they don't bother checking his identification. The uniform is proof enough. Maybe he waited for a big group, and the guard at the gate didn't read every name tag."

"How in the hell could they miss him?"

"Maybe the MP was busy and the Korean gate guard waved him past. Besides, a lot of GIs look like him. Husky, dark whiskers. When they're busy, a guy like that would've been easy to miss."

"Could be. They have enough to worry about. He may have even done it before the notice on him went out. Plus, when you're leaving and walk off post, they don't check you at all. Not on Yongsan Compound, anyway." Ernie thought about it. "Let's go ask that guy, what's his name?"

"Master Sergeant Mortenson Cleveland."

"Right. We can go to his office this morning once they open."

Inside the snack bar, Strange was waiting for us. We went to the serving line first, grabbed a tray and silverware, and at the steam table ordered breakfast. After we paid the weary cashier, we joined Sergeant First Class Harvey, NCOIC of the 8th Army Headquarters Classified Documents Section, at his table.

"Had any *strange* lately?" he asked.

"More than you'll ever know," Ernie said, plopping down his tray and taking a seat.

Strange frowned. "You're supposed to *share*."

"Says who?"

"Says the information I have for you guys."

"Give it to Sueño. I'm busy." Holding his knife in one hand and his fork in the other, Ernie tucked into his ham and eggs.

"What is it?" I said, maneuvering the front edge of a BLT into my mouth.

While I chomped, Strange grinned. "Better than you'll ever imagine," he said.

"How so?"

"Don't talk with your mouth full."

"Look, Harvey. We had a late night and we're both starved, so cut the crap and talk."

I seldom became short with him. Ernie was constantly, but not me. Somewhat rattled by my impatience, he sipped on his hot chocolate, wiped his thin lips with a napkin, and glanced around the snack bar to make sure no one was listening.

"Somebody got wind of the Provost Marshal sending you guys up there to talk to General Bok," he said, "to tell him to lay off the dames and not embarrass Eighth Army any further."

"Actually, we didn't tell him that. All we did was ask him about the women and let him figure out the rest on his own. But go ahead."

"So word came down from on high to leave General Bok strictly alone. No more CID agents, no more First Corps Commander up there. No matter how much he embarrasses Eighth Army. Hands off. That's the word."

"Why?" Ernie asked.

Strange spread his fingers. "Hell if I know."

"Who issued this directive?" I asked.

"Somebody high up."

"The Pentagon?"

"Or God or somebody. But whoever it is, the Eighth Army Chief of Staff jumped. He called your boss, Colonel Brace, and chewed him out for sending you guys up there in the first place."

"Oh, great," Ernie said. "He'll blame us."

"Shit always flows downhill," Strange said. "In fact, now the Chief of Staff's acting like the entire thing wasn't even his idea."

"*He's* the one who told Colonel Brace to send us up there?"

"That's the scuttlebutt."

"Typical," Ernie said, slicing into his ham and shoveling a huge chunk into his mouth.

"That stuff's bad for your cholesterol," Strange told him.

"So's two marshmallows with your hot chocolate."

"I'm back to one."

"Why? I thought you already hit your fighting weight."

"There's a new dolly at the headquarters building I've had my eye on. I want to be lean and mean for the encounter."

"You? Seduce someone? Don't make me laugh."

"She's already making eyes at me."

"You mean that new WAC? The one in Plans and Operations? The one who's nearsighted?"

"Yeah. What of it?"

Technically, the Women's Army Corps, the WACs, had been disbanded a couple of years ago. Now, women were integrated into all army units just as men were. But that didn't stop most GIs, and especially two reprobates like Ernie and Strange, from continuing to refer to them as WACs.

"Her lenses are thicker than your skull," Ernie said. "She can't see more than five feet in front of her."

"Then why'd she linger in front of the classified documents cage every day?"

"Do you talk to her?"

"No. But she stands outside."

"Talking to the honor guard, I'll bet."

"Well, they do exchange a few words."

"Even though neither one of those guys is supposed to talk."

"They're only human."

"So's she," Ernie said. "And she's got the hots for one of them, not you."

Sometimes, I thought Ernie went too far with his needling. He didn't have to crush Strange's pipe dreams.

"You never know," I said. "Maybe she likes the sophisticated type. After all, those Honor Guard soldiers do nothing but stand around all day."

"Looking sharp," Ernie added.

"That isn't everything," I said.

Ernie finally got the hint and shut up, carrying his empty plate back to the bus tray at the end of the serving line.

"What's her name?" I asked Strange.

"Haven't got that far yet."

"You don't want to push these things too fast," I said.

"No. I'll be careful."

"You want some more chocolate?"

"No. Like I said, I'm on a diet."

"It's making a difference already."

"You think so?"

"Sure."

Ernie returned to the table. "You ready to go save the world?"

I stood up. As we left, Strange said, "Watch out for Sarkosian."

I stopped and turned back to Strange. "How'd you know about that?"

He shrugged. "All his buddies are dead, your names and pictures showed up in the *Overseas Observer*. He's toast and he knows it, facing thirty to life at Leavenworth. Why wouldn't he try to take you down?"

"We're gonna catch him first," Ernie said.

"Everybody's talking about it at the head shed," Strange continued. "There've even been bets on how long you two are going to last."

"*Bets*?"

Strange nodded.

"Did you place one of those bets?" Ernie asked.

"What kind of guy do you think I am?"

Strange grinned. It was hideous, like a snaggletoothed marsupial eyeing carrion. Suddenly, I regretted having been kind to him. I grabbed Ernie by the elbow, and before saying something that might permanently cut off our source of classified information, we retreated from the 8th Army Snack Bar.

"I'm so pleased you gentlemen decided to join us," Staff Sergeant Riley said as we walked into the office. "Where in the hell have you *been*?"

"Out," Ernie said and headed for the coffee urn.

Miss Kim wasn't in yet, so I grabbed the UNC/USFK/8th

Army telephone directory off her desk. It wasn't much thicker than your average edition of *National Geographic* but printed on cheaper paper. I found the number of the Korea Bureau of the *Pacific Stars and Stripes* and dialed. When somebody answered, I asked for Mort Cleveland.

"He's not in."

"Why not? Does he keep bankers' hours?"

"Who's this?"

I told him.

"I'm Rob Futzmann, the Bureau Chief here. What the hell does the CID want to talk to him for?"

Futzmann was a Department of the Army Civilian, a DAC. There were plenty of them scattered around the headquarters.

"Come on, Mr. Futzmann," I said, "you know I can't tell you that. What I can tell you is that Mort isn't in any trouble. When do you expect him in?"

There was a pause. "Now you've got me worried."

"How so?"

"Mort was supposed to be in a half hour ago. Not only is he always on time, he's always early. One of the most dedicated newspaper men I've ever worked with. But he's late for the first time in the almost ten months I've known him, and now the CID calls. You're freaking me out."

"He's late."

"Yeah. As simple as that, but Mort is a Master Sergeant in the US Army. He's never late."

I gave him our office phone number and spelled my name for him. "I'm going out," I told him. "If he comes in, call and leave a message with our secretary, Miss Kim." She walked in as I mentioned her name. "She'll make sure I get it."

"Are you going to check on him?"

"Yes," I told him. "We're leaving now."

"A half-hour late?" Ernie said. "For Christ's sake, Sueño. You're too freaking nervous."

"Mort Cleveland is never late."

"There's always a first time."

"Yeah," I said. "I hope you're right."

Ernie shut up. He would never admit it, but I knew he was as worried as I was. In the Army, being late for work is a serious offense. A soldier can be court-martialed for it as a violation in the UCMJ, the Uniform Code of Military Justice; an offense known as "failure to repair." And the coincidence was real enough to get our attention. As soon as we were about to ask Mort Cleveland if he'd had any contact with a murderer, he hadn't shown up for work on time for what sounded like the first time in his life.

We flashed our dispatch at the western gate of Yongsan Compound, and after the MP waved us through, we sped into the village of Samgakji. Ernie parked the jeep and we hopped out and trotted across the street, entering the pedestrian lane where we'd been shot at before. Ernie reached up and touched the dent in the wall where the round from the M16 had hit.

"Still here," he said.

We ran through the shadowed lanes and reached the double-wooden gateway that led into Mort Cleveland's hooch. I tried the small door cut into the gate, but it was locked. Ernie pounded on the old lumber until it rattled.

"Mort!" he shouted. "Mort Cleveland. It's us. The two guys from the CID."

The small door creaked open, and the withered face of a little old Korean lady peeked out. Ernie and I rushed past her.

The door to Mort Cleveland's hooch was closed, and the light was off. The little old lady had followed us in. She waved her right arm and said, "*Kasso. Kasso.*" They've left. They've left.

I spoke to her in Korean and asked where they'd gone.

She seemed relieved to be able to communicate and told me that yesterday, early in the evening, another American had come and there'd been an argument. She hadn't seen it all because she'd been out at the vegetable market, but when she'd come home, Mort's wife was crying and clutching her little boy and Mort was bleeding. She pointed to the top of her head. Somebody'd called a PX taxi for them, and they'd gone over to the hospital on the compound.

"Did they come back?" I asked.

"Not yet," she replied.

"Did you see the man he argued with?"

She shook her head. He was already gone when she'd arrived.

Ernie and I thanked her. As we retraced our steps down the narrow lanes, we were as wary as an infantry squad on patrol. When we reached the dent in the wall, Ernie reached up and touched it again.

"For good luck," he said, kissing his fingertips.

And then we were out in the street running toward the jeep, keeping a double-arms distance from each other. As far as we knew, Sarkosian no longer had a weapon. But he'd proven a resourceful guy. Until we definitively knew otherwise, we'd assume he was lying in wait for us. Like a trained assassin.

-21-

We flashed our badges at the reception counter of the 121st Evacuation Hospital on South Post of 8th Army's Yongsan Compound. "Cleveland," I told the female medic. "Mortenson's the first name." She thumbed through a card file, stopped, flipped back, and said, "Which one? Senior or junior?"

"There's two of them here?"

"Two cards," she said, lifting them out halfway as if to prove it. "Master Sergeant Cleveland is in ward eighteen bravo. Junior is in the ICW."

"The Intensive Care Ward?"

"You got it."

"Which way is eighteen bravo?"

"That way," she told us. "But it's not visiting hours yet."

We ignored her last comment and rushed down the tiled causeway.

"It must've been Sarkosian," Ernie said.

"Maybe," I replied. "Either way, when the CIA appears in your life, it's a bad moon rising."

"They're not so bad," Ernie said, swerving around a medic pushing a patient on a gurney.

"What do you mean?"

"I mean they used to fly that pure China White in from Burma," he said, "for us troops in Vietnam, to raise money for their operations."

"Do you believe that?"

"*Somebody* flew it in," he said. "And I enjoyed that more than a Bob Hope USO Show."

"Better than Joey Heatherton?"

"Even her."

We reached Ward 18-B and checked the clipboard wired to the foot of each bunk. Finally, we found Cleveland's. We stared at unruffled sheets.

"Gone," Ernie said.

"I think I know where to find him."

We hurried toward the Intensive Care Ward.

Sitting beside a little boy in a big hospital bed were Mort Stevenson and Mort Jr.'s mother, Coco, both sound asleep, looking so peaceful that Ernie said, "I hate to wake them."

But we did. And as soon as Mort Cleveland's eyes popped open, he ignored the bandages around his head and stood up and leaned over his son. Coco woke up and joined him.

"What happened?" I asked.

He told us.

On the way back to the CID office, I considered Mort's story.

A dark man with a heavy five o'clock shadow and short hair had arrived in front of his hooch shortly after sundown. From the overhead floodlight, Mort had seen that he was wearing blue jeans and a tucked-in, red-checkered shirt with a button-down collar and a nylon jacket with a name embroidered on the front.

"Karim," he told us, pronouncing it correctly.

"You're observant," I said.

"I'm a reporter."

Mort told us that he'd received a few stitches in his head and the doctors were watching him for signs of concussion, but he had high hopes of being released this morning.

"Coco waited with you here all night?"

"Yeah. The nurses told her to leave but, you know, Korean custom. They eventually gave in and let her stay."

In Korean hospitals, the attention paid by staff to individual patients wasn't comparable to Western hospitals. Some of them didn't even provide meals. It was customary for family members to stay in the hospital with their loved ones both day and night, to watch out for them and perform routine chores like take them to the toilet, change their sheets, and make sure they received enough food and water.

"How do you figure Sarkosian found you?" Ernie asked.

"I'm not sure yet. But I suppose the same way you did."

"We got your address from Billeting."

Mort frowned. "So maybe somebody at the *Stripes* bureau told him."

"Could be. Or maybe he described you and asked some people in the neighborhood if they knew where you lived."

"Yeah," Mort said. "Koreans always know when one of us *miguk*s lives in the area."

"What'd he do once he found you?" I asked.

"He called my name, and I slid open the door and went outside on the porch. Mort Jr. followed me out and started to play. Karim was friendly at first, telling me he had a news story and wanted to contact the lady who wrote for the *Overseas Observer*. He asked if I could give him her whereabouts. I remembered you guys asking the same thing, and since this guy wasn't with law enforcement I got suspicious, so I asked him why he wanted it. That's when things went bad. His face twisted and he started sputtering, and then he accused me of screwing him up."

"He said that?"

"Yeah. His exact words were, 'You're fucking me up.' And then he did something I should've been prepared for but wasn't. He leapt forward and grabbed Mort Jr. I went at him, but he dodged me and held my son by the neck, swinging him in the air."

Mort closed his eyes in pain at the memory. Coco must've understood much of what he said because she started to cry softly and touched her son on his bare arm.

"Sarkosian was choking him," I said.

Mort nodded. "I backed off, holding my hands up so he wouldn't hurt him more. By now Coco was outside, and she was crying and pleading with him not to hurt Mort Jr., so I told him he could find Katie Byrd Worthington at the Bando Hotel downtown. He said that if I was lying, he'd be back to hurt the boy, and I told him I wasn't lying. He backed toward the gate, and at the last second he set Mort Jr. down and ducked backwards through the doorway. I ran after him, charging through the door as quickly as I could, but he fooled me. Instead of running away, he was waiting right outside the opening, and when I came out, he smacked me on the head with something."

"Something like what?"

"I'm not sure," Mort said, gingerly rubbing the top of his bandaged skull. "But it felt like a ball-peen hammer."

"But you hadn't seen the weapon before, when he was standing in front of your hooch?"

"No. He must've either had it in his back pocket or left it outside the front gate."

"Where it might've been stolen," Ernie said.

"Yeah," Mort agreed. "Sort of unlikely, huh? If he needed it for self-protection, he would've kept it on him."

"How about your boy?" I asked.

"I was dizzy, almost out, kneeling in the dirt. By the time I recovered, the guy was gone, and when I returned to the hooch, Mort Jr. was unconscious. At first I thought he wasn't breathing, but when I leaned in closer, there was a faint intake of air making his chest rise and fall. One of the neighbors called a PX taxi for us and we took it to the One-Two-One." The 121st Evacuation Hospital.

PX taxis were big Ford Granadas owned and operated by the Post Exchange on base. They were allowed to enter the US military compounds, unlike kimchi cabs.

Mort Cleveland looked at his son. "We've been here ever since."

"What's the prognosis?" I asked.

"That's what we're waiting for. The doctor should be in soon. In fact, I'm going to go find him."

Mort hurried off. Ernie and I glanced at each other. There wasn't much we could do here. I took a long look at the boy. Wires and tubes were attached to various parts of his body. Reddish welts covered his neck. His mother stared at us with pleading eyes, as if we could do something.

We couldn't.

Nothing except catch Specialist 5 Karim Sarkosian, the man who'd done this, and make sure he didn't hurt anyone else.

■ ■ ■

When we returned to the CID office, Staff Sergeant Riley was less than his usual charming self. Instead of asking us where we'd been, he personally guided us to the Provost Marshal's office, all the while sporting a self-satisfied grin. When we entered, Riley shut the door behind us.

We saluted Colonel Brace, who ignored us and continued to thumb through a stack of paperwork. Behind him, draped in all their colorful splendor, were the flags of the United States, the Republic of Korea, and the United Nations Command. Finally, Colonel Brace slid the paperwork aside, looked up at us, and said, "What did you do to General Crabtree?"

"What did we *do* to him, sir?"

"Don't make me repeat myself, Sueño."

"We didn't do anything to him, sir," Ernie said.

I waved him off. It was obvious that Colonel Brace was upset about something, and the best way for an enlisted man to act when faced with the wrath of a full bird colonel was with diplomacy. Ernie didn't have a diplomatic bone in his body. He understood this, clamped shut his jaw, and let me do the talking.

"I'm not sure I understand, sir," I said.

Colonel Brace shoved a blotter report toward me. Up top, it said that it had been issued by the 597th MP Company at I Corps Headquarters, Camp Red Cloud. I scanned the report and handed it to Ernie.

"He's acting the fool again," Colonel Brace said. "Storming

around in his command and control center at night, ordering units into the field for no apparent reason. Standing there, we're told, with his helmet and his flak jacket on but only his skivvies underneath."

"He's an intense guy," I said. "He probably woke up in the middle of the night, rushed outside, and forgot to put on his uniform."

Colonel Brace snorted. "He looks like a lunatic. And when the intel boys at the Command bunker here in Seoul questioned him about his decisions, he said that he was trying to save democracy. Imagine that," Colonel Brace said, glancing between me and Ernie. "Democracy. Here in Korea. Right in the middle of the Park Chung-hee regime. President Park is locking *up* people for promoting democracy. What does Crabtree think he's doing?"

Neither Ernie nor I had any idea, so we stood mute.

"What I want you to do," Colonel Brace said, "is go back up there. Talk to him. See if the rumors flying around headquarters are true."

"What rumors, sir?" Ernie asked.

Colonel Brace stared at him sourly. "That all this aberrant behavior, this obsession with Major General Bok and the ROK Army Third Corps, that it all has to do with that woman, that mistress. The one Bok's keeping up there. What's her name?"

"Estella," I said. I wondered how Colonel Brace knew about her, but there were likely others who'd been spreading rumors.

Maybe the MPs who transported the rest of the women back from the ROK III Corps headquarters. Or the women themselves.

"Yes, Estella. Can two general officers really be threatening each other with move-out alerts because of jealousy over a woman?"

Ernie and I exchanged glances. Should we tell Colonel Brace that this so-called mistress, this Estella, claimed to be an agent for the American CIA? Or was he already aware of that information and withholding it from us because we didn't have a need-to-know?

I could tell by Ernie's demeanor that he had no desire to make things worse by bringing it up, and neither did I. Let the bosses hash this out amongst themselves. We'd follow orders and try to keep our noses clean. Still, Sarkosian was running amok here in Seoul. If we left and traveled north toward I Corps, who knew what he might do next? I told Colonel Brace about Sarkosian's attack on Master Sergeant Cleveland.

"Unfortunate," the Colonel said. "I hope the child recovers. But one fugitive running around Seoul is something that with any luck, the KNPs will be able to deal with. Have you reported the incident to them?"

"I was just about to."

"Good, do that. Then get up to First Corps and talk to General Crabtree. If you have to, find this Estella woman and take her somewhere so these two guys quit fighting over her.

The Chief of Staff is fed up with their bickering and the stupid accusations they're making against each other."

"What sort of accusations, sir?"

"Never mind that. They're too farfetched to repeat. Just get between them and get this Estella issue resolved. And if you have to, remind General Crabtree that if this thing isn't settled immediately—and I mean *immediately*—the Eighth Army Commander will take decisive action. You know what that means."

"What, sir?" Leave it up to Ernie to make him say it.

Colonel Brace frowned and stared each of us down. Then he said in a low voice, "General Crabtree could be relieved of his command."

In the world of high-ranking officers, being relieved of your command was worse than being impaled on a wooden stake and left in the sun to be eaten by fire ants. And General Crabtree would have to kiss goodbye any hope of recovering his career.

Before we were dismissed, Ernie said, "This Sarkosian almost killed a dependent child. As it is, the child might not recover his full mental capacities."

Colonel Brace stared at Ernie. "Yes," he said. "What's your point?"

Here it comes, I thought. Ernie was about to spit in the punch bowl.

"Sarkosian has to be stopped, sir. I think it's more important than us babysitting two general officers."

Blood rushed to Colonel Brace's face. "Do you think I haven't considered that? I know what Sarkosian did, what he's capable of doing. But having two commanders with as much power as the First Corps commander and the ROK Army Third Corps commander threatening one another with move-out alerts and causing reciprocal division-wide chaos by the North Korean Communists on the other side of the DMZ is something that could erupt into *war*. Do you understand that? Millions of people could die. It has to stop right now."

"Then you shouldn't wait," Ernie said. "The Eighth Army Commander should relieve both of them *now*."

Colonel Brace looked down and took a deep breath. "Not my call," he said.

General officers with illustrious forebears or excellent political contacts in Washington DC were sometimes treated like coddled children, even at the risk of men under their command dying or wars breaking out. These two jokers, General Crabtree and General Bok, were being given one more chance to straighten out and fly right, a chance no enlisted man would receive in similar circumstances.

"We'll act quickly, sir," I said, and before Ernie could protest again, I hustled him out of Colonel Brace's office.

On our way north to I Corps, we stopped in downtown Seoul at the headquarters of the Korean National Police. Mr. Kill's second-in-command, Officer Oh, greeted us in the lobby, having changed from her usual blue summer uniform to her khaki-colored skirt and long-sleeved blouse. Her cap was something like a short-brimmed Australian campaign hat tilted at a rakish angle. She nodded to me and to Ernie and we followed her upstairs in the narrow elevator.

She led us down a long hallway to the office of her boss and mentor, Gil Kwon-up, Chief Homicide Inspector of the Korean National Police.

He sat at his desk speaking Korean into the phone. Officer Oh bowed to him and motioned for us to take seats on the leather-upholstered bench that sat next to the oblong coffee table of varnished mahogany. We sat while Officer Oh stood in the doorway, hands clasped behind her back, waiting for Kill to finish his phone call. When he did, he dropped the phone in the cradle, glanced at us, rose from his seat, and buttoned his coat.

"*Deitssoyo*," he said to Officer Oh, which meant "It's done," but in practice meant something more like, "That will be all."

Officer Oh bowed slightly, turned, and left the room. Mr. Kill sat on a leather-covered stool opposite us. In the center of the table was an octagonal box of wooden matches and two glass ashtrays. Mr. Kill knew that neither Ernie nor I smoked, so he didn't pull out the pack of Turtleboat cigarettes I knew to be in his upper-right shirt pocket. Instead, he said, "You've been busy."

I nodded. "Yes, sir."

"Your boy has evaded us so far," he said.

"Not our boy," Ernie said.

Kill studied Ernie. "No, I suppose not, since he's tried to kill you."

"And worse," Ernie said.

I explained what Sarkosian had done to Mort Cleveland Jr. Mr. Kill shook his head.

"He's been clever. And he's unpredictable."

"He has stolen money," I said. "He knows Korea, and he plans to take his revenge before we catch up with him."

"We'll see about that." Mr. Kill moved the ashtray slightly. I knew he wanted to finish this conversation so he could have a smoke. Most big shots in Korea or anywhere else wouldn't have hesitated to light up. It showed Mr. Kill's keen sense of politesse, which I found to be odd in a man who had reputedly locked up hundreds—some said thousands—of criminals in his almost thirty years as a cop. Sarkosian might be a first for us: both a murderer and a bank robber. But he was one of many for Inspector Gil Kwon-up.

"And you're having trouble up north," he said.

"Yes." I wasn't surprised that he was following the internal problems of the United Nations Command. There were hundreds of Korean employees who worked amongst the staff at 8th Army headquarters. More than a few of them, probably in key areas of responsibility, reported regularly to the Korean National Police. I never had the nerve to ask whether these informers were paid or if they did it out of patriotic duty. Maybe I'd find out another day.

"Your next stop," he said, "will be First Corps headquarters?"

"Yes," I said.

He nodded. "Be careful up there. Things are going on that even we aren't aware of."

We'd worked with Mr. Kill on a number of cases. Mostly from the GI angle, digging out information from US military bases and the business girls in the GI villages—places that were difficult or sometimes impossible for him to access. Usually, though, he knew the workings of anything high up in his own government, even if he didn't always choose to divulge it. That he didn't claim inside knowledge here somehow seemed to raise the stakes even higher.

"The situation seems pretty straightforward to me," Ernie said. "Two commanders, one leading First Corps and the other the ROK Army Third Corps, both want the same woman. A love triangle. Instead of duking it out like any sane person would, they keep posturing with combat alerts."

Mr. Kill smiled. "Yes, so it would seem."

"But that's not it?" I asked.

"It could be. But military intelligence in both our armies has their own motives and processes. And they're sometimes opaque to the rest of us in law enforcement."

"But you suspect something bigger's afoot?"

He nodded.

I wondered if I should mention Katie Byrd Worthington's conversation with Estella. But after all, the assertion that she was an American CIA agent had been made by a tabloid journalist. I had no way of confirming it. And I didn't want to look foolish by making such a bold and unfounded accusation. Not to mention that I might be mucking up US national security.

Ernie shot me a warning glance. Apparently, he didn't want me spilling too much either. Instead, I thanked Mr. Kill for his advice. He told me that he'd double the KNP patrols both in Samgakji, where Sarkosian was last spotted, and Itaewon, the main GI village in Seoul.

"Sarkosian would likely feel comfortable in either place."

"Maybe," I said. "But there's also probably a lot of GIs who've heard about him and what he did in Suwon."

"But they haven't seen his picture yet?"

"No. Not yet."

Aside from a direct recitation of the Associated Press story, both the American Forces Network Korea and the *Pacific Stars and Stripes* had downplayed the bank robberies, despite the many deaths that had occurred in the last few days. Their reasoning was that they didn't want to "damage Korean-American relations." Sarkosian had done enough of that on his own.

We thanked Mr. Kill and left the office.

-22-

On the road north, Ernie stepped on the gas and passed a truck laden with mounds of fat white Chosun radishes.

"What the hell was Kill going on about?" he asked.

"He was warning us to be careful."

"Big help," Ernie said.

"He probably has inklings of things he's not fully sure about and doesn't want unfounded accusations getting back to Eighth Army headquarters."

"Mr. Kill thinks we'd rat him out to Eighth Army?"

"Ernie, we *work* for Eighth Army."

"Maybe *you* work for them. I work for Ernie Bascom."

Ernie often talked about looking out for number one, but I knew that he'd be there in a pinch. In fact, when it came to violence, Ernie Bascom made damn sure he was never left out.

We passed through downtown Uijongbu, took a left where the road divided, and after about a mile, ran smack dab into the front gate of Camp Red Cloud, headquarters of the US Army I

Corps. A roadblock had been set up in front of the gate. Ernie downshifted and coasted to a stop in front of an armed MP wearing full combat regalia.

"What the hell?" Ernie said.

"Lockdown," the MP replied. "Nobody in or out."

"We have an emergency dispatch."

"Tough shit."

"No *tough shit* about it. Who's the Officer of the Guard? I want to talk to him."

"It's a her."

"Whatever. Bring her out here."

The MP shouted behind his back, and in about five minutes, a diminutive black woman wearing fatigues and the rank insignia of a First Lieutenant walked out of the guard house. As she conferred with the MP, he nodded toward us. Keeping her right hand on the hilt of her .45, she approached our jeep. I noticed that her name tag said Kramer.

"May I see your dispatch?" she asked.

We showed it to her. And our badges.

She shook her head. "Total lock down," she said. "General Crabtree's orders."

"You'd better check, Lieutenant," I said. "We were sent by the Eighth Army Provost Marshal, specifically to talk to General Crabtree."

Her forehead wrinkled in worry and she said, "Wait here."

She returned to the guard house, where I imagined she

was making a phone call to report that two CID agents from Seoul were here to interview General Crabtree. Ten minutes later, Lieutenant Kramer emerged from the guard house and walked toward us.

"No entry," she told us.

"That's bullshit," Ernie said.

She shook her head negatively. "No entry. But Command Sergeant Major Tapia told me to relay a message."

We stared at her.

"He wants you to meet him here in the village." She pointed at the street straight ahead of us. "There's a place called the Lucky Star Club. I've never been there, but they tell me it's hidden back in one of those alleys. He said be there at twenty-hundred hours." Eight P.M.

"You spoke to Screech Owl?" Ernie asked.

"Huh?"

"That's his first name. Screech Owl."

"What kind of name is that?"

"Apache," Ernie told her.

"Wow," Lieutenant Kramer said. "That's bold."

In front of the Camp Red Cloud main gate, crossed metal stanchions blocked our way, along with a chain link fence and a half-dozen MPs armed with M16 assault rifles. Still, I knew what Ernie was thinking. He hadn't given up on finding a way in.

"You sure you can't make an exception?" he asked the Lieutenant, using a boyish grin that was his version of charm.

"No can do," she said, standing back up to her full height.

"Then meet us at eight at the Lucky Star Club. I'll introduce you to the Command Sergeant Major. He's a legend in his own time. You'll like him."

She laughed. "Enough of that. You got your answer. Move out."

"Anything for you," Ernie said.

He turned the jeep around and we headed back to the bar district of Ganeung sam-dong. Ganeung Third District, which held more bars per square *pyong* than any other area in the city of Uijongbu. All of them catering to American soldiers.

Screech Owl was late. And First Lieutenant Kramer didn't turn up.

"Your boyish charm ain't what it used to be," I told Ernie.

"She's just playing hard to get."

"At this rate, you'll never have another story to tell Strange."

"Don't you worry, Sueño. I'll soon have more conquests than the sultan in *One Thousand and One Arabian Nights*."

"So you *have* read a book," I said.

"Mrs. Pettigrew in the fifth grade used to read it to us. Always put me to sleep."

The Lucky Star was a small club without any pool tables, which meant that its clientele was slightly more mature than average. Young NCOs rather than first-enlistment grunts. The juke box had some oldies but moldies on it, and I dropped in a couple of hundred-*won* coins. When I returned to the bar, Ernie had swiveled on his stool and was staring openmouthed at the front door.

"What sins did we commit," he asked, "to deserve this?"

Katie Byrd Worthington stood at the top of the short flight of steps, squinting and allowing her eyes to adjust to the dim light. She held her hand across her brow like a cavalry scout scanning the Great Sonoran Desert. Finally, she spotted us and scooted around an array of cocktail tables to join us at the bar. She waved to the barmaid and pointed to the bottles of OB in front of us. "*Hana*," she said. One. The barmaid reached in the cooler, pulled out a cold OB Beer, popped the top, and slid it in front of Katie. She offered a glass, but Katie waved it away. Sipping from the brown bottle, she glugged a couple of swallows, then set it down and wiped her lips with the back of her hand.

"Close your mouths, boys," she said. "You look like a couple of bullfrogs trying to catch flies."

"How?" I asked.

"How do you catch flies?"

"No. How did you find us?"

"Sergeant Major Screech Owl called me. Told me where you'd be."

"Why'd he call *you*?" Ernie asked.

"He needs me." She paused, eyes flashing mischievously. "*And* he needs the *Overseas Observer*."

"He needs you not to badmouth his boss," Ernie said.

Katie faked amazement. "Would I ever do that?"

"Damn right you would," Ernie replied, "to weasel your way into a story."

She leaned toward us conspiratorially and lowered her voice. "The good Sergeant Major needs our help."

"*Our* help?" I asked.

"Yeah," Katie replied, offended. "*Our* help."

"For what?" Ernie asked.

Katie sipped on her beer. "I'm not quite sure. It has something to do with Estella."

"The lucky star," I said.

"Huh?"

"That's what Stella means in Latin. Star."

"I don't know how lucky she is."

"Sounds like she's not very," Ernie said.

"I'll drink to that," Katie said. She finished her beer and ordered a round for all three of us, telling the barmaid that the two gentlemen would be paying.

Sergeant Major Screech Owl kept us waiting far beyond our appointed time and didn't show up until a half hour before the midnight curfew. He was wearing civilian clothes with a thick gray jacket and a winter cap with the earflaps pulled down. At the bar, he shook his head negatively to the barmaid and turned to us, "Outside. We need to talk."

As the others walked out, I chugged down the last of my beer and found myself settling with the barmaid. When I stepped out into the cold night air, all three of them were gone. I raced down the narrow street away from the lights of the front gate of Camp Red Cloud and found them in a narrow pedestrian pathway waiting for me. Once we were arrayed around him, Command Sergeant Major Tapia cleared his throat and said, "I think he's gone off his rocker."

"Who?"

"General Crabtree. It's that woman who did it to him. Ever since he met her up there at Third Corps, he's been acting weird."

"You're talking about Estella."

"Right."

"Weird in what way?" Katie asked.

"He hates General Bok. Ordering alerts every time Bok orders them."

"Practice alerts?" I asked.

"Right. The North Koreans haven't been doing much of anything lately. No provocative acts, no Division-wide approaches to the DMZ, nothing like the stunts they like to do to keep us off balance. In fact, the only thing they have done is go on alert in response to us going on alert."

"Purely defensive then," I said.

He nodded. "But Bok and General Crabtree are acting like a couple of schoolboys. I think Bok's fed up with it, worried that General Crabtree is badmouthing him up the chain of command. We did find anomalies in Bok's combat posture that need to be corrected, and if I were him, I'd be embarrassed about them. But all he has to do is fix them, and everything will be right."

"Anomalies like what?" I asked.

"His defensive positions are set too far to the rear. He needs to move them forward. Bok says he doesn't have the budget to construct new revetments and bunkers and other reinforced emplacements, but General Crabtree thinks that's bullshit. His operating budget is plenty big enough."

"Does he think Bok's pilfering money?"

Screech Owl shrugged. "Probably not. He's been spending tons of money preparing his tank battalions for withdrawal. You know, those new roads he's building. So when the North Korean attack comes, he'll be able to keep firing in a combat retreat, regroup on the southern side of the Taebaek Mountains, and advance in force on the oncoming Communist tank battalions."

"Makes sense, doesn't it?" Ernie asked. "We always assume that the North Koreans will have the upper hand at first. A surprise attack. They'll throw all their forces at us. But then we'll back off, counterpunch, and wear them down with precision firepower."

"That's the theory," Screech Owl said, hunching his shoulders against the cold. "I never liked it myself. I figure it's better to get them when they're right on the line. Lay everything on them on the DMZ, make them wish they'd never been stupid enough to attack."

"Okay," I said, interrupting. There were only a few minutes left before curfew, and I didn't particularly want to get into a detailed discussion about tactics. "I understand that General Crabtree and General Bok might have different points of view on how to handle any given combat scenario. And that this woman has come between them, but you said at first that you're worried General Crabtree has gone nuts. What did you mean?"

"I mean he's talking about attacking the Third Corps."

A momentary silence fell over the group. Katie, who'd been quiet so far, swiveled her hair from side to side, as I'd seen her do when winding up to let someone have it.

"You're saying," Katie said, "that because these two guys have some sort of problem comparing the size of their tank battalions, that it's the fault of an innocent woman? That it's Estella?"

"Yes," Screech Owl said. "Once she came on the scene, everything started going wrong."

"Sure. Blame the woman." Katie placed her hands on her hips. "What, exactly, did General Crabtree do to her? Did they just talk? Did they screw until they both passed out from exhaustion? Explain it to us, Sergeant Major, and don't be bashful. What exactly are you talking about?"

"She went to his room."

"Whose?"

"General Crabtree's. Estella snuck in there one night when he was staying at the Third Corps compound."

"How in the hell do you know?"

"I don't sleep much indoors."

"You sleep better outdoors?"

"Yeah. The way I grew up. That's why I took to the Army so well. I'm a field soldier. Pulling guard duty in the middle of the night doesn't bother me. I find it relaxing."

"So you were snooping?" Katie said.

Screech owl's expression was grim. He stared at her non-committally. "You could call it that."

"You feel protective toward General Crabtree."

"He's a good man."

"And she's an evil woman," she retorted.

He didn't answer.

"So did she spend the rest of the evening with the great General Crabtree?"

"Only a couple of hours. When she came out, I followed her."

"Okay. Come on," Katie prompted. "Give. What's the rest of the story?"

"She went to her room, I heard the shower running. About a half-hour later, she came out. Quiet. Thinking nobody was watching her. She went to General Bok's room."

"So that's what this is," Katie said. "You and a couple of crybaby generals offended because they've never encountered a woman who aggressively asserts her sexual needs. And because she didn't get off with General Crabtree and now she's going to try again with General Bok, you're blaming her for starting another Korean *freaking* War."

"I don't care who she screws," Screech Owl said.

"As long as it's not your boyfriend."

Since I'd known him, Screech Owl had always kept his expression impassive. But this time, it was as if it had crystallized into the face of a cliff. What Katie had just said, if spoken at an all-male barracks, would've been enough to not only start a fight, but a war. No soldier wanted his reputation tainted in any way by hints of homosexuality—not even in jest. Not to mention that "going queer," as it was often called, could result in arrest, court-martial, and a dishonorable discharge.

Katie fidgeted, realizing that she'd gone too far.

"All right," she said, "I didn't mean that. He's not your boyfriend. But you're looking out for him."

"I'm looking out for everybody," he said. "If those two keep screwing around with move-out alerts, the North Koreans are liable to think we're preparing a preemptive attack."

"And take the initiative," Ernie said, "by crossing the DMZ themselves."

Screech Owl nodded.

Footsteps shuffled at the end of the alley. At first, I thought it might be an MP coming to shoo us back to the compound since the midnight curfew was almost upon us. Then I realized that the sound was more than a shuffle. It was a pounding. A heavy pounding. Combat boots on the run. And then the siren sounded, a long wail like an ancient giant coming to life.

"Alert!" Screech Owl said.

And then we were all running. Screech Owl back to the compound. Ernie and I back to our jeep. When we reached the alley where we'd parked and locked it, Katie was right behind us, breathing heavily.

"You can't come with us," I told her. "We have to follow the Command and Control Communications van and try to find General Crabtree."

"Right. That's why I'm going with you."

"They might move out right up to the DMZ," I said. "And we'll have to follow."

"Good. I always wanted to see it."

She climbed into the back of the jeep.

Ernie and I looked at each other. "You gonna drag her out?" he asked.

"I was hoping you would."

He shrugged. "In for a hundred *won*, in for a thousand."

Ernie slipped behind the steering wheel and I jumped in the passenger seat. When he started the engine and pulled forward, Katie patted him on the back. "Good boy. Wait'll you see tomorrow's *Overseas Observer*. You're gonna love it."

"I'm not gonna be in it, am I?"

"No. That's why you're gonna love it."

When the Command and Control Communications van emerged from the front gate of Camp Red Cloud, Ernie fell in right behind. Because of the manic confusion of every move-out alert, nobody seemed to notice another military jeep following like a compliant duckling behind the mama duck up front.

The convoy headed east toward the northern end of Uijongbu until it reached a major intersection. Combat MPs had already arrived and were stopping what little civilian traffic there was and waving through the I Corps convoy. We zipped through the main intersection of Uijongbu, then past the two- and three-story high-rise apartment buildings on the northern end of the city, and soon we were passing dark rice paddies and quiet farm communities, heading north. It was a few miles later, when we reached the city of Pocheon, that things went nuts.

The combat MPs had screamed past the convoy on the dirt edge of the road and were now blocking the center of town, closing the intersection with the main highway in order to expedite our movement. But instead of picking up speed as they passed through Pocheon, the convoy slowed.

"What's the hold-up?" Ernie asked.

We were stopped long enough that I hopped out of the jeep

and ran up on a berm along the edge of a rice paddy and tiptoed to see what was going on ahead of us. I ran back to the jeep and climbed in.

"The Command and Control van is up there," I said. "Stopped. They're moving the portable stanchions, from the south side to the north."

"Why?"

"Hell if I know."

It was odd, not heading toward the DMZ during a move-out alert. Instead we were turning away, in the general direction of the extreme eastern limits of the city of Seoul. A minute later, the convoy started to move again. Up ahead, headlights paraded steadily south.

"For Christ's sake," Ernie said.

"What?" Katie said, pounding her fist lightly on his shoulder. "What does this mean?"

"It means," I said, "that General Crabtree is going to set up his First Corps defenses, and his headquarters, on the northeastern edge of Seoul."

"Why?" she asked.

"To protect the city."

"From what?"

"Not the North Koreans," Ernie said.

"How do you know?"

"If this was a real invasion, the North Koreans would've already sent their air force south. We'd already be receiving incoming. More importantly, they would've unleashed their artillery. It's dug into the sides of the mountain ranges near the DMZ. They roll it out on railroad tracks and the artillery pieces are huge. Massive guns, some of them almost as big as the Washington Monument. By now, we'd not only hear the rounds flying overhead, but we'd see the flashes of light from the explosions taking Seoul apart piece by piece." He waved his hand to our left and our right. "As you can see, everything's quiet."

"So maybe the protection of Seoul is General Crabtree's assignment in case of war. Maybe this is all practice," Katie said.

Ernie hit the big intersection and was waved south by an MP with a flashlight.

"No way," Ernie said. "At first, the MPs were set up to guide us north, as would be normal. But somebody must've ordered them to stop, and now they're redirecting us to the south. Also, every unit has reinforced fire positions close to the DMZ, placed in advance at strategic points. There's nothing like that on the northern edge of Seoul."

"Why not?"

"It doesn't make sense militarily. If the North Korean tanks get that far, they're going to take Seoul and we'd already be pulling our surviving units south of the Han River, to regroup and make a stand."

"So there's no plan for going where First Corps is going?"

"No."

"Then what in the hell is General Crabtree doing?"

Ernie didn't answer. He was following the convoy through narrow roads that were mostly unlit. I turned in my seat.

"General Crabtree is going to set up a defensive position somewhere north of Seoul."

"Against who?" Katie asked, almost crying.

"You already know."

"Against General Bok," Katie said. "The ROK Army Third Corps is attacking Seoul. He's planning a coup. That's what Estella was trying to tell me."

"What'd she tell you?" Ernie asked.

"She said that she was there to help him do what he was destined to do."

"But she didn't explain what that was?"

"No," Katie said, shaking her head in confusion. "I thought it was some sort of political grooming for his eventual run for the presidency. And while she was at it, that she would make sure he wouldn't abuse more women. Wouldn't bring them up there for more parties for him and the big shots he was wining and dining. I thought we were sisters, trying to protect one another."

"Not likely," I said. "When one dictator tries to displace another dictator, a lot of people die. Many of them, maybe most of them, women."

"Not to mention children," Ernie said.

"So what's the US Army going to do?" Katie asked. "Are they going to reinforce Crabtree and stop Bok?"

"Probably not," I said.

"*Not*? What are you talking about? They *have* to."

"It's an internal problem in the South Korean government. The US doesn't want to be seen, at least not out in the open, as picking and choosing winners. North Korea already claims that the South Korean government is nothing but a puppet of the Yankees. The official stance of the US government is probably going to be to stand by and let them fight it out."

"As long as the winner," Ernie added, "hates the Commies as much as the Pentagon does."

Katie looked back and forth between us. "You guys are *crazy*. I thought we were here to defend democracy."

Ernie shrugged. "Don't blame us."

"And General Crabtree," Katie said, pulling out her notebook. "He hates Bok. Allowing him to take over the country is certainly not what he would choose."

"That's why Eighth Army wanted to stop Crabtree," I said, thinking out loud now. "But the honchos didn't want to relieve him and admit how serious the problem had already become. Maybe they didn't know how quickly Bok was going to act. That he'd already been moving ammunition to the rear and repaving roads to allow his tank battalions to move faster. They kept hoping that General Crabtree would come to his senses and stop acting on his own and start following Eighth Army's orders."

"Which were to do *nothing*," Katie said, scribbling more furiously now.

"Yes. But Bok seized the moment. He didn't wait for those opposed to his plans to close ranks. He acted with audacity."

The convoy ground to a halt. Ernie tapped on the brakes, sliding on the muddy blacktop.

"Uh oh," he said.

"What's the hang-up?"

"Probably a roadblock."

"Bok's soldiers?"

"Who else?"

Along with other people in the front and the back of us, we climbed out of the jeep. Ernie elbowed me and pointed. In the distance, illuminated by the light of a three-quarter moon, I could barely discern the outline of a row of hills. "What?"

Katie stood next to us, squinting forward also.

"Along the lower edge of those hills," Ernie said. "What do you see?"

They were so dim I almost thought I was imagining them. "Red lights," I said. "Very dim lights."

"Exactly. It's hard to see them from a distance. Emergency lights for vehicular travel during blackout conditions."

"Like combat," Katie said.

"Exactly."

"Christ," she said. "There's got to be thirty or forty of them."

"That's Bok's lead force," Ernie said. "And his advance commandoes are already blocking the road."

"The Third Corps tanks will have a clear path into Seoul," I said.

"Not clear."

"What's going to stop them?"

Ernie looked at me. "What do you think the rest of the ROK Army is doing right now? Sitting around with their thumbs up their butts?"

"They'll confront them before they enter the city?"

"Or after," Ernie said. "Wherever. It's going to be a helluva fireworks show."

Katie thought about it. "God*damn* it! What do these boys think they're doing, playing these games? People are going to *die*!" She looked back and forth between us. "Well, don't just stand there. We need to get to Seoul."

"Why?"

"Estella. She told me that if anything went wrong, she would meet me at a Buddhist statue, near that big gate downtown."

"Guanghua-mun," I said.

"Yeah. That's it. She promised me a full briefing."

"A briefing?"

Gunfire erupted up ahead. Everybody crouched low, most of the GIs aiming their weapons forward.

"We better move now," Ernie said, "before the road behind us is blocked."

We piled back inside. Ernie started the jeep, pulled out of line, turned around, and rolled slowly back down the road in the opposite direction of the other vehicles in the convoy. The last vehicle in the row was an MP jeep. An armed MP stood in our way, his M16 leveled straight at us.

Ernie stopped. Another MP approached us from the side. He glanced at me and Ernie and Katie Byrd sitting in the back.

"What unit are you with?" he asked.

I showed him the dispatch.

"You're CID, right?"

"Right."

"Just got a radio report. General Crabtree wants you to hold where you are."

"Why?"

"I don't ask *why*." He pointed the barrel of his rifle at Ernie's temple. "Turn off the ignition." Ernie turned off the ignition.

The other MP was speaking on the radio. He waved at our MP and flashed him a thumbs-up.

"What's that supposed to mean?" Katie asked.

"Hell if I know."

Less than two minutes later, two men, winded, ran up to the side of our jeep. They peered in. I recognized them both: Lieutenant General Crabtree and Sergeant Major Tapia.

"Make room!" Crabtree yelled.

I leaned forward and they pulled up the back of my seat. Both men clambered in and squeezed into either side of the tiny rear compartment, with Katie sardined between them.

Perspiration running off his face, Crabtree said, "Thanks for the ride. I just turned the Command vehicle over to the XO." The Executive Officer of I Corps. He turned to Katie. "Estella called and told me she designated a rendezvous point between you and her if something went wrong."

"Yes."

"Where is it?"

Katie crossed her arms. "Why would I tell you?"

General Crabtree reached for his .45. Screech Owl leaned across them both and held on with both hands to General Crabtree's right wrist. For a moment, the two men struggled.

"That'll do no *good*!" Screech Owl yelled. "Calm down. Let me see if I can work this out."

General Crabtree took a few deep breaths, raised his right hand, and set it on the top of the back of my seat in plain view. "Go ahead then," he dared. "Try to reason with her."

Screech Owl turned to Katie. "It's important that we talk to Estella."

"I want to be there," Katie said. "I want to hear everything that's said, and I want it all on the record."

"Is that all you can *think of*?" Crabtree roared. "That damn rag of a tabloid you work for?"

"It's not a rag," Katie argued, chin tilting up.

"Sir," Screech Owl said. "You said you'd let me handle this."

Exhausted, Crabtree nodded his head. "Okay," he said, waving his hand. "You handle it."

Screech Owl turned back to Katie. "If we let you in on the story, when would you publish it?"

"Not till next Sunday. This week's edition has already been put to bed."

Screech Owl spoke in an appeasing voice to General Crabtree. "See, sir? It'll all be over by then. Ancient history. Nothing to worry about."

Rubbing his forehead with his right hand, Crabtree flicked the fingers of his left hand as if in acquiescence.

"Okay," Screech Owl said. "Then it's settled. You take us to Estella, we talk to her, you get to listen, and then you can publish a week from tomorrow in whatever rag you want."

"It's *not* a rag," Katie repeated.

"Everybody ready?" Ernie asked.

When no one protested, he started the ignition and we slowly rolled forward. This time, the combat MPs stood back and let us pass. To our right, the clatter of tank treads on pavement rumbled across acres of rice paddies.

The intersection in downtown Pocheon was dark and deserted now. Ernie turned left, heading back toward Uijongbu, and as he did so, I noticed a kimchi cab with its overhead light turned off pull out of an alley and follow us at a distance of about fifty yards. Whoever it was, I thought he was bold, since we were well into the midnight-to-four A.M. curfew. It was about two in the morning.

I leaned my head out the side of the jeep to see if he was still following, but he was a little too far to tell now. I thought I saw him through the low-lying fog, but I wasn't sure.

"What?" Ernie asked.

"Just a kimchi cab," I replied.

"Probably trying to sneak home."

"I suppose."

-23-

At Uijongbu, we turned left, and about ten miles later we reached the northernmost edge of Seoul. At every ROK Army roadblock—and there were plenty of them—we had to get out of the jeep, show our identification, and produce our emergency dispatch. So far, we Americans were viewed as neutral in whatever dispute was going on between the units guarding the capital and General Bok's III Corps. Still, everyone was frisked, including Katie. She screeched at the ROK Army soldier and slapped his hands away, which amused him to no end. The others made fun of the assaulted soldier as he held his wrist in mock pain.

By the time we reached downtown Seoul and the area in front of Guanghua-mun, the Gate of the Transformation of Light, the city was eerily quiet. We climbed out of the jeep and looked around.

"Why no tanks?" Ernie asked.

"Too early," General Crabtree said. "Besides, Bok's heading

for Gukbang-bu." The Ministry of National Defense, which was on the southern edge of the city. "That'll be his first objective. He'll take over that and then the Korean Broadcasting System, and once he has Park Chung-hee surrounded in the presidential palace, he'll announce the creation of a new government."

"And during all this, Eighth Army's keeping its hands off?" I asked.

"That's the policy."

"But you don't agree with it," I said.

"No way in hell."

"Why not?"

"Korea needs to move forward, not backward."

Before I could ask what he meant by that, small arms fire erupted on the eastern edge of the city.

"Damn," Crabtree said. "They're moving faster than I thought."

"We don't have much time now, sir," Screech Owl said.

General Crabtree nodded, thinking it over. He scanned the area around the two-story-tall edifice of Guanghua-mun.

"No sign of her," Screech Owl told him.

"No. Maybe she's on her way. Or maybe she was stopped. No way to be sure."

More explosions in the distance, a deeper rumbling sound.

"Tanks," Ernie said.

Screech Owl and Crabtree's eyes met. They came to some

sort of agreement. The general turned toward us. "Estella's late. I can't wait for her." He placed his hands on his hips. "I was going to ask her to try to get this thing called off somehow. But there's no more time." He glanced around at the dark buildings surrounding us, sighed deeply, and said, "Here's what we're going to do. You three stay here." He motioned toward me and Ernie and Katie Byrd Worthington. "We're taking the jeep."

"That's *my* jeep," Ernie said. "The tuck and roll alone cost me twenty thousand *won*."

Every payday, Ernie slipped the head dispatcher at the 21 T-Car motor pool a bottle of Johnny Walker Black to keep this jeep set aside for him and to keep it tuned up, topped off with gas, and maintained in Indy-500 condition.

"It's not your jeep," Screech Owl growled. "It's the Army's jeep."

Ernie reached in and plucked out the clipboard. "But my name's on the dispatch."

"A general officer can countermand that."

General Crabtree interrupted. "No time for this now. The Sergeant Major and I have to reach Gukbang-bu, and fast." He turned to Katie. "If you make contact with Estella, tell her she has to stop this. Too many lives are at stake."

Screech Owl snatched the dispatch out of Ernie's hands, turned, and stepped toward the jeep.

Furious, Ernie shot him a look, but he knew he was powerless against the order of a general officer. "Okay," he said, as if he were making the choice. "But don't lose that damn gearshift knob. I paid good money for it."

It was one of his most prized possessions—the grinning face of a red devil glowing in the dark.

"You got it," Crabtree said.

They climbed into the jeep. General Crabtree behind the wheel. Sergeant Major Screech Owl in the passenger seat.

After they drove off, Katie said, "Come on. We have to find Estella."

"I thought she told you to wait here for her?"

"Yeah. But in case she was late, she gave me directions."

"Why didn't you tell Crabtree?"

"Pooh on him."

"You don't trust him," I said.

"He's a man, isn't he?"

It was a long hike from Guanghua-mun to the Buddhist shrine on the side of Inwang Mountain. It wasn't much of a mountain, but rather a steep hill linked to the wall of jagged precipices lined with stone defensive walls guarding the northern reaches of Seoul.

Huffing and puffing, we climbed the last few stone steps to the large wooden platform on which the Buddhist shrine sat. Candlelit paper lanterns hung from rafters. In the center, a placid Buddha with a pleasingly plump belly smiled contentedly at us.

"The same one we saw at ROK Army Third Corps," Ernie said.

There were many types of Buddha, the Gautama Buddha being the most recognizable in image. Based on what I'd seen, the Maitreya Buddha was the most popular in Korea. This one was smooth and bronze, smiling slightly with his right ankle crossed over his left knee.

Katie slipped off her shoes, stepped up on the varnished flooring, knelt, and bowed. Ernie and I stood at the edge of the foundation, first glancing around to see if we were alone, then turning and gazing into the crater of the city. Through the fog off to the east, we could occasionally see flashes of red light, accompanied by muffled booms.

"Tank fire," Ernie said.

"Christ. These guys are getting serious."

"They've *been* serious," Ernie said.

A muffled rat-a-tat-tat of small arms accompanied the tank explosions.

"It's mostly aimed one way," Ernie said. "The poor guys defending the city are outgunned."

The other ROK Army tank battalions, of which there were many, were arrayed thirty miles or more north along the DMZ, facing the North Koreans. No one had expected a force of South Korean soldiers to turn on their own comrades and attack the capital.

Discipline in the South Korean army was absolute.

Soldiers had been beaten, tortured, and thrust into solitary confinement for the pettiest of offenses. A few had even been executed. As a result, orders were followed without the type of second-guessing and questioning that was so prevalent in the American army. And soldiers were kept isolated on their bases from broader Korean society. Often, they didn't hear radio newscasts or watch television. The information they did get was written down by their commanding officers and read to them by senior NCOs as they stood at attention in unit formations.

So far, Bok's tank battalions had held up well. No one had wavered in the performance of what they considered to be their duty. Although many on the outside would have considered this so-called "duty" to be armed insurrection, even treason.

I turned to Katie. "When is this Estella supposed to get here?"

Just as I said it, a figure appeared out of the mist and walked slowly into the light of the overhead lamp. Katie rose to her feet and stepped in front of the Buddha, and the two women embraced. Arm-in-arm, they walked toward us.

Katie introduced us, using our full names, as polite as I'd ever seen her. The name given for the woman was Estella, only that. She had long curly black hair, and wasn't tall, but slender, with an even-featured face with flawless skin that complemented a noncommittal stare. Her narrow, dark-brown eyes added to her beauty.

I shook her cool hand.

"Are you going to tell us what's happening?" I asked. "Who you are?"

She pulled her hand back. "You'll find out soon," she said, her English barely accented.

"You mean after the coup? After General Bok takes over?"

When she didn't answer, Ernie interrupted, impatient now. "Are you American CIA? Is that it? You guys just got tired of Park Chung-hee? Thought it was time for somebody a little more to your liking?"

"Not the CIA," she said calmly. "It's bigger than foreigners meddling in our affairs."

"But . . . *you're* a foreigner," I said.

"No." Her eyes flashed with an icy anger. "I'm *not*." She looked around at all of us, including Katie, who seemed to have taken an almost reverential posture toward her. "Come," Estella said. "The temple extends up the side of the hill. I'll show you."

She turned and walked away from the fat bronze idol, following a flagstone pathway that wound in a circuitous route up the hill. After about fifty yards, she pushed through an old wooden gate and held it open for us to follow.

We ducked beneath a low overhang.

A courtyard extended into the side of the hill, ending at a light-green stucco wall. At the doorway, we slipped off our shoes and stepped up onto wooden flooring. Estella led us through another door, a sliding one made of teak that was embossed with one phoenix rising after another. Inside sat a brass pot on a small diesel space heater. Beside it, leaning forward on a rocking chair, was an old man. He wore slippers and a white shirt covered by two or three sweaters with collars of soft fur. A felt blanket covered his knees. He looked over at us as we entered, a smile creasing his round face.

Estella bowed and said something to him I didn't understand, and I realized that she was speaking Japanese. The old man nodded, grinned at us again, and said in Korean, "*Anyonghaseiyo*?"

Estella followed his lead and started speaking Korean, less than fluently, I thought, and with an unusual accent. "This is my friend Katie," she said. "The one I told you about. She'll make sure our story is told to the world."

The old man, still smiling, nodded toward Katie, clearly entertained by having so many young people in front of him.

"These two men," Estella said, "are from the US Army. So far, they know nothing about our plans. Before I explained it to them, I wanted them to meet you first."

The old man nodded and reached out a withered hand. Both Ernie and I stepped forward and shook. His palm and his fingers were smooth, and as cold as if they'd been stored in a freezer.

"His name is Yi Il," Estella said. Yi the First. "He is third cousin to the late Crown Prince, last surviving heir to the Chosun Dynasty throne."

"Okay," Ernie said curtly. "Are we supposed to bow or something?"

"No, that won't be necessary. Not until his investiture."

"'*Investiture*?'" Ernie said.

"When they crown him king," I whispered.

"Oh, for Christ's sake." Ernie blew out air, pissed with all the formality. "Okay now, Estella. We've put up with your mystery. Are you going to tell us what the hell is going on, or what?"

"Don't be rude," Katie said.

"What's rude about wanting to know why we're being led around by the nose?"

"Swearing in front of someone you've just met is *rude*!" Katie insisted.

"I don't give a shit if it's rude," Ernie replied. He threw his hands up. "Will somebody tell me what's going on here?"

Katie was about to say something else, but I spoke first. "I think I know."

Ernie turned to me, open-mouthed. "Well then, *what*?"

Katie and Estella studied me, surprised.

"This gentleman," I said, motioning toward the grandfather, "has just returned to Korea after a long absence." I paused, taking a deep breath, wondering if I was about to make a fool of myself, and yet not giving a damn. But it had all clicked suddenly. His Buddhist faith. The young Japanese-speaking woman treating him with reverence. The probable backing of General Bok by what was left of the old-money elite here in Korea, fueled by their barely hidden disdain for upstart President Park Chung-hee and dissatisfaction with his brutal and corrupt regime. What powerful force could overthrow that regime with arms alone? There was only one thing that could change Korea's political fate, wrenching loose the iron hold of its authoritarian leader without tearing the country apart: tradition.

"This gentleman, Mr. Yi Il," I continued, "is a member of the royal family. A man with a claim to the title of heir to the throne of the Chosun Dynasty. Only now back in Korea after being held for decades in Japan."

"Not *held*," Estella said. "Exiled."

I was right then. I took another deep breath and continued. "General Bok and some of the prominent Korean families who support him want to restore the monarchy."

Tears glistened in Estella's eyes. "Yes," she said.

Katie pulled out her notebook and started scribbling.

"This guy's a *king*?" Ernie said, motioning toward the old man.

Without looking up from her notebook, Katie said, "Show some respect!"

"He's related to kings," I corrected. "When the Japanese took over in 1910, they kidnapped the Korean crown prince, Yi Un. In Japan, they later forced him to marry a woman of Japanese royal blood."

"They didn't *force* him," Estella said. "It was love."

Ernie ignored her. "Why?" he asked.

"To forge an official liaison between Korea and Japan. But they never sent the crown prince back. There was more anti-Japanese sentiment amongst the Korean populace than they had bargained for. And after the Sam-il Movement, the remnants of the Korean royal family were held in Japan for good."

On March 1st, 1919, the entire country had erupted in strikes and protests called the Sam-il Movement, *sam-il* for March first. The Japanese army had put it down brutally, murdering many Korean patriots and spurring an already deep-seated resentment.

"It's not like that," Estella said. "Misguided trade unionists and socialists were behind the uprising. The Korean people loved Tennō."

"Who?" Ernie asked.

"Tennō," I said. "The Japanese emperor."

"Loved the Japanese emperor?" Ernie scoffed. "Not according to the Koreans I talk to."

Katie stopped scribbling. "*You* only talk to bar girls and strippers."

"Yeah," Ernie said. "So?"

The old man seemed upset by our conversation. Estella rushed toward him, comforting him, speaking in Japanese, offering him a warm refreshment. I heard the word *ocha*. Tea.

"Okay, fine," Ernie said. "So we know why Bok's trying to pull this off. Take over the government and put the royal family back into power. But you can bet he'll be the main man in charge. He'll be the one pulling the strings in South Korea, no question."

"Not only South Korea," Estella said. "The entire country, even the Communists up north will rally under the Chosun banner. We'll be united again."

"Fat chance," Ernie said.

Katie shoved her notebook and her pen in one of the pockets of her jungle fatigue jacket. She stepped toward Ernie and said, "Will you shut the hell *up*? Can't you see you're upsetting the crown prince?"

"Well, good," Ernie said. "Right now, ROK Army soldiers are shooting and killing other ROK Army soldiers." Ernie pointed to the frail old man in the rocking chair. "*He's* responsible for that. Comrade killing comrade. Brother killing brother." He waggled his finger at Katie's nose. "I don't know about you, but I'm going to do whatever I can to put a stop to it."

"Bully for you," Katie said.

Ernie turned to me. "Where'd Crabtree say he was going?"

"To Gukbang-bu," I said. "The Ministry of National Defense."

"We need to commandeer a vehicle. Get over there and tell him about all this Chosun Dynasty bullshit, let him know who's behind all this mumbo jumbo."

"It's *not* mumbo jumbo," Katie said. "It's important to people."

"Yeah," Ernie said. "People stuck in the past."

Being aware of who was behind the coup and what their motives were might not make much of a difference, but on the other hand, it could make all the difference. At least then the South Korean military could guess which other military leaders felt sympathy toward the cause and who might've already expressed an interest in a restored monarchy. With that knowledge, they'd be better able to anticipate the next blow from a turncoat. We'd stumbled into valuable intelligence, and it was our responsibility to make sure that it got into the right hands.

The tank fire was coming closer. Certainly, the Capital Guard knew by now that they were caught in a full-on battle. Making our way across the city would be dangerous. Still, it had to be done.

"All right," I told Ernie. "Let's do it."

"I'm going with you," Katie said.

"No you're not," Ernie said. "People are shooting out there."

"I don't care. I'm *going*. Try to stop me."

Ernie looked at me for support.

"No, way," I said. "This is our military duty, and we're going to have to move fast. Write whatever story you want, publish whatever photographs you want. We might not even be around to see them."

Ernie and I started toward the door. I hadn't taken more than two steps when a deep commanding voice bellowed out "*Chong-ji*!" Halt!

We turned.

Estella stood behind the rocking chair, having twisted it to face us. From beneath the felt blanket, the old man had pulled out a pistol. An antique, maybe a German Luger. But whatever it was, its barrel looked just as deadly as that of any other pistol. Slowly, Ernie and I raised our hands.

"You're not going anywhere," he said in perfectly accented English.

Estella stepped forward, keeping out of the line of fire, and deftly collected first my .45, then Ernie's.

We sat on the wooden floor, Ernie and I glancing anxiously at one another. Outside, the gunfire had grown more intense, the sporadic report of tank blasts rumbling up the hillside. Katie continued to write rapidly in her notebook, occasionally asking me a question about Korean history and Japan's colonization of the country. Often, she'd follow up with, "Are you sure?"

I always answered the same way: "Look it up."

I told her that the last Korean king had had numerous wives and many offspring. Most had been taken to Japan during the annexation. After World War II, only a tiny fraction had returned. Most had stayed in Japan, but others had gone elsewhere in the world.

"This guy," I said, nodding toward the old man holding a pistol on us, "might be a crown prince, or he might be a third cousin twice removed. Either way, all General Bok wants is a figurehead."

"A symbol of Korean unity?"

I nodded.

Katie continued to scribble.

After a half-hour of cooling our heels, Ernie said to Estella, "How about some chow? A guy could starve to death around here."

"Be patient," she said.

"Oh, sure, the world's falling apart around me, and I'm supposed to be patient."

"The world is not falling apart," she said. "It's being rebuilt."

"How's that?"

I hadn't expected an answer, but she began to explain, her soft, melodic voice filling the cramped room.

According to her, the ascendants of Korea and Japan had been part of a massive empire called Koguryo. They had dominated Manchuria, what was now northern China, along with the northern reaches of the Korean peninsula. Proof of this was the hundreds, maybe thousands of mound-like tombs spread throughout what was now wilderness, reaching deep into Siberia. Eventually, Koguryo broke into factions, and some of its people moved south into the Korean Peninsula, a small portion going as far as to settle on the island of Honshu, eventually spreading throughout the Japanese archipelago. This was so long ago, she said, that many of the customs and art and language had since changed, becoming distinctly different from the Korean mainland. Though both languages, Korean and Japanese, shared a common grammatical structure, they had deviated profoundly and were now unintelligible to one another.

Ernie's eyes glazed over. Katie stopped taking notes. Only I was alert, peeved that she was repeating an old Japanese line: that they were the true inheritors of the great Koguryo Empire. A warlike state that had once been so powerful it threatened the existence of China itself.

The old man had been listening intently to Estella's speech. She switched from Koguryo to telling us how her father, the son of the armed man in the rocking chair, had been invited during the fifties to go all the way to Monaco to attend the wedding of Crown Prince Rainier and Princess Grace.

"It was there that he met my mother," she said, smiling as if she had personally experienced the moment. "She was royalty, too, from Spain. Basque country. It was love at first sight."

The old man's eyes closed. The hilt of the Luger slipped from his fingertips. The moment I'd been waiting for. I launched myself from my sitting position and leapt.

Estella screamed.

The old man was surprisingly spry. He reeled backward, the gun falling away, but then recovered and clutched the side of my neck, digging his fingers deep into my flesh and squeezing. I jerked away and fell backward, but as I did so, I kicked forward with all my strength. The rocking chair tilted wildly. I scrabbled on the floor for the Luger, but didn't find it, and when the old man hit the ground, I pinned him with a thud.

The bony old man beneath me lay still. I rose slowly, not feeling right about manhandling such a frail person.

Ernie threw the felt blanket aside, searching for the pistol. I was standing now, and Estella pushed us out of the way to get to Yi Il. "What have you done?"

"Where's the goddamn *gun*?" Ernie said.

We stopped looking around, then realized that Katie had backed up against the wall. In her small hand she held the Luger, pointed right at us.

She motioned with it. "Check him!"

I did, kneeling and touching the side of the old man's head, feeling for a pulse and at the same time leaning forward in front of his mouth. Then I felt it. Both a pulse and warm breath emitting from his throat. I stood back up. "He's okay."

Estella straightened the rocking chair, and Ernie and I helped the old man back into it. While Estella adjusted his sweaters and shook out the felt blanket, Ernie and I turned to Katie.

"Put the gun down," I said.

"Not yet."

"What? You want to help these people take over the ROK government? Is that it? More Korean soldiers dead? Maybe a civil war? Maybe North Korea taking advantage of the chaos and launching another invasion? Millions going off to sacrifice themselves, like in the first Korean War? Is *that* what you want?"

I was angry, and I knew it. Katie kept the pistol aimed directly at my chest.

"What I want," she said, "is the story."

"What story?"

"All this," she said, waving her hand. "The horror and pain and unbearable wounds. I want it all. I want to be the only one. The first reporter who scoops the world and lets them know what the great powers have wrought in this tiny country. I want them to bow down to *me*."

We both stared at her. For the first time since I'd known her, moisture seeped around the edges of her eyes.

After a pause, Ernie surprised me. He spoke in a gentle voice. "You want to come with us," he said.

"Yes," Katie replied. "I want to see all of it."

Ernie and I glanced at one another. We both turned to her and nodded at the same time.

"Deal," I said.

She grinned, wiped her eyes with the back of her free hand, and flipped the pistol around, expertly I thought. She offered the handle to me.

"Keep it," I said.

We ordered Estella to tell us where she'd stashed our .45s.

She did, crying all the while and begging us to consider the fate of the country, as if that weren't what we were doing. Neither of us spoke as we strapped the shoulder holsters back across our chests. We checked the weapons. Both loaded. One round in the chamber, seven in the magazine.

"Enough to stop a coup?" Ernie said.

"Can do, easy," I replied.

As we left, Katie followed, gun still in hand.

-24-

Ernie pointed his .45 at the temple of the kimchi cab driver. "We go," he said.

Perspiring, the man nodded rapidly.

At zero-four-hundred hours, the end of the midnight-to-four curfew, the first kimchi cabs had appeared on the street. These were the go-getters, the intrepid few. Most of the city remained indoors, and the buses—as far as I could tell—weren't running. Everyone had heard the gunfire that night, and even though things were quiet now, whispers of a military attack against the city must've spread from home to home like a virus. But these cab drivers had bills to pay, children to support, families to feed. Even if you were part of the invading army, they'd be out trying to hustle a fare from you.

Ernie sat up front in the passenger seat, his .45 trained on the driver. Katie and I sat in back.

"*Odi*?" the driver asked. Where?

"Gukbang-bu," I said. The Ministry of National Defense.

"Gukbang-bu?" he said, swallowing.

I confirmed.

He started the engine and the little Hyundai sedan rolled forward.

"Why there?" Katie asked, already writing.

"You heard where General Crabtree and Screech Owl were going," Ernie said.

"I *know*," Katie said. "I'm not stupid. But I wanna hear it from your mouth."

"For the record?"

"Yeah, for the record. You got a problem with that?"

"Will you two knock it off?" I said.

"Tell *her* to knock it off," Ernie replied.

"He's a butthole," Katie responded.

If we hadn't been in such a precarious position, I would've told them to get a room.

A ROK Army checkpoint waved us to a halt. I wondered if they were Bok's or ours. As we approached, I was relieved to see that according to their insignia, they were local constabulary troops, not ROK Army III Corps.

As Americans, we were neutral here. After all, the coup was an internal Korean problem, and both sides would be doing their best to curry American support. Shooting a couple of CID agents along with a freelance reporter wouldn't do much to advance that cause. That was my reasoning. But of course, I could be wrong.

Ernie showed his badge to the Sergeant of the Guard.

"*Odi ka*?" he asked gruffly.

I leaned forward. "Gukbang-bu," I replied, hoping that was an answer that wouldn't lead him to arrest us.

His stern face showed no reaction. He fondled Ernie's badge, then tossed it back. He wriggled his fingers, and I turned over my badge and Katie her passport. Taking his time studying them, he asked, "*Wei Gukbang-bu ka*?"

Why are you going to the Ministry of National Defense?

This was a little trickier. It was possible that these guys weren't local troops at all. Maybe General Bok had gotten hold of some of their patches and had them sewn onto the uniforms of his own troops. It would be a good ploy to ferret out those opposing the coup. I decided to make our mission seem as innocuous as possible.

I told him in Korean that we'd gotten stuck in northern Seoul last night during curfew and were supposed to return to our compounds as soon as possible. But we were afraid to go there directly due to the gunfire we'd heard and wanted to stop at the Ministry of National Defense first to make sure it was safe to proceed.

He was surprised at my language ability, though he struggled not to show it. I also knew he was putting on a show for the troops standing behind him. He was the man in charge, and as such, he had to look decisive and all-knowing. My tone, I hoped, had been properly obsequious.

Apparently, it had. He turned to his men, grinning slightly, and then back to us.

"*Musop-da*?" Are you afraid?

"*Aju*," I said. Very.

Then he said, "*Tambei isso*?"

I knew we had him. The damn thing was that since neither Ernie nor I smoked, we didn't have a cigarette between us. Katie sensed what was happening. She reached into the folds of her loose jungle jacket and pulled out a pack of Kools. She handed them to me. I in turn handed them to the Sergeant. He returned my badge and Katie's passport. Sticking the valuable American tobacco in his chest pocket, he stepped back, cradled his M16 rifle in the crook of his arm, and waved us forward.

The cab driver stepped on the gas but had apparently forgotten to put it into first, and we stalled. Still perspiring, he twisted the key in the ignition, grinding metal gears against metal gears, and finally coaxed the little cab into starting. Slowly, we rolled forward.

"You don't smoke," I told Katie. "Why'd you have a pack of Kools?"

"Old trick I learned in 'Nam," she replied. "Always have something with which to offer a bribe."

"We owe you," I said.

Ernie snorted.

■ ■ ■

The Ministry of National Defense was under siege, surrounded by what must've been an entire battalion of tanks. Across the street, we crouched behind a window on the third floor of an office building that had been hastily abandoned.

"No way we can get in there," Ernie said.

"Nor do we want to," I replied.

"I thought you wanted to tell them about this royal family card Bok's playing?"

"I do. But we won't do anybody much good if we're blown to pieces by a tank round."

"Don't worry. They'd use small arms fire on us. They wouldn't waste a tank round."

"Reassuring."

"Thought so."

Katie crouched next to us, her notebook and pen out. "So what are you guys going to do?"

Ernie turned toward her. "Any suggestions?"

"Yeah. You could help General Bok overthrow the Park Chung-hee regime. It's brutal, the elections are rigged, and there's no freedom of speech here. About time somebody kicked them out."

"No way I'm getting involved in that," Ernie said. "All I really want to do is convince these jokers to stop shooting at each other. South Korean soldiers killing South Korean soldiers doesn't do anybody any good."

Before Ernie finished his sentence, a volley of tank rounds

was unleashed. Mortar and brick dust exploded from the ten-foot-high walls surrounding the Ministry. The front gate, made of reinforced steel, twisted like an arthritic claw and folded inward. After another volley, the tanks rolled forward, knocking down the gate, firing at the soldiers inside the guard shack. A half dozen of them ran outside, trying to get away. Mercilessly, the tank pursued, spitting machine gun fire. Rounds hit their mark. One by one the soldiers went down, their backs ripped open, blood spilling into the dirt and dust.

"Bastards," Ernie said.

Katie peeped over the ledge of the window, wide-eyed.

More tanks poured through the opening, accompanied by crouched infantry soldiers with their rifles pointed straight forward. Automatic fire erupted from within the Ministry. Attacking soldiers went down. More tank fire erupted out of steel barrels, and great gaping explosions of dust and brick and metal smashed into thick protective walls. More rounds spit from second- and third-story annexes flanking the main edifice. More soldiers fell face first onto pavement. More tank treads rolled across twisted metal and fallen bodies. The infantry filtered in past the tanks and fanned out, entering the building from all sides.

Katie gripped my arm. "Isn't General Crabtree in there?"

"I think so," I replied. "And Sergeant Major Screech Owl."

She turned to me. "They'll be killed!"

I nodded and turned away.

"We can't just sit here and let them die," she protested.

"What the hell do you expect us to do?" Ernie said.

"We have to do *something*."

"You're the one who kicked Screech Owl in the balls."

"I've had a change of heart," she said.

I spotted something. "Look! Over there. Out of that side gate."

On the western edge of the walled compound a pedestrian gate had been opened, and Korean soldiers were streaming out. Amongst them, identifiable in the pre-dawn light with their height and olive drab uniforms, were General Crabtree and Sergeant Major Screech Owl Tapia. They headed down a side alley near the building we were in.

"Come on!" I yelled. We ran toward a window at the end of the hallway. From there, we could see the gaggle of loyal troops regrouping and one of the Korean officers shouting orders.

What the men on the ground couldn't see, but we could from our vantage point, was another squad of General Bok's infantry approaching from the far side. They were about two blocks away, advancing carefully, afraid of an ambush.

"They'll be trapped!" Katie grabbed my arm again. "We have to save them."

"Come on." We ran down the cement stairwell and out of the building. Once we emerged onto the narrow street, Ernie didn't even slow down. He knew that he'd only beat the approaching assault troops if he sprinted at full speed, which he did. When he rounded the corner, we lost sight of him.

By the time Katie and I reached the same intersection, Ernie had spotted Lieutenant General Crabtree and Sergeant Major Screech Owl. They were about a hundred yards away, jogging toward us, Ernie waving them in. Katie punched my arm.

"Look!" she said, pointing down another alley. "Bok's soldiers."

There was no time for hesitation. Within seconds, those troops would emerge out of the narrow pathway and take us all into custody, if they didn't shoot us outright. The alleyway was a few feet up from where we stood, so if Ernie and the other two could reach this corner and sprint down the road we'd come from, they'd have a straight shot at freedom. But if the ROK troops arrived first, they would have a straight shot at all of us, and I had no doubt that they wouldn't miss at such short range.

"I have to slow them down," I said.

"How?"

I slipped off my shoulder holster and handed it to Katie along with the .45. "You still have the Luger. Can you use this, too?"

"What do you think I was doing in 'Nam? Knitting?"

"As soon as Ernie and the others reach this corner," I told her, "get them the hell out of here."

"What about you?"

Before she could finish the sentence, I was already running toward the mouth of the alleyway. When I entered it, I had my hands straight up and walked directly into the phalanx of General Bok's ROK Army III Corps troops.

They frisked me, quickly realizing I wasn't armed.

"What are you doing here?" the lead officer asked me in English.

"I'm lost," I told him. "I need to go back to my compound."

He squinted at me, furious. With the back of his hand, he shoved me aside. "*E sikki*," he said. "*Na ka!*"

It seemed rude, ordering me around like a dog. Also, I didn't particularly like being pushed, but at least I hadn't been shot. And I'd accomplished what I wanted to do, which was stall them until the others could get out of their way.

He ordered his formation forward and, as the other troops tromped past me, every second or third soldier straight-armed me as their commander had, pushing me up against the dirty brick wall. When they passed, they turned right toward the Ministry of National Defense. After they departed, I straightened myself and had just started re-tucking my shirt into my pants when I heard footsteps. I glanced right. That's when I froze.

It was her.

■ ■ ■

Doctor Yong In-ja reached out and touched my hand.

"I've been worried about you," she said.

"And I've been worried about *you*."

She laughed. "No need." She let go of my hand and tapped the Soviet-made AK-47 strapped over her right shoulder. At the end of the alleyway, ready to move out in any of three different directions, stood a group of men similarly armed.

"Your infantry squad?" I asked.

"Party workers," she said. "Free men. Something difficult to find on this peninsula."

She'd told me before what her group, known as the South Cholla Workers Union, stood for: a third way. Not a military dictatorship like in South Korea, nor a massively brutal Communist tyranny like North Korea, but a free state. Ruled in a democratic way, sensitive to the autonomy of various regions of the country. Respecting differences that stretched back to the Middle Ages and before. Like those of South Cholla province, where she was from. They used a slightly unusual Korean dialect, had alternate customs and holidays, and, most conspicuously, harbored a fierce sense of independence, especially vis-à-vis the authoritarian rule that emanated from the capital city of Seoul.

"Why'd you come up here?" I asked. "You're taking a big risk."

The South Cholla Workers Union had long since been outlawed by the South Korean government, and as one of their leaders, she'd be arrested on sight.

"We've been monitoring General Bok," she said.

"And me," I replied, remembering the fleeting glimpse of someone I thought to be her that night near Samgakji.

"Maybe a little," she replied. "To survive, we have to be ready for however this conflict turns out. Park Chung-hee will probably put down the insurrection. That's what we expect, and if things turn out that way, he will become even more oppressive."

"And you want to show him that you're still here and still active."

"Exactly."

"But if Bok wins?"

"We want to show him that his new regime, backed by massive influxes of Japanese money, will not conquer us. It didn't work before, and it won't work now."

She meant the Japanese colonization of Korea from 1910 to 1945. A dark period when the resilient people of South Cholla had never given up their struggle.

I also knew she didn't want the North Korean communists to win in this perennial battle for the hearts and minds of the Korean people. The first thing they would do if they ever took over South Korea was eliminate all hint of opposition. Especially opposition that took the socialist positions of Doc Yong's group. The Commies only pretended to be for the workers and for the people. The truth was that they were for themselves, and themselves alone.

The men at the end of the alley seemed to be getting impatient. Doc Yong noticed it, too.

"How's Il-yong?" I asked.

"He's healthy. Smart, like you."

"No. Like you."

"I show him your picture, remind him that he's half American, and I teach him the best parts of America. The ideals. The quest for freedom."

"When he's older," I said, "will you make sure he studies the Gettysburg Address?"

"Yes. I will." She realized that I was struggling not to tear up.

"Why do they keep us apart?" I asked. "It's just . . . torture."

Someone hissed in urgency down at the end of the alley.

"I have to go," she said.

"I know."

The men were still watching, so instead of embracing, I squeezed her hand.

She smiled, turned, and ran toward them.

I sprinted back to the intersection where I'd left Katie, but she was gone. I kept running down another block and then another until someone whistled. A shrill, reedy sound, like some sort of desert bird. Command Sergeant Major Screech Owl Tapia emerged from the darkness. He motioned for me to follow.

I did.

-25-

Katie returned my .45 to me, and then the five of us commandeered another kimchi cab and made our way to what General Crabtree called Hanguk Bangsong. Korean Broadcasting. It was a radio station midway between Guanghua-mun and Seoul *yok*, the city's train station.

When the ROK Army soldiers guarding the ground floor saw the stars on General Crabtree's lapels and the stripes on Sergeant Major Screech Owl's sleeves, they came to attention. A nervous lieutenant called upstairs and received permission to let us up. The elevator wasn't working, and after five flights of stairs, we were all slightly winded.

She was waiting at the entrance to the studio. Estella, who bowed to General Crabtree and studied him carefully. He, in turn, couldn't take his eyes off her.

We were ushered in. Crabtree's guess had been right. General Bok was here, along with the old gentleman, Yi Il, the erstwhile crown prince, who no longer had his rocking chair but was sitting in a comfortable-looking leather chair in front of a large stainless steel microphone. Bok turned when we entered.

"Ah, General Crabtree. Good of you to come." He motioned toward a six-foot-long control panel with plenty of buttons and knobs and blinking yellow and green lights. "As you see, we're just about to begin our broadcast."

Crabtree stopped in front of him. "You can't do this, Bok."

General Bok frowned, his dark eyebrows twisting upward. "And why not? Is it American policy to promote a brutal dictator like Park Chung-hee? Is it America's place to see our country divided, as it never has been before in its five-thousand-year-old history? After all, it was *your* decision after World War II that led to the split. It was *your* decision that mandated that American troops accept Japan's surrender in the south, below the thirty-eighth parallel, and Soviet troops accept Japan's surrender in the north."

"A poor decision," Crabtree said. "I admit that. And we Americans have regretted the division of Korea ever since. But this," he said, gesturing toward the old man, "this is no way to solve anything."

"And why not? Reinstating the Chosun Dynasty, the royal family Yi. All Koreans, north and south, will rally to that banner. I can deal with the north. I've been speaking with them for years, both at ROK Army Third Corps and through more informal contacts amongst members of the prominent families in Japan and on either side of the DMZ."

Bok must be delusional, I thought. The power of prominent families in North Korea must've disappeared by now. Maybe a few had survived, those who had thrown in their lot with the Communists early on and maintained total loyalty toward Kim Il-sung ever since. Whomever Bok had actually been speaking to in North Korea was probably a Workers' Party apparatchik controlled by the regime.

Bok continued, still addressing General Crabtree. "Besides, you're a foreigner. What could you know about what's good for this country?"

Crabtree took a half-step toward him; they stood nose to nose. "I know that right now, right this minute, Korean soldiers are killing other Korean soldiers. And why? For some cockamamie idea about bringing back the past, picking up with a system from a century ago. It won't work, I tell you. If the Commies up north have led you to believe that they'll go along, they're playing you. All they're really after is chaos in the south so they can *attack*."

Bok shoved his nose up until it was almost touching General Crabtree's. "*Let them*!" he said. "Then we can fight it out once and for all. *Settle* this." He slashed his hand downward in a diagonal motion like it was a sword. "One side will win, and one will lose. But in the end, we'll be one country again. One country and one people, like we were meant to be."

Estella hurried forward. She gently touched Crabtree's elbow, smiled up at him, and coaxed him back a few steps.

The General's face softened. Soon she had him a few feet away, motioning to swivel chairs around a short conference table. He refused to sit but didn't return to Bok.

Meanwhile, as they'd been arguing, a technician had been fiddling with knobs and dials. I watched him, trying to figure out what he was up to.

Bok spoke to the old man, Yi Il, leaning forward and explaining the important topics he wanted him to discuss, but the old man appeared to be struggling with his handwritten Korean script. Estella left General Crabtree with Katie and Screech Owl and hurried toward the man she'd called her grandfather. As the three of them—Bok, the old man, and Estella—pointed at the script and discussed it, I realized they'd switched to Japanese.

The technician, nervous at the tension in the room, took advantage of the delay and hurried over to a small table with cups and a thermos on it. While he poured what smelled like barley tea, I continued to study the control panel. There was one metal switch close to the microphone that was larger than the others, and conveniently placed so whoever was speaking could reach it easily. Checking to make sure that no one was watching, I leaned forward and flipped the switch. A red light came on. Below it was a Chinese character. I couldn't be sure, but I believed it said "On."

The three of them continued to discuss the script, speaking in sibilant Japanese. I wondered if the sensitivity of the microphone was enough, so I found another knob with numbers on its edges and twisted. On a scale of one to ten, it now read eight.

I returned to General Crabtree. He was perspiring, and Screech Owl was close to him. When I reached him, he said, "You're both armed?"

As if he'd conjured up a pack of genies, a half-dozen Korean soldiers entered the broadcast room, and the same lieutenant who'd allowed us up the stairs ordered his men to hold us at rifle point while others stepped forward and reached for our .45s. Screech Owl was about to fight them. So was Ernie, but I said, "Hold on. I think we've got something else working."

"What?" Crabtree asked.

"You'll see, sir. But there's no sense getting ourselves killed when it won't ultimately do any good."

He nodded, seeing the logic in that.

Crabtree gave the order, and the four of us allowed ourselves to be disarmed. The Korean soldiers didn't bother to check Katie Byrd Worthington. She kept fiddling with her camera and taking shots, asking people to pose and reaching into her generously pocketed jacket for more film and flashbulbs. One pocket held a bigger bulge. The Luger.

Bok took a break from coaching the elderly Yi Il. He shouted an order and had us taken outside.

I hung back for as long as I could, listening to them speak Japanese. Watching the technician, still frightened and preoccupied, gulping down tea. He hadn't yet returned to the control panel.

The lieutenant and his armed guards held us downstairs in the lobby. I sat as close as I could to the front door. Every time another soldier walked through, I heard the words emitting from the metal speaker in front of the building. Japanese, not Korean. A crowd was beginning to gather. People were mumbling amongst themselves, not happy to be hearing the language of the colonizing power broadcast outdoors for everyone to hear. Private conversations were one thing. A public display was another.

Most people in the States didn't realize the extent of Japanese Imperial oppression in Korea. Some had heard of "comfort women," forced into prostitution for the Japanese troops. Some had heard of the forced labor, Koreans being taken from their country and transported to frigid northern islands to slave in coal mines. Or young men being transported into the remote wilderness of Manchuria to risk their health and even their lives chopping away at the endless forests. But as terrible as all these were—and they were terrible—there were some things Koreans considered to be even worse.

First, the Japanese had taken away their language.

In the years after the Sam-il uprising, the Japanese policy had become one of erasing all elements of Korean culture. Its goal had been to turn Koreans into obedient, second-class subjects.

The Korean language was banned in schools. All education was delivered in the new national language, Japanese.

Second, the colonizing authorities decided to re-register everyone in the country under a Japanese name. This was a major blow to a country that honored its ancestors so highly. Almost all Korean holidays centered around visiting ancestral grave mounds and having picnics to commune with the dearly departed. Confucian filial piety ran deep—it was not only a virtue, but a part of the country's cultural marrow. To take a Korean's family name was to take their identity. Which was the plan. To strip Koreans bare of their cultural touchstones and rebuild them into faithful subjects of the Japanese emperor.

It didn't work. Although they were forced to show loyalty in public and participate in the economic life of the Japanese empire, Koreans never lost their identity—or their hatred of those in power, which grew under the boot of the Imperial Japanese Army.

Communicating primarily in Japanese, General Bok, Estella, and the old man were going over the entire speech. Bok coached the wannabe crown prince on the correct pronunciation of some Korean words with which he was unfamiliar. Bok, in his fluent Japanese, exhorted the old man to muster all the sincerity of which he was capable. Or at least, that was how it seemed to me. Even though I couldn't understand exactly what was being said, except when they briefly switched to Korean, it sounded like Bok was giving the old man a locker-room-style halftime speech. And Estella repeatedly soothed her grandfather in her soft voice.

Outside, the crowd was growing larger. A few of them occasionally lobbed a stone toward the speaker that was spouting the offending language. Finally, the dim-witted lieutenant seemed to realize what was going on, but before he could do anything, the speaker was briefly turned off and then back on again. Three notes rang out from a xylophone, calling for everyone's attention. An officious voice in Korean, maybe the technician's, announced an important address from Major General Bok Jung-nam. All citizens take heed!

Bok spoke for ten minutes, basically talking about the valor of the ROK Army III Corps troops, how President Park Chung-hee had agreed to sign his resignation, how the country would be united under the banner of the Chosun Dynasty, and how for the first time in almost a hundred years, all foreign troops would be expelled from the country.

Instead of cheering, the crowd outside seemed confused. Some of them were murmuring amongst themselves about the long discussion they'd heard in Japanese. Someone shouted, "What about the Japanese? Will they be allowed in?"

Others jeered. More rocks were thrown.

Bok, unable to hear any of this from his studio, introduced Yi Il, heir to the throne of the Chosun Dynasty. Haltingly, the old man began to read his speech. Even I could tell that many of the words were mispronounced and the rhythm of the sentences didn't sound right. At one point, the old man faltered so much that Estella's voice chimed in softly in the background, apparently repeating how to say a word in Korean. Then the old man asked her a question. Just two or three words, spoken in Japanese, but it was enough to enrage the crowd. People were shouting now. "We don't want a Japanese king taking over our country!"

Rocks smashed into the windows. Rotten onions and loose heads of cabbage hit the front door. A contingent of guards pushed their way outside and shoved the mob back. But more people had joined, apparently excited by the sporadic gunfire in the city, many probably having listened to the amateurish radio broadcast.

With the front doors open, Screech Owl noticed it first.

"Gunfire," he said.

"Yeah," I replied.

"But coming from the north now."

"The Second Corps," General Crabtree said, standing up and walking toward the front door. "They're moving in to save the city."

"Bok's plan," I said, "is that the people will rise up and support him."

"Not now. These people are mad as hell." Crabtree turned to me. "What's gotten into them?" he asked.

I told him about switching on the mic early, while they were preparing in Japanese.

"That's enough to piss them off this much?"

I nodded. "Think about it. What if this happened in the States—someone went on national broadcast and told us we had a new president, but he started speaking and he wasn't an American?"

Crabtree grunted. "Fat chance anyone would let that go through."

"This is a hundred times worse. Everyone listening in a few minutes ago knows that the figure at the head of this coup is more in tune with the country that brutally colonized them for decades than Korea. Royalty or not, they don't want anything to do with him."

The ROK Army guards were approaching full panic. The mob outside was growing faster than they could push them back. No one was watching us.

"Time to leave," Screech Owl said.

"Yes," Crabtree said. He put his hand on his Sergeant Major's shoulder. "You lead these people back to Yongsan Compound."

"What about you?"

"I've got to go upstairs. Try to reason with Bok. Stop more bloodshed."

"And you want to talk to Estella," Katie said. She'd sidled up to the two men while they weren't looking.

"What is it with you?" Crabtree said. "Don't you ever give up?"

"Not as long as there's a story."

"Well you've got your story," he said, motioning to the mob outside. "But if you want to ever see that in print, you'd better follow the sergeant major and get the hell out of here."

"Do you love her?" Katie asked.

Crabtree paused. "I don't know."

Katie jotted something down. "I'll take that as a yes."

"Go now," General Crabtree said, shooing us away.

Ernie and I didn't need much coaxing. At any moment, that mob would overwhelm the Korean soldiers and break down the front door. They might be angry at the memory of Japanese occupation, but when you're pissed off and trying to protect your country, any foreigner will do.

Crabtree sprinted up the stairs.

Ernie, Katie, Screech Owl, and I made our way out the back door of the building and hurried down an alleyway, heading south toward Yongsan Compound. On the way, radios were turned on, sitting on window sills and propped atop stools in doorways, volume full blast. For a while we heard General Bok talking, trying to convince people that restoration of the monarchy was the only way to reunite the country. Eventually, he changed to screaming at his ROK Army III Corps commanders, ordering them to reposition to the northern edge of the city to stop the advance of the ROK Army II Corps. Finally, we heard shouts and crashes and then screams. Men cursed in Korean, Bok screeched something, and a couple of gunshots rang out.

A few seconds later, the broadcast went dead.

-26-

Just after dawn, the city was already filled with looters.

The Korean National Police were nowhere to be seen, and the Army itself—no matter what corps you were from—had abandoned all discipline. Soldiers in fatigues carried gunny sacks full of oddly shaped items, or in some cases, boxes filled with stereo equipment or television sets, most of the electronics made in Japan.

"They're not taking the Korean-made stuff," I told Katie.

"Made in Japan is higher quality?"

"That's what they think."

She scribbled that down. When we finally reached Namdaemun, the Great Southern Gate, we knew we were close. Maybe a mile and a half. A straight shot down a tree-lined lane that ran through the residential area of Huam-dong. There were no kimchi cabs out now. And Ernie's jeep, along with its custom-made tuck-and-roll, had been abandoned during the chaos of the attack on the Ministry of National Defense. Even the most intrepid taxi drivers were no longer trying to hustle; they were just concerned with protecting their property.

Oddly, no one had menaced us in any way. Even groups of young local thugs, holding clubs and knives, ran right past us.

"Looting fever," Ernie said. "They can rob a *miguk* any time. But how often can you break into the Cosmos Department Store and get away with it?"

"A red-letter day," I agreed.

Screech Owl ranged a few yards ahead of us, keeping a sharp eye out for danger. The alleyways that emerged onto the main road were narrow, and I kept wondering what Sarkosian might do if he managed—especially in this chaos—to get hold of a weapon. So Screech Owl wasn't the only one keeping a wary eye out for the unexpected. Although how we'd protect ourselves now that we were no longer armed, I wasn't quite sure.

Finally, we reached the last intersection.

The traffic light wasn't working, but we looked both ways, and then the four of us darted across the road. From there, it was a long block past the entrance to the small US compound of Camp Coiner on the right and the ROK Marine headquarters compound on the left. At the end, at the top of a gradual rise, stood the back gate to the 8th United States Army's Yongsan Compound. From here we could see helmeted MPs and the Korean contract-hire gate guards. And behind them an extra contingent of armed soldiers, armored troop transports blocking the way.

"Safety," Katie said.

An eerie feeling ran up my spine. I glanced around as we hustled for the gate, but in the end, we made it. Safety on the US compound at last. We showed our IDs and were allowed in.

So much for a premonition.

It was still early morning when we returned to the CID office and discovered that Miss Kim wouldn't be coming in. Eighth Army had announced that no local-hire employees should report to duty that day because of the rioting. Riley had switched from the khaki uniform he usually wore into fatigues, along with full combat regalia. He wore his steel helmet, even indoors, the leather strap securely buckled beneath his chin, web gear with ammo pouches stuffed with magazines, and his M16 rifle leaning against his desk within an arm's reach.

"What? No hand grenades?" Ernie asked.

"Don't be a wiseass, Bascom," he replied. "Who knows what these Commies are up to?"

"Commies? What Commies?"

Ernie headed toward the serving counter, and when he realized that the metal coffee urn was empty, he shook it in disgust. "How can a guy be expected to fight World War III without coffee?" he asked.

"There's instant in the cupboard," Riley growled.

"How about hot water?"

"You'll have to heat it yourself."

Which Ernie did by filling a bronze pot Miss Kim usually used for tea and placing it atop an electric burner.

Riley turned to me. "Where's your report?"

"You're not going to ask if we were hurt or if we suffered any combat trauma? Nothing?"

"Knock off the bullshit, Sueño. Colonel Brace wants that report, and he wants it *now*."

So after Ernie and I each had a cup of Folgers Instant Crystals, I sat down to type my report.

Without asking permission, Katie Byrd picked up the phone to make a call and discovered that the 8th Army Public Affairs Office was about to organize a press briefing. She waved as she hurried out the door and spent the rest of the day at the meeting, being apprised on what the honchos knew—and were willing to publicly release—about General Bok's coup.

Ernie found the copy of the hot-off-the-press issue of the *Overseas Observer* that Riley had managed to finagle early that morning from the PX and thumbed through it contentedly. Until he came to page three. "You're kidding me, right?" With the back of his hand, he slapped pulp.

"What?" I said, looking up from my typewriter.

"That broad Katie. What won't she do next?"

I rose from behind the field table and gazed over Ernie's shoulder.

"She's not only got an article about Sarkosian being on the lam, but to counterbalance it, she's got this sappy love story between General Crabtree and Estella. 'The Lady on the Line,' she's calling her. Trapped on the DMZ just a few yards from North Korea, unable to reunite with the man she truly loves."

"No photo?"

"She's promising that next week."

"Well, she took plenty today."

"Yeah," Ernie said, "Crabtree and Estella will be another Romeo and Juliet before she gets through with them."

"If they survived that mob at Korean Broadcasting," I said.

By mid-afternoon, word was that the tide had turned. The loyal troops of the II Corps were sweeping through the city now, mopping up the remnants of General Boks' III Corps, most of whom were surrendering immediately. As far as the fate of General Bok, Crabtree and Estella, and Crown Prince Yi Il, we didn't know yet. What we did know was that Park Chung-hee had issued the order for his soldiers to shoot looters.

"On sight," Riley said, feigning aiming his rifle. "The ROKs aren't screwing around."

"They usually don't," Ernie said.

The next day, as things were settling down in the city, Ernie convinced the head dispatcher at 21 T-Car to loan him a tow truck and a driver and he went to Gukbang-bu in an attempt to retrieve his jeep. When he returned to the office, he was downcast.

"A total loss," he said. "Crushed by a goddamn Third Corps tank." He opened his palm. "This was all I could salvage."

The red devil face on the gearshift grinned up at me.

Replacement vehicles were at a premium at the motor pool now, so Ernie and I took a kimchi cab to downtown Seoul to the headquarters of the Korean National Police. We waited less than five minutes to be ushered into Mr. Kill's office. He was distraught, sitting at the coffee table, for once lighting up and smoking in front of us.

"A disgrace," he said. "A national embarrassment." He looked at us. "Why can't we resolve our political differences without resorting to violence?"

I spread my hands. "You're not the only ones."

"No, we're not." He shook his head. "But we thought we were making such progress."

"You are," I said. "It was put down within hours."

"If they hadn't been so amateurish, they might've pulled it off. Imagine that. Accidentally broadcasting a conversation in Japanese. Had they really thought the Korean people had forgotten colonization?"

"Yeah," I replied. "That wasn't smart."

"No." He stubbed out his cigarette.

"Any word on what happened to General Bok?" I asked. "Or General Crabtree?"

"Not yet. Second Corps fired on the building. Direct hit as far as we can tell, but it's still a mess. Our people are sorting through it."

"They haven't identified the bodies?" Ernie asked.

"The morgue is jam-packed. It will take time."

We sat silent for a moment. Mr. Kill fiddled with his shirt pocket, visibly tempted to light up another *tambei*, but in the end, he resisted the urge.

"Sarkosian," he said.

"Any leads?"

"No. That's the thing. You'd think that with us posting his photograph in every KNP office in the country and having patrol officers here in Seoul carry a copy of his picture in their pocket, we would've spotted him by now."

"Clever guy," Ernie said.

"Yes. And we can't discount the possibility that during all this, he might've gotten ahold of a firearm."

My thoughts exactly. "So what do we do?" I asked.

"My men are still dealing with the arrested looters and the bodies caught in the crossfire. As soon as that dies down, maybe in a couple of days, I'll send out the bulletin and photograph again, emphasizing how important it is to find him. He and his gang are responsible for the deaths of at least five Koreans, maybe more. Some of the victims in the last robbery are still in the hospital, and in this confusion, I haven't received updates."

"You'd think a burly foreigner like him would stand out pretty easily," Ernie said.

"You'd think. But Seoul is becoming more cosmopolitan. And if he's spending money freely, people have a tendency not to, how do you say it?"

"Kill the golden goose," I said.

"Yes. He's sitting on at least two thousand dollars."

"That will buy a lot of silence," Ernie said.

"But not enough," Kill said. "We'll get him."

Ernie and I were both thinking the same thing: if he doesn't get us first.

Since we were downtown, we decided to check in with Katie at the Bando. I used the house phone in the lobby to dial her room. It rang about six times before she picked up.

"What?" she said.

"It's me," I said.

"*Me* who?"

"Sueño," I replied.

"Why the hell are you calling me so early?"

"It's almost noon."

"For you, maybe. For me, it's four in the morning."

"Late night?"

"Filing stories like crazy, mailing rolls of film. This story is spreading beyond just our little *Overseas Observer*."

"Which story?"

"The one everybody wants to read about. The one with the princess and the love-struck general. Roll over Willy Shakespeare. Katie Byrd Worthington is on the way."

"Have you talked to them?"

"Since we last saw them?"

"Yeah."

"No. Have you?"

"No," I replied.

She was silent for a moment. "So you think maybe they didn't make it?"

"I think maybe not." I wondered how much to tell her, but then I figured, what the hell. "According to Mr. Kill, the Korean Broadcasting building was shelled by the ROK Army Second Corps artillery."

"*Ugh*," she grunted. "Much left?"

"Not much."

"Christ," she said. "Guess they really were star-crossed lovers."

It had been obvious General Crabtree had a soft spot for Estella, but I'd never seen that feeling reciprocated. "Were they really lovers?" I asked.

"Who the hell cares? If I say they were lovers, then they were lovers."

The truth, I thought, might be buried for good under rubble.

"You haven't heard from Sarkosian, have you?"

"Not a word."

"Maybe we could find you a room on the compound," I said. "It might be safer there."

"And let Eighth Army lock me up if and when they feel like it? No way, José."

"He's out there somewhere, Katie," I told her. "And in all this chaos, he might've gotten ahold of a gun."

"Hey, a person can get killed crossing the street." I heard her reach for something on her nightstand and then set it down with a metallic thud. "And a person can die from lack of sleep. Will you quit worrying, Sueño?"

"Not in my nature," I replied.

"Talk to Ernie. He'll explain how."

With that, she hung up.

-27-

The rest of the week went by quietly—the Korean government methodically putting itself back together—and then the biggest event of our lives took place on Sunday when the new issue of the *Overseas Observer* hit the stands.

Ernie and I sat in the 8th Army Snack Bar, going over the paper with Strange.

"Too bad about Crabtree," Strange said. "He was a bold dude."

The big headline in this week's issue was about Lieutenant General Abner Jennings Crabtree and Major General Bok Jung-nam, as well as the woman known only as Estella and the self-proclaimed Crown Prince Yi Il. All of their bodies had been found amidst the rubble of the Korean Broadcasting building. Katie played it up big. How the two lovers had been separated by international politics and had almost restored the rightful monarchy of the Chosun Dynasty when the violent put-down of the attempted coup cost them their lives. Katie knew full well that Estella and Crabtree had been at cross purposes, with her aiming to overthrow the current government and him wanting to stop her. But Katie wasn't about to let minor details get in the way of a good story.

To make sure the GIs read it, Katie managed to have the story wrapped around a particularly busty pinup girl.

"Oh, brother," Ernie said. "Old Katie Byrd really laid it on thick, didn't she?"

"She's not so old," Strange said.

Ernie looked at him. "How do you know?"

"I've seen her," he replied. "She's good-looking. Once you get past the blue jeans and the jungle jacket, I'll bet she has a nice body."

"One you'll never see."

"Neither will you," Strange said, "if the head shed gets its way."

"What do you mean?" I asked.

"I mean they're trying to figure out who to blame for this coup."

"Who to *blame*?" Ernie said. "They already know who to blame. General Bok and Estella and that old guy who claimed to be the prince. They're who to blame. And they're all dead."

"Not that simple," Strange said, sipping contentedly on his hot chocolate, enjoying the fact that he'd gotten a rise out of

Ernie. "The Park Chung-hee government is going over Third Corps with a fine-toothed comb, looking for traitors. And finding plenty. There'll be trials, maybe executions."

"So? What's that got to do with us?"

"Eighth Army is wondering who put them up to this. Who coordinated between ROK Army Third Corps and the US First Corps to open an easy pathway between the DMZ and Seoul."

"An easy pathway?" Ernie asked. "General Crabtree did everything he could to place himself between Bok and Seoul. He just didn't have enough troops or enough warning. Ask Screech Owl."

"Oh, yes. And the good Sergeant Major. He's being interrogated under oath as to *his* part in all this."

"He did his best to stop the coup and his best to protect General Crabtree."

"Crabtree's dead."

"Yeah. But before he died, he ordered Screech Owl to return with us to Yongsan Compound."

Strange spread his hands as if in surrender. "There you go."

"What?" Ernie asked. "What do you mean, 'There you go'?"

"It's not what *I* mean. It's what the honchos mean. They're wondering why you two and Screech Owl abandoned General Crabtree."

"He wanted it that way. Besides, what were we going to do? Stop Second Corps artillery from blowing up the building?"

"You could've done something."

Ernie leaned back in his chair, exasperated. "No matter what you do in this army," he said, "you're always wrong."

Instead of medals, I thought, they only gave us grief.

The next morning at the CID office, Staff Sergeant Riley got busy chewing us out for the black market statistics going to hell while we'd been worrying about ROK Army III Corps and the bank robberies. "You two get your butts over to the Commissary and PX," he told us, "right now. And start making some arrests. At least four today. Minimum. And four every day for the rest of the week."

"Take a hike," Ernie told him.

The phone rang. Miss Kim picked it up, identified herself, and listened. Then, with her slender hand, she covered the receiver. With a worried look, she turned to me. "Geogie," she said.

I rose from my seat and walked toward her. She held out the phone. I took it, nodded to her in thanks, and said, "Sueño speaking."

The voice was raspy, hoarse, as if it had been swallowing sand all morning. "If you tell anyone," it said, "she will die."

Sarkosian.

"Where are you?" I said.

"Get a paper and pencil."

Miss Kim could apparently hear. She slid a ballpoint pen

and a lined pad in front of me. Behind me, both Riley and Ernie had grown silent.

"Shoot," I said, immediately regretting the choice of words.

"The Tonam-dong district," he said. "A warehouse numbered 284-15. There's only one door. It will be open tonight. Twenty-three-hundred hours *exactly.* No one but you and your partner. And remember, you cross me, she dies."

He paused, and it sounded as if he were moving away from the phone. Then some rustling of what might've been linen or cloth and a long gasp, as if someone was desperately gulping air. And then, "Tell him to go *fuck* himself, Sueño!"

Katie Byrd Worthington. And then the male voice again.

"You still listening?"

"Yeah," I said.

"Go to Camp Mercer. In my wall locker, I have a passport. I want you to bring it. Understand?"

"Understand."

"Repeat the address to me."

I did.

"Don't come early, don't come late. *Exactly* twenty-three-hundred hours. You got that?"

"Got it."

"No weapons. No guns, no knives, no nothing. Just you two, unarmed, with my passport."

"No money?" I asked.

"Hey, wiseass, I'm setting the rules here. You just keep your goddamn mouth shut!"

I pulled the receiver away from my ear. All eyes in the room were on me.

"Okay," I said. "Just the passport."

"You don't bring it, she dies. You're late, she dies. You bring any cops, Korean or American, or anybody other than you and your partner, she dies. You *got* it?"

"Got it," I said.

"Don't be late."

He hung up.

Ernie and I looked at each other. Miss Kim started to cry.

Tonam-dong was a hilly and tightly packed area of Seoul, one of the oldest districts in the city. Only a mile or so northeast of the royal palaces and the presidential residence, but the neighborhoods quickly dropped off from opulence to abject poverty. Once you hiked up the steep hills, few of the narrow alleys had been paved. When it rained, they turned into sucking muck. When it snowed, they froze into rocky ridges laced with deep canyons. There were warehouses that weren't much more than stucco buildings, one or two stories tall, with high windows barred by rusty iron. There were also industries, but they were usually housed in wooden lean-tos with signs overhead advertising bicycle repair, plumbing supply, or window glass cut to specifications. We also spotted a cobbler, repairing shoes in the open air.

The shops were lit by single bulbs hanging naked from wooden rafters. Or in some cases, by the sizzle of welding equipment.

"People still repair shoes?" Ernie asked.

"Around here, they do," I said.

"I thought people threw 'em away and bought the new fashion."

"If the PX manager had his way, that's exactly what they would do."

Both Riley and Miss Kim had been sworn to silence. Not even the Provost Marshal knew about this nighttime mission. Also, neither Ernie nor I had checked out a weapon. We weren't in a hurry to, anyway, since a Report of Survey had been initiated on the two .45s that had been taken from us by General Bok's troops in the Korean Broadcasting building. We'd given them up for good reason, but that didn't stop a whispering campaign from swirling amongst the 8th Army MPs. Many felt that surrendering your weapon was the equivalent of surrendering your balls. They claimed they wouldn't do it even unto death. Of course, most of these guys had never done anything more dangerous than escort a drunken GI out of a nightclub, so I took their philosophies lightly.

Ernie was taking it harder.

What worried me was that tonight he might try to compensate for the damage done to his macho reputation. He might try to kick someone's ass. Which sometimes came in handy, but with Katie Byrd's life at stake, violence had to be carefully calibrated.

The afternoon trip to Camp Mercer had been uneventful, and the Commanding Officer there had taken the right steps—Sarkosian's personal effects had been sequestered under lock and key. With him standing next to us, we had searched through Sarkosian's duffel bag and his field gear and a leather briefcase he owned. I breathed a sigh of relief when we found the passport. It was still valid, and he could still theoretically use it at Kimpo International Airport. Except for the fact that when he presented it to Korean customs authorities, he was sure to be arrested. Security in public places, especially transit points, was much higher in South Korea than it was in other countries. They'd been dealing with North Korean terrorism since the end of the Korean War.

Bombs went off at unexpected times in South Korea: on land, in the air, and at sea. The government made heroic efforts to try to prevent that from happening: eyes-on, open-bag inspection of all luggage, an official check and double-check of passports and visas, and running names and faces against most-wanted lists.

As we walked up the muddy hill of Tonam-dong I patted the document again. Ernie glanced at me, nervous himself. "Will you quit fiddling with that thing?"

"I wonder how he plans to get out of the country."

"Maybe pay some fisherman to take him to Japan."

"Maybe. Risky, though. They might take the money and turn him in anyway."

"It'd serve him right."

Our plan wasn't much. We'd been afraid to reconnoiter the area earlier in the evening, which was something we should've done according to basic MP procedure. But our best chance of keeping Katie alive was to follow Sarkosian's orders, turn over the passport to him, hope for the best. Other than that, we'd play it by ear. Ernie and I knew enough to keep space between us so in case Sarkosian had a weapon, he wouldn't be able to hit both of us if he fired. We had no plan other than that, but I was hoping, perhaps naively, that no plan was the best plan here. We'd improvise. And if Sarkosian made the slightest mistake, we'd make him pay. Part of me hoped it was with his life.

But Sarkosian probably did have a weapon. We'd gone to the Bando Hotel earlier in the afternoon and gotten the manager to let us see Katie Byrd's room. All her personal effects were still there except her multi-pocketed jacket, her camera bag, and her trusty Nikon. I opened the drawer and found nothing, unsure whether to feel relieved or concerned that the Luger was gone as well.

"Why didn't she shoot him?" Ernie asked.

"I bet she didn't have the chance," I said.

I wondered if he'd caught her by surprise, or there was some other circumstance in which Katie had been taken. No sign of a fight—had she gone willingly, been allowed to pick up her things, maybe even snuck the gun with her somehow? It was that, or Sarkosian had gotten hold of it.

As we tromped through Tonam-dong, we received some strange looks from the locals in the area, but not many. At night, it was dark up there, without many people out. Only the very occasional streetlamp cast a dirty yellow glow, and people had their own problems to worry about. They glanced at us, shoved their hands deeper in their pockets, and kept walking.

I used my flashlight to study the numbers, and after turning right down one alley and left down another, we ended up doubling back into a cul-de-sac. I finally spotted the white numbers in faded paint on rotted wood: 284-*bonji*, 15-*ho*.

This was the one.

We listened. The building behind the wooden gate was tall, more than one story high, almost two. The walls were whitewashed stucco and slathered with grime. We waited for a while, listening, hearing nothing.

Ernie checked his watch. The dial glowed green.

"It's time," he said.

I nodded. He stepped forward and turned the handle. Slowly, the gate creaked open. No one there.

"Shall we?" Ernie said.

We went in to the empty courtyard.

-28-

A brick sidewalk wound around the edge of the building, then continued up onto a low cement stoop. Another door, this one of solid steel.

Ernie tried the knob. It lurched open.

Darkness. We stepped inside.

"I have a flashlight," I said, speaking loudly to announce myself to whoever might be there. "I'm going to turn it on."

"Belay that," someone said. A gravelly voice, only a few yards away. Ernie and I just about jumped out of our skins.

"Close the door," the voice said.

"We'll all be blind," I said.

"I said, close the goddamn door."

I glanced at Ernie. Almost imperceptibly, he nodded. I reached back and slowly closed the door. It clanged shut with a metallic ring.

"Now," the voice said, "step toward the sound of my voice. Exactly six steps. Count them out."

We hesitated.

"*Do* it!"

We did, stepping forward slowly, carefully, feeling for a hole or booby trap. What we didn't do was count them out. In this large, empty room, our footsteps reverberated. That should be enough. The only piece of information I had gathered in this otherwise sensory-deprived world was that I could roughly pinpoint where Sarkosian was, especially if he moved or said anything.

We finished the sixth step.

"Six!" I said.

And then, as if a nova from deep space had exploded, light sliced into our eyes for a fraction of a second. Ernie and I crouched, covering our faces. A flash bulb!

"The passport!" Sarkosian shrieked. "You, Sueño. Reach out your right hand, with the passport in it. Do it. *Now*!"

I couldn't see anything except pinwheels spinning before me, but I stood back up to my full height and reached for the passport. Before holding it out into the darkness, I had the presence of mind to say, "Katie. We have to see Katie."

"Passport first," he said.

"No. Katie touches my hand, she speaks so I know it's her, and then I let go of the passport."

There was a silence as if he was thinking it over and then murmuring. Katie's voice. Feet shuffled toward us. And then arguing. "My camera. I want my goddamn camera."

Leave it up to Katie Byrd Worthington to make demands at a time like this.

Sarkosian said something I couldn't make out, and Katie said, "Fine. Keep the flash attachment. Just give me the damn camera."

It dawned on me that part of Sarkosian's plan had been to have his eyes fully adjusted to this darkness before we arrived. It gave him the advantage of being able to at least make out shapes while we were totally blind. Before the flash went off, my eyeballs had begun to make the adjustment they'd told us about in night-fighter training. I had begun to spot pinpricks of light here and there throughout this space, started to orient myself within it. But now, after the flash, I was as blind as Mr. Magoo.

"Hand it to her," Sarkosian said.

"What? The passport?" I asked.

"Yeah."

"First I want to touch her hand."

"Go ahead."

I reached out, circling my hand in the void. Finally, I touched fingertips, and a small hand clutched mine. "Is that you, Katie?"

"It ain't Santa Claus."

"What do you think?"

"I think you should give me the *goddamn* passport."

I wanted to ask her if he was armed but didn't think it was

wise right now. Ernie had shuffled a few feet away—ready, I knew, to spring at a moment's notice toward the sound of Sarkosian's voice. By now, he'd probably slipped his brass knuckles over his fist.

"Okay," I said. "Here it is."

Katie let go of my hand and grabbed the thick document.

"My *camera*," Katie said.

"All right, goddamn it."

Apparently, he handed Katie her precious Nikon camera. Sarkosian grunted. Fingers shuffled through pages of paper.

"Let me go," Katie said.

"Not until I make sure this is my passport," he said.

Maybe ten feet away from us, a dim light shone in the darkness, a penlight covered by a hand. Still, for a split second, it illuminated Sarkosian's face like the latest Hollywood Technicolor technique. He was pointing the Luger in my direction.

Ernie moved. Startled, Sarkosian twisted and fired at the sound. Something hit the ground and rolled—Ernie, diving for cover. Then the light went out. The gun fired three more times in rapid succession. I was crouched on the ground now, rushing to the left, away from Ernie but still toward Sarkosian. If one of us could reach him, we'd have a chance, but the odds were slim. The gun fired once more, and as it did, something swished through the void.

Something heavy. And then a clunk, like rock on wood.

Katie was screaming. "Son of a *bitch*. How dare you lock me up? *Me*? I'll teach you, you sonofabitch!"

I charged forward blindly. I felt Katie's body and pushed past her, then stumbled over something big and heavy on the floor. I knelt, groping with my hands. Sarkosian. I felt the stubble on his beard. Ernie bumped into me.

"Got him," I said, reaching for my handcuffs. "He's down. Find a light."

Within seconds, overhead fluorescent bulbs buzzed and flickered to life. Katie and Ernie and I all covered our eyes with our palms. I glanced down. Sarkosian was out cold, lying on the ground in front of me. I kept my knee propped securely on his back and fumbled with the cuffs, and seconds later his big hands were securely fastened. I checked his carotid artery. Heart beating strong. Plenty of air escaping from his mouth. So much, I was surprised he wasn't snoring.

"What'd you do?" Ernie asked Katie.

"You assholes almost got in my way," she said. "When he gave me my camera"—she held the Nikon up in the air—"I swung it around by the strap and bonked him a good one. Almost didn't work because of you guys stumbling around in the dark."

I noticed a lead pipe lying beside Sarkosian's thigh. He'd possibly been planning to brain Katie with it. Or us.

"Why the darkness?" I asked.

"He figured you'd bring guns, even though he'd said not to.

If it came to a shootout, he'd be able to escape." Katie pointed. "Down there."

Behind Sarkosian was a small wooden door, the kind Koreans sometimes had in warehouses to slide crates from one room to another. I walked toward it, pushed it open, and peeked through. Metal rollers led down to a lower level.

"Is there another door down there?" I asked.

"Yeah," Katie replied. "That was how he was going to escape. Down that ramp, out the back loading door, and he'd emerge on the opposite side of the hill. A completely different neighborhood."

"And he would've left you lying here," Ernie said to Katie. "Probably with your head bashed in."

"No way," Katie replied. "He never stood a chance."

"Please. Once *we* got here, he didn't stand a chance," Ernie said. "We saved your butt."

"Huh. You think Katie Byrd Worthington couldn't have gotten away from this moron? All you guys did was make it harder for me."

"Sorry we interfered," I said.

Katie grinned. "I forgive you. In fact, I'll let you make up for it by buying me a cold one."

But Ernie wouldn't let it go. "So how'd he capture you? You were armed. Had a little lapse in concentration?"

"No way. I found *him*."

"*You* found *him*?"

"Of course. I wanted to interview him. All it took was brains and a little good old-fashioned shoe leather. I went to places where foreigners other than GIs hang out. Like those *hagwons* that teach conversational English. I talked to one person who led to another, and eventually I found Sarkosian hiding in some old *yoguan*. And what better way to get him to open up than to let him think he'd gotten the better of me?"

She smiled and waved her notebook, letting it fall open, showing pages of notes.

"But the Luger," I said. "You could've gotten us *killed*!"

"Huh." She shrugged. "No great loss. Still, I wouldn't do that, even to you two. Before I found Sarkosian, I made sure the Luger was filled with blanks."

Ernie knelt and picked up the weapon. He fiddled with it for a while until he was able to pull out one of the cartridges. He held it up to the light and examined it. "This isn't a blank. Look at this," he said, fondling the tip. "Full metal jacket."

For once, Katie Byrd looked surprised. "Imagine that," she said finally. "The guy who sold me the ammo swore they were blanks." She shook her head. "Just shows to go ya', can't trust anybody these days."

"Ain't that the truth," Ernie replied.

Then he staggered toward the wall, gripped a support beam, bent over, and upchucked a full day's ration of army chow.

-29-

Eighth Army didn't know exactly what to do with Sarkosian. Sure, he'd misappropriated government vehicles and government weaponry and wasted government-issued ammunition, not to mention being absent from his assigned duties. But the sum total of all those charges would've gotten him nothing more than a Bad Conduct Discharge and two, maybe three years in the stockade.

The Status of Forces Agreement between the US and the Republic of Korea, however, stipulated that the ROK had jurisdiction over all crimes committed on their territory unless both sides agreed to turn the prosecution over to the US Army for court-martial, which was often done in low-profile cases. But in this case, the outrage of the Korean public made turning it over impossible. In the end, the SOFA Committee decided that the ROK judicial system would maintain jurisdiction.

They, of course, charged Sarkosian not only with bank

robbery, but also with murder. More than one convicted killer—just ask Mr. Kill—had gone to the gallows. But the Korean government faced an unusual problem with Sarkosian. It had to do with the US taxpayer, who for decades had been financing the American defense of the Republic of Korea against its Communist neighbor to the north. Did it really make sense to have a story appearing in Stateside newspapers concerning an American serviceman in South Korea being hanged by the neck until dead?

The other side of the equation was domestic political blowback. Korean citizens wanted justice, or even revenge against this man. But Park Chung-hee had to keep a wary eye on the seven hundred thousand Communist soldiers just thirty miles north of their capital. The attack on Seoul via the III Corps coup that had just happened had revealed the weaknesses within his own regime; this was no time to put military support from the US at risk.

Sarkosian's trial wasn't covered in the Korean press, on the orders of Park Chung-hee. The AP and UPI, of course, did cover the trial, as did the *Overseas Observer*. Katie Byrd Worthington not only sat in the press section during the trial, but for at least a couple of hours, she was sworn in as a witness. Kidnapping was added to Sarkosian's list of charges, almost as an afterthought. Katie didn't mind since she used the threat of refusing to testify as leverage to coerce the Korean prosecutor into allowing her an exclusive interview with Sarkosian.

The *Observer* editors dedicated almost twelve column inches to Sarkosian's rant. It was quite a screed. He still blamed Ernie and me for having "messed him up," as Katie put it, cleaning up the vulgarity so it would be allowed in print. And he still swore that someday he would take his revenge. Which could never happen if he were subject to the same punishment any Korean criminal would for similar charges—which would certainly be death. But Sarkosian was not only an American, but a US Army soldier, and so after the guilty verdict, the Korean court sentenced him to time in a Korean prison: a total of eight years.

"Eight years?" Ernie said, incredulous, as we sat in the 8th Army Snack Bar. "With all that blood on his hands?"

"They don't want to hang an American soldier," I said. "And they sure as hell don't want him locked up in Korea forever. They want to get rid of him. If the Korean government had their way, they'd send him back to the States now and never look at him again."

"How are the families of the dead taking it?"

"Not well," I said. "Not from what Mr. Kill tells me. Some of them are threatening public demonstrations to protest the light sentence."

Strange approached. As he sat down, Ernie and I both stopped talking. For once he brought his own cup of hot chocolate.

"You think he'll be able to pull it off?" he asked.

"Who and what are you talking about?" I said.

"Sarkosian. Do you think he'll be able to keep his vow to murder you two when he gets out?"

Ernie barked a laugh. "Guess we'll find out in eight years."

"In eight years," Strange said. "By then, he'll speak Korean better than Sueño here."

"Yeah," I said. For that, if for nothing else, I envied the man.

-30-

Miss Kim stood on a crowded bus on her way to work when a tightly folded note was pressed into her hand. She turned quickly, but whoever had passed it to her had already slipped through the crowd and proceeded to hop off the bus at the next stop. She wasn't even sure if it was a man or a woman.

The note had my name on it. In the CID office, when we were alone, I unwrapped it and flattened it out. Written in English was a time and a place.

I thanked Miss Kim, and she was kind enough not to ask who it had come from.

There was no signature on the note, but I knew who'd written it.

I sat on a bench in Children's Park on the side of Namsan Mountain on the southern edge of Seoul. Toddlers played on swings and clung to merry-go-rounds, and young female attendants waved their arms and called to them when any of them started to wander away. Nobody paid much attention to the lone *miguk* on the bench. I'd been there ten minutes. A woman wearing a long overcoat, a pulldown wool cap, and a scarf covering her mouth strode behind me. She didn't say anything, but when she entered the tree line at the edge of the playground, I stood and followed.

Deeper in the woods, she stopped and pulled the scarf from her face. We hugged. I squeezed her so tightly I was worried I might hurt her. I loosened my grip and stood back and studied her. Doctor Yong In-ja.

"You're taking a risk," I said. "Again."

"So are you."

"All they'd do to me is accuse me of consorting with a Red and pull my security clearance."

"And push you out of law enforcement."

I shrugged. "Worse things could happen." I glanced around the wooded area, seeing nothing. "I'm worried about them catching *you*."

The Park Chung-hee government had used General Bok's attempted coup as an excuse to crack down on everyone and anyone who had ever opposed it. Hundreds of suspected dissidents had been taken in for interrogation, even torture. Dozens, our military intelligence thought, had already been "disappeared." That was, buried somewhere in a shallow grave. Doc Yong, as leader of the revolutionary South Cholla Worker's Union, was high on Park Chung-hee's list for elimination.

She paused, searching my eyes. "Maybe someday, Korea will be a free country, and those of us who strive for a third way, a way outside of both brutal communism and blood-sucking capitalism, will be heard. Maybe we'll have leaders on both sides of the line who don't crave every last drop of power, who won't murder those who disagree with them."

"That could be a long time," I said.

She stared at me. "Yes," she replied. "Until then, you still cannot try to find me or Il-yong. You know that will lead them to us."

I did know. The Korean National Police, and the Korean CIA, had informants everywhere. An American GI, out of place in a province or a town with no US military bases, asking questions, dropping names, searching for someone, would attract every cop in the area.

"You stopped them," she said.

"Stopped who?"

"General Bok and that pretend heir to the throne of the Chosun Dynasty. You were there with them in the Korean Broadcasting studio." She must've had spies in the KBS building. The resistance to Park Chung-hee was silent, but widespread. "You switched on the sound," she continued, "so everyone could hear him speaking Japanese, so everyone would realize this was a ploy by the Tokyo industrialists and their Korean collaborators."

"I didn't do anything important," I said. "The Korean

people stopped them, by rising up against them instead of for them."

"Did your superiors order you to foil the coup?" she asked. "Or did you decide on your own?"

"My superiors," I said, "don't know anything about the mechanisms of Korean society. And they care even less. As long as there's an anti-Communist government in power, they're happy." And then I realized something. "Those European women who were taken to Bok's Third Corps Headquarters—did your organization have anything to do with them?"

"We had to find a way to expose Bok to the world," she said. "What easier way than through sex?"

Sex, GIs, and the *Overseas Observer*, I thought. The perfect trifecta.

"I thought you wanted Park Chung-hee to be overthrown."

She shook her head negatively. "Not by Bok. He only wanted to bring back the elites who'd done well under the Japanese, like his own family. Park needs to be removed from power, but through a democratic process."

She grabbed my hand. "I'm worried about that man, the bank robber. He said he's going to kill you."

"He'll be locked up for a long time."

"But if he escapes—"

"Don't worry. He won't."

"I hope not." She pondered it for a moment, and the smooth planes of her face wrinkled with concern. Finally, her face brightened. She squeezed my hand. "Before you go, there's someone I want you to see."

As if on cue, ten yards downhill, a man stepped out from behind a tree—a man I hadn't seen before. He pulled someone gently behind him. Someone small.

"Il-yong," his mother said, motioning with her hand for him to come closer.

The little boy hesitated, bright brown eyes opened wide. Then he stepped forward and then he was running. I knelt. He stopped next to his mother and grabbed her mittened hand. She knelt as well.

"This is your father," she said, motioning toward me.

He looked up at her, slightly confused. "*Abeoji*?" he said in Korean. Father?

"Yes," she said. "Your father."

He turned his bright eyes and studied me. From head to toe, it seemed. His sweet face remained noncommittal.

I offered my hand. "Hello, Il-yong," I said. "I'm your father."

He continued to stare, unmoving.

"Go ahead," his mother said. "Shake his hand, the way I taught you."

He worked up his courage and stuck out his hand. I shook it, holding on a little longer than I probably should have. Suddenly, he jerked his hand back, grabbed the folds of his mother's coat, and buried his head into her side.

She kissed him and comforted him. The man standing next

to the tree shuffled. Doctor Yong In-ja looked at me, her eyes wide and moist.

"We have to go," she said.

"When will I see you again?"

She shook her head. "No way to know."

I choked at the madness of it all. I would gladly have put in our marriage paperwork so she and Il-yong could get their visas and leave this place. But the Korean government would never let her go. One of the reasons for the so-called "security check" on marriage licenses was to make sure that the potential Korean bride had been neither a Communist nor a member of an opposition group. The South Korean authorities would not only deny her application for marriage, they would arrest her to boot.

But more importantly, even if we could get them out, she didn't want to marry me. Yong In-ja was committed to her comrades in South Cholla. Leaving with a foreigner would take her away from the cause that she'd dedicated her life to.

She must've sensed my frustration and waited a moment for me to calm down. Finally, she said, "When he's older, what do you want me to tell him?"

I pondered the question, keeping my eyes on Il-yong, knowing my stare embarrassed him but unable to look away. "Tell him that I would never have left him, nothing would've made me leave him, if there'd been any other way."

She nodded.

"Say goodbye to your father," she told Il-yong. He stared at me with wide eyes but said nothing.

Then she stood and pulled along the now bashful Il-yong. They walked together toward the waiting man. Backs toward me, the three of them filtered through the copse of trees and disappeared down the leaf-covered hillside. I remained kneeling, listening to the crunch of their feet on the papery foliage until the sound faded into a silent infinity.

ACKNOWLEDGEMENTS

Thanks to translator, interpreter, and actor YunJung Elena Chang for her wise counsel on Korean cultural and linguistic issues. Any mistakes are mine alone. Also kudos to Coco Cugat Garcia and the folks at the Yongsan Legacy Project for helping to memorialize the US military headquarters on Yongsan Compound which existed in Seoul from 1945 until 2018. Their work was invaluable to all of us who were privileged to serve there.